MW01167309

THRESHOLD

A
KEY MURPHY
THRILLER

I hope you enjoy
The Adventure.

KEVIN BARRY O'CONNOR

Copyright © 2022 by Kevin O'Connor
Published by WIN, Ink

First paperback edition March 2023

Title Production by The Book Whisperer

ISBN 979-8-9867131-3-7 (paperback)
ISBN 979-8-9867131-2-0 (ebook)

www.kevinbarryoconnor.com

For those that lost someone to the pandemic, for all of us that lost some piece of ourselves to the disease, may we remember how interconnected we are. And to the army of those on the front line; medical professionals, scientists, teachers, first responders, mental health professionals, and volunteers – you remind us that kindness and compassion remain the great healer.

Threshold: the magnitude or intensity that must be exceeded for a certain reaction, phenomenon, result, or condition to occur or be manifested.

CHAPTER 1

TUESDAY, AUGUST 31, 2021
IONA, SCOTLAND

"Mr. Murphy, one last question." The BBC reporter paused. Her eyes narrowed, serious, yet there was mischief in them. "Someone shot you in Jamaica two years ago. You told the world that you and Dr. Murphy were going to, and I quote, 'kick their ass.' When will that happen?"

Blood rushed to my face. My jaw tightened and my hand formed a fist. I caught my reaction and settled myself. I was the beneficiary of a recent genetic discovery known as the Ancestral Memory gene. This gene caused me to experience the actual memories of an ancestor. It led the love of my life, Arin Murphy, and I to find the missing pages of the *Book of Kells* and one of the most significant lost treasures in Christendom. We had turned the treasures over to Ireland at a ceremony in Dublin in 2019. Our faces were on almost every TV, newspaper, and magazine worldwide.

We had gone on a three-week press tour. Our last stop was Arin's birthplace, Kingston, Jamaica. The government had prepared a hometown hero's welcome. Some welcome; I was shot as we exited the airport, the bullet grazed my arm. A text message followed: *If we wanted you dead, you'd be dead.*

The reporter said something, far away, distant. I felt Arin squeeze my hand, and I shook off the recollection.

"Did you just experience a memory from your ancestor?" The reporters' eyes were wide and beaming.

I returned her excited look with a smile. "No," I lied. "I was thinking about the incredible history that happened right here."

I swept my hands over the landscape of this tiny island of rocks and hills and mystery. Iona had once been the monastic home of one of Ireland and Scotland's most important saints, Columba, also known as Columbkille. It was here that Irish monks began creating the *Book of Kells*, my ancestor Aedan its guardian.

Arin and I sat to the left of a tall Celtic cross, the reporter just two feet away. I gestured to the church, its gray and weather-beaten stone walls only thirty feet from us. "It's believed that Saint Columba's original monastery was here, on the same grounds. The Scriptorium, where the monks created the *Book*, was just there." I pointed to the open space to the west of the church. "The Scriptorium sat about twenty yards from the monastery, a circular design with three hundred and sixty degrees of light."

The air was autumn crisp, the sky cloudless, a magnificent blue, the surrounding water reflected the broad and boundless heavens.

"Thank you, Key, but back to my question."

I guess my waxing poetic was not exciting for TV.

"Covid has changed everything," I said. "We don't know if the threat still exists or if those people are still alive. If they are, I would tell them to rise to the new reality and focus their money and talents toward helping people."

"And if they don't?" the reporter asked, "if they threaten you again?"

Arin's fingers tightened around my hand. I saw fire in her eyes and felt certain that something provocative was forming in her mind. The reporter leaned toward her, hoping, I assumed, that she had struck a nerve.

"Dr. Murphy?"

Arin, a now famous anthropologist, put her hands on her lap and folded them, which I've seen her do before she gives a lecture. Her lips formed a slight smile, the gap in her teeth showing. Her eyes softened.

"Our foundation for children has been our focus during the pandemic." Arin's Jamaican accent was melodic and friendly. Her dark curls framed her face.

The reporter's shoulder slumped; she went from the edge of her seat to leaning back, deflated, I thought, at the lack of sensationalism.

"But," Arin continued. "As Key once famously said, 'Jamaicans don't scare easy.' We can always find time to kick ass if necessary."

The interview wrapped up, our first live, in-person TV event since Covid restrictions had loosened. The world remained enthralled by our story. Arin and I were the embodiment of a modern fairy tale, a reminder of the magic of life and love amongst the daily, gnawing presence of death.

With Arin's hand in mine, we skirted around the church and stopped at an overhang, looking down at the beach below us, the calm lap of the ocean washing over the sand and pebbles. The neighboring island of Mull was but a mile away. A cove was visible almost directly across the water.

"Aedan had hidden the seafaring boat there. He waited until dawn for his true love to join him for the journey to Ireland."

3

"And I've been waiting two years for you to kiss me on this magical island where it all began." Arin reached her hand to my face. I cupped mine behind her neck and we drew to each other, our lips softly meeting, as if for the first time. She pulled in tighter, the firmness of her body pressing against mine.

A deafening noise broke our trance as a helicopter passed over, landing twenty yards away. We watched a man step down: trim, muscular, gray on his temples accenting his cropped black hair. He ran under the rotors, removed his sunglasses, and stopped inches from us.

"What are you doing here? What's going on, Padraig?"

"Yer phones are off for hours." His face was lined, tense. "You're needed in Philadelphia."

"Oh my God." Arin squeezed my forearm, her voice pitched high. "What's wrong?"

"Everyone's fine."

"Why didn't you just send somebody to get us?" I asked. Padraig Collins was one of the wealthiest men in Europe.

"I'm the only one trusted with this message." The roar of the helicopter made it almost impossible to hear. Collins leaned closer. "There's reason to believe there will be a terrorist attack in Philadelphia."

"What?" I felt like I was going to fall backward. This made no sense. "What's it have to do with us?"

Arin looked at me, then at Collins. "Details, Padraig. Tell us."

"There's someone you need to meet that has information," Collins shouted. "She has the Ancestral Memory gene, just like you, Key, and she won't talk to anyone but the two of ye. They'll explain when you get there. My jet is waiting for you in Glasgow."

I took Collins by the arm.

"Padraig, tell us now. What are we walking into?"

His eyes narrowed, a slight tremble, something I've never seen from him before. "On Saturday evening, there will be an attempt to assassinate the Vice President of the United States."

CHAPTER 2

P adraig Collin's jet had ferried us from Philly to Glasgow less than twenty-four hours ago. We were to visit my parents in Dublin for several days, but the gods of chaos had a different plan. Arin had reclined her chair into sleeping position, a pillow and blanket enveloping her as we sped above the clouds. I longed for sleep, but the turbulence in my mind kept me wakeful despite the smooth ride home. I did the one thing I hoped would settle me as it so often had. I gazed upon this remarkable woman and wondered at my fortune.

As the magical mystery tour of Arin played on in my mind, it was interrupted by the haunting sound, the 'pftt' of a silencer, as I replayed watching Collins kill a man that was about to violate Arin. Collins had saved me the trouble, but he had put us in the predicament in the first place. To his credit he's spent the last two years making up for it.

. . .

I took my phone off airplane mode as we landed. It chimed with a message from Detective Buck McCoy, my best friend: *Meet me at Dr. Garcia's office. Text me when you are on your way.* I assumed Buck was in the middle of whatever was going on. It was 7:43 in the morning. I replied we would be there in twenty minutes.

It surprised me to see the lobby buzzing with people so early. Dr. Sylvia Garcia's company, Futuro Biologics, occupied the top four floors of a large building in University City. The University of Pennsylvania and Drexel University were the center of the West Philadelphia universe, and Garcia and Futuro had become two of the constellation's brightest stars. It was Dr. Garcia who discovered the Ancestral Memory gene, and Futuro was becoming a giant in the biomedical and gene-editing world. Arin and I went to the security desk on the ground floor. A Philadelphia police officer stood to the side of it.

"Dr. Murphy, Mr. Murphy, follow me, please." At least he didn't stumble over our matching last names and say Mrs. Murphy, like most people do, assuming we were married. We shared a Murphy ancestor in common from hundreds of years prior, who had left his mark in name and the legacy that had bound us from the start.

The officer led us on to the elevator. A few moments later we exited into the brightly lit reception center of Futuro. A large rendition of Dr. Garcia on the cover of *Time* magazine was mounted on the wall behind the reception desk. Next to it was a photo of Dr. Garcia standing between Arin and me. She stood all of four-ten, but she towered in intellect. The receptionist greeted us and told the officer to bring us back.

We followed him toward Dr. Garcia's office but stopped short at the door marked Evaluation Suite. A second officer stood at the door and opened it on our arrival. I followed Arin in, feeling like Pandora's Box had just swung open.

A woman stood.

"Key, it's good to see you again." The Philadelphia Police Commissioner reached her hand towards Arin. "Dr. Murphy, I'm Commissioner Thompson."

Buck sat across from her. He stood; his detective's badge was on his belt, his Glock holstered.

"I understand you just arrived from Scotland and have not been briefed," the police commissioner continued. "I need all of you, including our special guest, at a meeting in an hour. Detective McCoy will bring you up to speed. The officer who met you in the lobby will escort you."

The Commissioner walked to the door and left the room.

Arin and I turned to Buck.

"What the eff is going on?"

Arin planted a kiss on his cheek.

"Is Sylvia in there?" She waved her thumb toward the inner room. Dr. Garcia had been a mentor for Arin at University and was a close family friend. Arin's family was one of the wealthiest in Jamaica and a major investor in Futuro. Her brother Joseph was the Chairman of the Board.

The door swung open.

"I thought I heard the voice of my angel." Her short arms went up, and Arin bent into them, exchanging kisses on each cheek.

"Mama Sylvia, I missed you."

We hadn't seen her in a few months. Arin and I had become the face of Futuro. Our shares in the company funded our children's foundation. The better the company did, the more kids we helped. Pushing into her late seventies, she looked more vibrant than most people my age.

"She won't tell her story to anyone until you're here," Dr. Garcia said.

"We don't know who *she* is. We know nothing," Arin

looked at her famous mentor. "All we know is that she has the Ancestral Memory gene."

Dr. Garcia shot a look at Buck.

"They just got off the plane. I haven't had a chance to tell them anything," Buck said.

Dr. Garcia tugged at an earring then looked back at the door.

"My neurologist is just finishing an eval of her. I'm late for a videoconference, so I'll make it quick. She has lesions in her brain. She's highly functional most of the time but seems to be in decline. Her neurological activity is off the charts. Her scans are even more active than yours, Key, and that's saying a lot. This also means that she is short-circuiting, if we want to phrase it that way. Simply put, she can either go into a memory or just black out. It's hard to tell which."

"OK, but I still have no idea what's going on."

Dr. Garcia, as always, a force of kinetic energy, a proud daughter of Galicia, Spain, stepped to within inches from me. She looked up and I leaned forward.

"You will soon. I will leave you with this. She's extraordinary. And fragile. She has studied every word of every video with you and Arin. I believe her memories will increase now that the two of you are here." Dr. Garcia stepped back and turned to Buck. "And this knucklehead won't tell me what's really going on. Says he'd have to kill me if he told me."

She took Buck by the hands.

"See you later, handsome," she added as Buck kissed her on the cheek—Dr. Garcia, part of our extended and strange little family.

She opened the door and stopped. "The neurologist will let himself out the other door. This room is yours for however long you need it."

The room went quiet. It was a soothing space, earth tones, not a single thing on the walls. It reduced stimuli before a brain scan. As I turned to Buck for an explanation, the door to the eval room opened. I had been expecting a bedraggled and broken woman. Instead, I was staring at a fireball of energy. Her jet-black hair was in a ponytail. Freckles dotted her cheeks. Her face was the map of Ireland, as my mother would say. Her large green eyes stared back at me.

Buck made introductions. "Arin, Key, say hello to Cat Fahey, former Marine Corps Captain. We served together in Iraq."

I felt naked as her eyes scanned me then Arin.

"I can't believe I'm finally meeting you." A smile spread across her face as she stepped forward and extended her hand. I had gotten used to not shaking hands, but I instinctively met hers.

"Dr. Murphy." She reached out to Arin for a handshake. Arin responded with a fist-bump.

"Please, call me Arin."

"I've watched some of your anthropology lectures online. It's so good to meet you," the Marine said.

Buck tilted his head to the conference table and sat. We joined him.

I looked at our guest. To become Captain, you have to be a badass. For a woman to make it, she would have to lead a team of male badasses. As I was assessing her, I could see that she was assessing me, her eyes not leaving me, some mental calculations forming, it seemed.

"Tell us what's going on," I said.

Arin sat down next to me, folding her arms and leaning them on the conference table.

"First, I need to give you and Arin some background about Captain Fahey," Buck said. Buck was my best friend, like my older brother. His sister Tanya and I grew up together. Two Black kids, one pale red-headed Irish kid, our families thrust together by fate. Tanya's death still rattled me.

"Buck, stop with the formal Captain stuff." Cat's

demeanor quickly shifted from vibrant to distant; shadows played over her eyes. Her mouth pulled tight and it seemed like she lacked the will to hold herself up. Buck was about to speak, but I put my hand up. I wanted to hear about her ancestral memories.

"Tell me about them," I said.

Cat had tilted her head and shoulders downward, but her eyes lifted. I recognized the look: the weight, the confusion. I had lived it.

"The memories. Tell me," I said gently.

Cat glanced at Arin, who nodded in reassurance. Arin and I had been through this so many times. People experiencing the memories frequently believe they are having a mental breakdown. It takes time to adjust.

"We'll get to that," Buck interrupted, "there's a far more urgent matter, as you know. It's why I need you here." Buck tapped his knuckles on the table. "We have a problem, and you, little brother, the memory whisperer, might be the only one who can solve it."

I said nothing. Something about Cat's ancestral memory must be a blockbuster. I folded my hands and waited.

"Cat believes a terror attack will occur at the Made in the USA Festival in Philly this weekend."

Collins had told us this. Even so, my stomach tightened. I shook my head to rid it of confusion.

"I don't understand how we fit in."

"You will, but first you need to know why Cat is legendary. She's one of the most respected situational awareness experts in the military. Ever. Her ability to read body language and non-verbal signals put her in the elite." Buck patted my shoulder. "Reminds me of you."

I had a quick mental rush of images from playing football at Penn State. I could read a play before it started, as if I had been in the opponents' huddle. The little tics and micro-movement of their eyes had announced their intent.

Cat jumped in, "But, Key, I'm damaged goods. PTSD. I suffered some combat-related hearing loss—possible brain damage. I've had a hard time holding a job. Can go days forgetting to go to work, shower, sometimes I forget to eat. Been homeless for stretches. I'm making progress getting my life back, but the memories are so intense, and I'm ... I don't know the right word."

"Obsessed," Arin added. "I get obsessed, and I don't even have them. I have the gene, but no memories, not yet. Key tells me what it's like."

"I'm completely obsessed. Especially now. One of my Marine buddies heads security at the Philadelphia Museum of Art. He hired me as one of his assistants. The art museum is the staging ground for the Festival. Six weeks ago, I noticed two guys walking the grounds, first near the Azalea Gardens, then in front of the museum, at the bottom of the steps by the Rocky statue. I picked them out. They were doing surveillance, I'm sure of it." Cat paused and gave Arin and me a nod.

"There was nothing actionable," she continued. She stared at the empty wall for a moment, her head nodding. "To everyone else, they were just two guys. I saw them again last week. One was at Eakins Oval; the other was on the bottom tier of the art museum steps. I watched as they gave a hand signal to each other. It was the sign of a violent white supremacist group."

I looked at Buck. He acknowledged me and gave me an almost imperceptible tilt of his head. I'd seen this a million times. It meant listen up: this is the real deal.

"That's when Cat told me about it," Buck said. "I called my colleagues heading up the police security detail for the Festival. They checked with the FBI. There has been very little chatter and minimal threats. All the chatter is about Chicago. The President is giving a Labor Day speech there."

I had sat at this very table, had been in the evaluation

suite, probes on my head, neurologists analyzing the tests, learning that I was a freak of nature.

"Arin, what do you know about the Festival?" Cat asked.

"Not much. I've heard of it, that's all."

Cat pulled in a deep breath and noisily released it.

"It's one of the largest hip-hop, rock, and rap festivals in the U.S. They canceled it last year because of Covid. Some of the biggest names in music will be here. Closing out Saturday night will be the first woman, the first Black woman, to hold the office of Vice President." This elite warrior paused, shifted in her seat, and looked at me, unflinching. "Key, I believe they intend to kill her."

I knew this was coming but hearing it from a decorated Marine still rocked me. And then I thought of Arin. Like the Vice President, Arin was mixed race.

"You believe that there is something in your ancestral memories that will help you?"

Cat nodded. Her body shifted, altered. Her muscled shoulders relaxed, and I could hear a faint sigh escape this hardened Marine.

"Yes. But I don't know what it is. That's why I need your help."

Arin leaned across the conference table.

"Cat, I want you to tell us everything. Every detail. Nothing is insignificant."

Cat nodded as tension once again stiffened her muscles. Her necklace dangled, the words *Semper Fi*, "always faithful", hung visible over her shirt.

"Thank you." A forced smile. "But if they threaten the VP, I will find them and kill them. She doesn't die on my watch."

I watched as her shoulders sagged forward and her back rounded. This was not the same woman who came through the door a few minutes ago. I knew the feeling; the fear that if you told anyone about your experience, they would think you were nuts. Despite the fact that she had sought us out, the very act of confession, of admission, is a tightrope walk.

"Sit up strong, Cat. You are not crazy; you might just save the world," I coaxed her.

The transformation in her was immediate; back ramrod straight, hands clasped, resting on the table. Captain Fahey was in the room. She concentrated on me to the point of discomfort.

"An explosion in Iraq had knocked me unconscious." She sat up straighter as the words came out. "A man reached down to help me to my feet. The vision was blurry, dreamlike, but I could tell he was kind, tall, strong."

The room was eerily quiet now, as if we were all holding our breath in anticipation. Cat closed her eyes, conjuring something or someone.

"The vision recurred frequently," she whispered. "I assumed it resulted from the trauma. As the visions became clearer, I saw it was a Black man and wondered if it was Buck."

I turned abruptly to Buck.

"I was there." Buck uncrossed his arms. "Led the rescue team. Nine received serious injuries."

"Nine? Who's Nine?" Arin asked.

Buck pointed to the Marine vet.

"Her team called her Nine, as in a cat has nine lives. She got them out of so many tight spots she became a legend. The attack she referred to was in Mosul. She had read the scene and stopped the convoy. The enemy exploded the device remotely and she was a little too close. Cat saved a lot of lives that day."

"Much respect," Arin said.

"There's something else," Buck interjected. "I was supposed to lead that convoy. My team got reassigned. Cat replaced me."

Everything slowed down in my brain. Cat almost died. By

Buck's admission, she was the best of the best. Which meant Buck almost certainly would have died. There would not have been the three of us sitting here talking to Cat. Whatever was about to unfold would not have involved us. Without Buck, there would be no conversation with Cat. No revelation.

Cat's chin had dropped to her chest, and her left hand brushed from her forehead to the back of her neck. She looked up, a slight blush on her freckled cheeks.

"Cut it out," she said. "I wasn't being a hero, just doing my job. Buck would've done the same."

"Bullshit," Buck leaned sideways toward her, "and you know it. I couldn't read that situation like you. Woulda just walked straight into the explosion."

Cat kept her head down, eyes to the floor.

"This is my family, Cat." Buck took Arin's hand in his and reached to take mine. "They got me, I got them. If I say, 'I got you, Cat,' that means they got you too. Understand, Captain?"

It took a long moment, then her head slowly rose and her eyes gained focus, meeting Buck's. A nod and what I took to be a slight smile.

"If it wasn't for your story, Key, I would have never put the puzzle together. I kept lying to myself. Not me. I'm Cat. No PTSD for me. But trauma doesn't let go. It just whoops you whenever it wants. The images intensified a few months ago. I assumed it was just the PTSD."

"Sounds familiar to me, Captain," I offered.

She gave me a stern look.

"If we're family, then drop the Captain stuff. Please call me Cat."

"OK, Cat."

"I watched the interviews with you and Arin over and over," she continued. "Key, you mentioned Buck several times during interviews. I hadn't seen Buck since Iraq.

Looked him up. He put me in touch with Dr. Garcia. I have the Ancestral Memory gene."

Dr. Garcia had discovered a gene that had mutated in about two percent of the world's population. This gene allowed a person to see and experience the memories of an ancestor. Of course, most people experiencing such memories thought they were insane, hallucinating, hearing voices and seeing events from another time. The discovery of the gene created an explosion in Ancestral DNA testing and gave stories like mine scientific validity. The memories of my ancestor Aedan led Arin and me to find the missing pages of the *Book of Kells*.

Cat stared at her hands as they rested on the table. Her eyelids blinked and her head drooped. Her arms were folded on the table and her head clumsily fell into them, softening the impact. Arin rose to her feet.

"She's OK," Buck said. "As Doc told you, it's either a memory or short-circuiting. Cat said it's been happening more frequently."

In almost two years of working with people with the gene, I had never encountered someone blacking out. I'd had some intense episodes myself, but nothing like this. I leaned closer to examine her face, trying to note any activity. Suddenly, her eyes blinked several times before focusing on me. She sat up straight, taking in the room and the three of us staring at her.

"I'm so sorry," she said. "This blacking out thing is weird."

"We are here to help. No apologies needed," I assured her.

Her head was nodding, more like a nervous tic. She didn't seem to know what to do with her hands.

"You see, that's just it. You already have." She turned her head to face Arin. "You too, Arin. Both of you have saved my life."

"I don't understand, Cat." Arin eased herself onto her seat.

Cat straightened and put her hands in her lap.

"As I said, I've watched the videos of all your press conferences and interviews. When I was at my worst, your stories lifted me." Her chest rose, a deep breath. "I desperately wanted to eat a bullet. You are the reason I didn't."

Arin wiped her sleeve across her eyes.

"I told Buck I'd only tell my story to you two. I've told no one else, not even Dr. Garcia." Cat forced a smile.

I wanted to reach across and give her a reassuring touch, but I kept still, letting her move at her own pace.

She laid her palms flat on the cherry wood conference table and leaned back in the chair.

"Recently, the vision and memory changed from blurry to clear. As I've heard you say, Key, it went from still photo to full-on video. The Black man reached down. He wore dapper nineteenth-century gentlemen's clothing. He was tall, handsome, in his late twenties. The man on the ground, the man whose eyes I was seeing through, grasped the extended hand. He said, in an Irish accent, 'They are coming to kill you, Frederick.' The tall man responded, 'I suppose, Martin, that we should do something about that.'"

Cat looked expectantly at Arin and me. I had no clue what she was getting at. I waited for her to go on, but Arin was halfway out of her chair, her fingers absently tapping the table.

"Did Buck say your last name is Fahey?"

"Yes."

"Martin Fahey was a famous Irish abolitionist. Do you know who the Black man was?"

Cat Fahey nodded.

"His name was Frederick Douglass."

CHAPTER 3

A rin's jaw quivered; her fingers held the side of her face. "You're sure?" she said in barely a whisper. "Frederick Douglass?"

"I'm sure."

Arin slowly rose from her chair. She took the few steps to the beige-colored wall and brushed her fingers along it. Her back was to us, lingering there silently. She made a slow turn, her eyes on Cat.

"Tell me; tell me everything," Arin said, as if she was addressing an oracle.

Cat smiled. "I will, gladly, the little I know so far. But I need to do something first. I'll be back in a moment." She stood and entered the evaluation room.

"This is amazing." Buck watched Cat exit the room. "But we're in some serious shit."

"Brother, you live in serious shit twenty-four seven. I just visit it sometimes." Arin was pacing. Her brain must have exploded when she heard the name Frederick Douglass. Jetlag was lurking on the outskirts of my brain, meanwhile. I took a deep breath, hoping to clear the fog.

"Give it to me straight. Why am I here?"

Buck was a decorated soldier, and a decorated super-cop. At thirty-eight, he had six years on me and a ton more experience. I stood for a moment and stretched my back, longing for a strong cup of coffee.

Buck folded his arms, top teeth biting down a bit on his lower lip.

"So, I walked into the meeting with the top brass, said I have credible intelligence from a military legend with PTSD, recently homeless, now working security at the art museum. She spotted some guys giving a white supremacy hand signal, and her ancestral memories are trying to tell her something about a terrorist attack this weekend." Buck gave a sarcastic grin. "As you might imagine, it didn't go well."

"Why was the Commissioner here?" Arin asked, still pacing the room.

"She wanted to meet Cat and Dr. Garcia. She had read Cat's profile. If there's the slightest chance that Cat might help with the VP, she'll take it. Leave no stone unturned, that's her modus. But she wants Homeland Security to get on board with receiving your help."

"Therefore, the meeting that the Commissioner asked us to?" Arin asked.

Buck nodded.

"And, what, you expect me to convince them?"

"Hell no. I expect you to wow them, blow their fucking minds. Not too much to ask." He gave me the Buck look. He asks, I do. I ask, he does. My anchor. As I'm his.

The sound of a soulful blues harmonica stirred me from my thoughts. Long piercing notes followed by rhythmic chords, then back to a sonic-scape that could break your heart.

"Cat plays when she's stressed," Buck whispered. "She says it calms her, centers her thoughts. Kind of like some people run for a cigarette. And by the way, she's staying at the house for a few days."

Arin's eyebrows rose.

"Not like that; she's in the guest room," Buck answered.

The three of us had been living in my parents' house since the lockdown, and they were stuck in Ireland. Arin and I spent much of our time coaching and evaluating people with a documented Ancestral memory. Arin's experience as an anthropologist and mine as someone with the mutated gene proved invaluable. We unlocked some exciting history and helped people navigate and tell their story. But nothing like this. Nothing like Frederick Douglass.

Arin sat beside me. We listened intently as Cat poured her heart into the blues. I imagined she was channeling the spirit, the energy, the souls of people who have been through the neuro scans, their brains wired for explorations of neurons and memories. Though the door was closed, the piercing notes bounced from wall to wood, straight into my core. I found myself simultaneously haunted and elated by the music.

Cat came back into the room.

"That was beautiful. I hope you'll play some more," Arin said.

Cat took her seat and stared at her hands, the harmonica beside them.

Arin opened the recording app on her phone and placed it in front of her.

"Are you OK with that?"

Cat nodded.

We had interviewed many people about their ancestral memory stories, but I had never seen Arin this excited. Her eyes had grown wide. She was biting down on her lip; antici-pation seemed to ripple through her.

"Could you tell where they were?"

"Dublin," Cat answered.

Arin grabbed the edge of the table to steady herself.

"This is remarkable. Martin Fahey exhorted Douglass to leave the U.S. for fear of being captured by his owner. He was not yet a freeman. They departed for a speaking tour to England and Ireland in 1845."

"You have verified that Martin Fahey is your ancestor?"

Cat nodded.

"What I call the 'initiating sequence,' the first memory, normally repeats for some time. For me, a sword swept near my throat. It was visceral. I would frequently jump back to dodge it. It took a few months before the memories turned into full scenes." I paused for a moment and recalled the experience.

"For you, it was the hand reaching down?"

Cat nodded.

"A few times per month at first. Then a few times per week."

"Was it only the hand? Any other features?" Arin asked.

Cat looked at Arin as she answered. "Two months ago, the view expanded. It was as if a camera had a tight frame around the hand, then slowly, with each new view, the frame widened until, finally, the two hands clasped. Around six weeks ago was when the other details emerged."

"Do you know how Martin knew there was a plan to kill Frederick Douglass?" Arin seemed to hold her breath as she waited for an answer.

Cat tilted her head and spoke directly to Arin. "Daniel O'Connell told him."

Arin's eyes widened. Her lips tried to form words, but nothing came. Finally, she let out, "Oh my God," as she backed away from the table and began pacing the room again.

I turned to Buck. His blank look told me he was as clueless as me.

"Time out." I formed a T with my hands. "I don't know what's going on."

"Who's Daniel O'Connell?" Buck asked Cat.

Cat turned to Arin.

"You're the expert."

Arin continued pacing, not noticing us. I stepped to her. She looked up at me and then at Cat and Buck. It was as if Cat's words had just penetrated her consciousness. Arin reached up, squeezed my shoulders, and bounced on her tiptoes like a schoolgirl who had won a contest.

"Captain Fahey, damn, you are full of surprises," she said. "O'Connell is perhaps the greatest figure in modern Irish history, known as The Liberator. Although he fought for Catholic emancipation, he was the fiercest and most famous anti-slavery voice in the world. Frederick Douglass considered him a hero."

"Cat," Buck broke in, "how is any of this going to help us figure out what's happening with the terrorists?"

"I don't know." Cat's eyes blinked wildly for a moment. Her fingers kneaded deeply into her shoulder, working out some kink or thought. "Something is lurking on the edges, trying to warn me. The memories intensified when I saw those two guys give the white supremacist call sign."

"For me to help, I need context. I don't know much about O'Connell or Douglass." I gestured to Arin. "Professor Murphy, enlighten us."

Arin clasped her hands. "Douglass was an escaped slave from Maryland. He'd moved to New Bedford, Massachusetts, and had published his book, *Narrative of the Life of Frederick Douglass*. He was becoming a renowned speaker on the abolitionist circuit. Bounty hunters were combing the north for escaped slaves. His white abolitionist colleagues believed Douglass would be back in chains if the bounty hunters found him. They convinced him to leave for a speaking tour in Ireland and England. And that's when—"

There was a knock on the door. The police officer stuck his head in and addressed Buck.

"The Commissioner just texted me. We need to leave."

I watched Cat as the worry in her eyes transformed.

"Let's get out of here." She was on her feet.

Marine on the move.

CHAPTER 4

A rin leaned forward, her hands on her knees, and continued the history lesson as the police van took us to our destination.

"O'Connell was a Member of Parliament and played a major role in the passage of the Slavery Abolition Act of 1833, banning slavery throughout the British Empire. Douglass was aware of this. He had worked among the Irish on the docks in Baltimore, his earnings paid to his owner. It was from there that he had planned and had made his escape."

The van turned left onto Pine Street, the shops and cafés coming to life as we sped by. The seats ran lengthwise on the right and left sides of the vehicle. Arin leaned forward just as a pothole jolted us. She gripped her seat then continued.

"It wasn't long after Douglass arrived in Dublin that he attended an O'Connell speech. He wrote extensively about it. Imagine this twenty-seven-year-old slave standing in the hall, likely the only Black person there, taking in these shocking words from a white man."

"This is my favorite quote from his speech that night." Arin closed her eyes and began reciting O'Connell. "'I have been assailed for attacking the American institution, as it is called, Negro slavery. I am not ashamed of that attack. I do not shrink from it. I am the advocate of civil and religious liberty all over the globe, and wherever tyranny exists I am the foe of the tyrant; wherever oppression shows itself, I am the foe of the oppressor; wherever slavery rears its head, I am the enemy of the system, or the institution, call it by what name you will.'"

Arin opened her eyes and engaged the three of us.

"O'Connell didn't know Douglass was in the crowd. When he learned of his presence, he called him to the stage, where this young man stunned the audience with his oratory, his powerful tales of slavery, his ability to move the soul. He was on his way to becoming a threat to the status quo."

We traveled north on Seventh Street and made our way around Washington Square, a stately tree-dotted park with a statue of our nation's founder. The eternal flame at the Tomb of the Unknown Soldier flickered as it always had. As Arin was about to continue, the van slowed and made a right turn. A black-suited man stood behind the security barriers and nodded to an invisible figure in the security booth. The gate rose. I recognized where we were: the Federal Building, the Philly home of the FBI.

The van rolled forward until it was behind a wall. Another man in a black suit opened the door, turned, and walked. We followed him into an elevator for a swift ride to the ninth floor. When the silver doors slid open he turned right in the hall. He opened a door and we stepped into a conference room where four people sat at the table. Commissioner Thompson was the first to stand, followed by Deputy Commissioner Francisco Cruz. I had met and served under both during my short stint as a consultant to the Narcotics division. We were introduced to the final two: FBI Special

Agent Di Stefano, trim, athletic, likely handpicked from Special Forces, and Secret Service Special Agent Williams. Williams's lips looked like they were tattooed into a permanent scowl. His rust-colored goatee framed his mouth. He remained standing as the rest of us took our seats, pacing four steps, turning back.

FBI agent Di Stefano, in his early forties, smiled, most noticeably toward Cat.

"We need to jump right in," he began. "Captain Fahey, we've been briefed on what you have told Detective McCoy." He tilted his head toward Buck. "We'd like to hear it from you."

Cat fixed her eyes first on the FBI man and then on the Secret Service agent. Her silence raised the tension in the room. As Di Stefano was about to speak, Cat looked at the two men.

"What game are you playing here?" she said.

Di Stefano pulled back in his chair.

"What are you talking about?"

"The nanosecond glance you two exchanged when we walked in, signaling the game was about to begin. Mister Intimidating, skulking behind you. His assignment, bad cop, leaving you, Agent Di Stefano, to play good cop. Your natural role. Army Ranger, am I right? The negotiator, big smile but tough as nails, the Mullahs respected you." Cat chiseled her stare into the FBI agent. "Why are we playing this game?"

"There's no game, Captain." Williams placed his hands on the chair he stood behind.

Cat lifted her gaze to him. She sat completely still, trance-like. Williams tried to ignore her.

"*Fi 'ayi wahdat kunti,*" Cat said, the recognizable sound of Arabic.

Agent Williams's chin pulled tight, his thin lips making a straight line, his eyes narrowing.

"*Ant taelam 'anani la 'astatie al'iijabat ealaa dhalika,*" he answered.

"Then I had you wrong: not Special Forces. You were a spook." Cat stood and leaned on the back of the chair, mirroring the agent's hands and posture. "You followed the money, terrorist money, and the Secret Service grabbed you to do the same domestically. Am I close?"

Agent Di Stefano turned in his chair to Agent Williams. Williams pointed at me.

"It's not just you I'm worried about, Captain. It's him."

That took me by surprise.

"What?"

"Explain yourself," Commissioner Thompson commanded.

His shoulders tightened. Williams stroked his goatee, then jutted his hand forward in my direction.

"Do you expect us to believe all this ancestral memory bullshit? Your ancestor showed you where to find the treasure. Really? Any two-bit con artist could make that up, could plant the treasure. Trust me, I've seen way more sophisticated cons than that, yet here you are, the darling of the media."

Commissioner Thompson slapped the table.

"I vouch for Key. If you don't like it, we'll head back to Police Headquarters and have this discussion without you. Am I clear?"

"Let *me* be clear," Williams retorted harshly, "the life of the Vice President is in my hands this week and I will not tolerate nonsense."

Cat burst out laughing. She turned to rest her butt on the table and look straight at the Secret Service agent.

"You're a piece of work, acting all alpha male." She clapped her hands and laughed a bit more. "You're testing us."

"Damn right," he shot back. "You have some serious problems and I don't know if I can count on you."

Cat pushed off the table and stepped toward the agent.

"That's legit. Past few years have not been my best. But to be honest, I found the two supremacists. You didn't."

Cat slowly backed away.

FBI Agent Di Stefano cocked his head toward his colleague, a slight smile escaping.

"I told you."

I had been watching Arin the whole time. She could go all Rambo on these guys, or all Socrates. A flip of the coin.

"Gentlemen." She smiled, all Jamaican charm and melodic accent. Her fingers were laced together, resting on the conference table. She glanced at the photo of the President and the FBI Director on the wall, then turned like a trial lawyer to Di Stefano and Williams. "It's established science. There is no controversy about the existence of the Ancestral gene. Could someone try to fool us? Of course. They have tried. The barrage of protocols weeds them out." She turned to Di Stefano. "The FBI has taken an interest in the research. Key and I have consulted with the agency. But you already know that."

"Hold on," Agent Williams said. "With all due respect, I don't know why you're here, Dr. Murphy. None of you have security clearance for this." He pointed his thumb toward Buck. "Including the Detective. I want your statements, and then I want you to get in the paddy wagon and go home."

Arin leaned closer to Commissioner Thompson. *"Maybe him mother neva teach him nuh fi be rude?"*

I looked in amazement from Arin to the Commissioner. I was not expecting Arin to speak Jamaican Patois, or the Commissioner to understand her. Then I remembered that the Commissioner's grandparents were born there. The Commissioner was trying hard not to laugh.

She said to the agents, "They have clearance."

"Excuse me?" Williams folded his arms. "No way."

The Commissioner pressed a button on her phone.

She spoke quietly, waited a moment, and began again. "Mr. Secretary, thank you for taking my call earlier. Your agents have legitimate concerns about involving our guests in this matter. I hope you can put their minds at ease."

She pressed a button, putting the phone in speaker mode.

"Gentlemen," Commissioner Thompson said, "I have the Secretary of Homeland Security."

There was some background noise, the phone muffled, hands over the receiver, then a voice.

"Agents Williams and Di Stefano, if our guests ask a question, answer it. And listen closely to what they say. If they tell you something, listen even closer."

A reluctant, "Yes, Sir," sounded from Williams and Di Stefano.

"And before I go: Captain Fahey, I read your file. I have asked the Pentagon to return you to temporary active duty. By law you don't have a say in it, but after all that you've given, if you decline, I'll respect it."

Her cheeks flushed. The tendons in her neck protruded. I could see the swallow in her throat. "It's an honor. Thank you, Sir."

"Welcome back, Captain Fahey. You are now on active duty. I have asked the Pentagon to assign you to liaison with Agent Di Stefano. Dr. Murphy, Key, whatever insights you have, let them be known."

The Secretary went silent. His breathing came across the speaker. "Listen to me—all of you. When I was an operative, I learned to distrust the big, logical stories. I put people behind bars or in graves because of the slightest cracks, the smallest of lies. The security apparatus will go after big and small. But it might miss the tiny cracks. I pray that you won't."

The line went dead before Cat could respond, but the rise in her chest, the clarity in her eyes, the determination in her fisted hands and clenched jaw told me that she was rising. Experience had taught me what she could not yet know:

she'd second-guess her memories, her instincts would thrash and battle her current fierceness. She might need another nine lives before this was over.

"Let's get to work." Commissioner Thompson's jacket was on a hanger behind her. Four stars adorned the collar of her white dress shirt. She nodded to the other officer at the table. "Deputy Commissioner Cruz, please."

I liked this guy; he was always good to me. I was nearly shot two years ago during a drug raid, and afterward he walked into the squad room and said to me, for all to hear, 'What's the difference between a donut and a cop? Donuts are supposed to have holes in them. Don't be a donut.' With that, he had laid a box of donuts in front of me and left the room.

"A right-wing group called 'The One-Six' filed for a permit to hold a rally on Saturday, the day the Vice President comes to town," Cruz began, no joke on his lips this time. "That's a new name for us. It's in support of the January Six insurrection. Our lawyers fought it; their lawyers won." Cruz let that settle with us for a moment. He was in full dress, three stars lining the top of each shoulder.

"They wanted it at City Hall. We pushed back hard. At least fifty percent of everyone arriving for the Festival by public transport will exit the subway at City Hall. We wanted them at the Constitution Center lawn, a mile in the other direction." He shook his head, worry evident on his creased face. "The judge allowed them to use Love Park. How's that for irony?"

Fifteenth Street separated City Hall and Love Park, the city founder, William Penn, looking down from his statuesque perch atop City Hall. I kept my eyes on Buck. He would assess this far better than I. He knew the police contingencies for critical situations, and his eyes told me this was not good.

Cruz drummed his fingers. "Agent Di Stefano, please take it from here."

Di Stefano had a file folder open in front of him. He

glanced down, then at Cat.

"The two men that you saw at the art museum, we have identified them from the surveillance videos. Patrick Boland and Lewis Walsh. They are not your everyday Proud Boys, Oath Keepers, Klansmen, white supremacists."

The agent scanned the page before him, then tapped his index finger on the white sheet.

"Boland has a PhD in History. Walsh has a Doctor of Divinity. They are both listed on the permit application. It seems they are the white-collar advance team for some of the nastiest militia groups on our radar. They don't look like the stereotype. They are smart, well dressed, and surprisingly charming. And they are Aryan Nation to the core."

At this, Agent Williams finally took his seat, his alpha male bluster set aside. He leaned back in his chair and ran his hand over his goatee yet again.

"Captain," he addressed Cat, "these two are smart and professional. We must consider the possibility that they wanted you to see them."

His words washed over Cat as she closed her eyes. I assumed she was summoning her ancestor, looking in the recesses of memory for any crumb of insight. She focused on no one, just bobbing her head up and down.

"You might be right, Agent Williams. Which means I'm being played."

It seemed as if Cat had stopped breathing, eyes closed, no motion. Not a sound in the room.

A moment later, she opened her eyes.

"They were very relaxed, just two friends in conversation. No one would suspect that they were doing reconnaissance. They stood out to me because they didn't want to stand out. They were using very subtle gestures. It was like they were measuring the area with their eyes, pretending to be tourists but discussing details."

Cat reached for her water glass and took a long drink, her

look far away.

"The one in jeans was at Eakins Oval. He turned to this friend who was on the art museum steps. Before they gave each other the white supremacist hand signal, the one at the Oval pointed his index fingers at the corners of the museum. The one on the steps nodded."

"That's it?" Commissioner Thompson asked. "Any idea what that means?"

"It means they were marking a spot." Everyone turned to Buck. "Or they want us to think that."

"Why?" asked the Commissioner.

I jumped into the discussion. "Cat, if they were playing you, that means they knew you worked security and were aware of your abilities." On the wall behind the agents was an enlarged map from City Hall to the Museum of Art. I stepped to the map and pointed at Love Park. "How many people are they expecting at the Love Park rally?"

"The permit limits them to three thousand," Cruz answered from across the conference table.

"Three thousand militiamen on the day the Vice President will be there?" Arin looked horrified.

"How many at the Festival?" My finger was on the Benjamin Franklin Parkway.

"Sixty thousand," answered Cruz. "Normally, it's eighty thousand. We limited the number to sixty because of Covid."

I tapped the area just above the Swann Fountain at Logan Square, the park that's smack in the middle of the Benjamin Franklin Parkway and a potential bottleneck.

"Is this the main entrance to the Festival?"

"Yes," Di Stefano said.

I turned back to the map and imagined standing at Eakins Oval. The monument to George Washington sat directly across from the art museum. I placed my forefingers on opposite sides of the museum.

"They could create an incident at these points that drives

sixty thousand people stampeding to the exits, with three thousand stoked-up insurrectionists waiting."

"Fuck," Arin let out, then looked embarrassed.

"In the confusion and chaos stands the Vice President." Cat was tapping her fist on the table while looking down at her feet. The drumming of her fist grew louder, faster, incessant, until she moaned and fell limp in her chair, her head tilted to the right.

"Give it a minute," I said. "She is in a highly sensitive state. As am I."

I was now standing inches from both agents. At six-three, I was looking down at them, and they were looking up at me. Williams rubbed his forehead.

"What the hell does that mean?"

"It means that our brains work furiously to make connections, see patterns, see the things that are not normally visible."

"For Christ's sake," Williams said at the top of his voice, "do I have to listen to this babble? I'm not fooled by your act."

I tilted downward, close to his face, and spoke softly in contrast to his brash voice.

"You can say whatever you want about me. I really don't care." I gestured to Cat. "She's a hero, doing the best she can. Back off."

"Listen up," Buck inserted himself, talking to Williams. "Two years ago Key helped us bust a drug ring in six months that we had been trying to nail for years."

Alpha male was back. Williams turned gruffly to Buck.

"I read the file. Beginner's luck. That's all that was."

"Cat took one look at you and deduced your background. Knew you spoke Arabic, had been CIA," Buck said.

"Guys." I put a hand on each agent's shoulder, sensing it would piss off Williams. "We have four days. We are on the same team. And you need us. I know this will sound crazy,

Agent Williams, but it's possible Cat's unique memories will reveal something that will help. And even if that doesn't happen, she's the one who spotted Boland and Walsh. Let it unfold."

Williams looked like he wanted to throw up.

I took my seat. Arin had Cat's hand in hers. No one was better with people that had ancestral memories. I knew; she had remained my guide.

Cat's head finally lifted, her eyes slowly taking us in. She seemed pleased that Arin was holding her hand.

"Martin told Douglass, 'They are coming for you, just not in the way we think. We are missing something, Frederick.'"

Commissioner Thompson looked baffled by Cat's pronouncement. She seemed ready to speak to Cat but addressed the group instead.

"There is a task force meeting at 4 p.m. at Eakins Oval. I want all of you there."

Williams couldn't contain himself.

"What did we just witness? A seance? Ma'am, there are high-level security issues that will be discussed."

The Commissioner shot him a look, clear in its meaning, then ignored him.

"Detective," she said to Buck, "you'll oversee our guests' needs and security. If anyone gives you a hard time, you have a direct line to Deputy Commissioner Cruz." Commissioner Thompson took her hat in hand. "You will need to sign consent and confidentiality forms. They are waiting in the van for you. We will issue you an ID pack so you can enter the Festival grounds."

"But, Ma'am," Williams inserted, "I have direct respon-sibility—"

"Yes," she cut him off, "you have direct responsibility for the safety of the VP. Other than that, you are in my house." She put her hat on. "Now put your dick back in your pants. The pissing match is over."

CHAPTER 5

The van was waiting for us. We signed the waivers and confidentiality agreements. The agent handed Arin, Cat and me our ID packs. They also issued Buck an ID pack. His detective's badge alone would not get him access to the task force meeting.

"Let's walk. I want us to see City Hall and Love Park with fresh eyes." I led our little foursome up Arch Street: a former Marine with PTSD, a narcotics cop, a Jamaican professor of anthropology, and me, world-famous for communing with my ancestor, Aedan, who's been dead for twelve hundred years. The bad guys didn't stand a chance. Or so I hoped.

The Federal Building sat at the eastern end of Chinatown, which was as much a part of the fabric of the city as the Italian Market in South Philly. It's always been known as Chinatown, but the Pho shops, sushi restaurants, and Korean barbecues were a testament to the demand for all Asian food. Sidewalk markets selling melons, mangosteen, cabbages, and kimchi vied for the tight spaces of concrete as humans scurried about them. I didn't know if you could use the word "cacophony" for scent, but if you could, it was that.

As we reached Tenth and Arch, Arin stopped at the corner and stared at the elaborate forty-foot-tall Chinatown Friendship Gate.

"That's stunning," she said.

Cat had sidled up to her as the southern exposure played its light on the golds, reds, greens, and blues. The symbols and carvings looked alive: dragons and tigers, rose petals and lotus flowers, thousands of years of lore and story given form. I'd seen it so often I barely noticed it anymore. It's funny how we see the common anew when someone else experiences its grandeur. Like Arin. My eyes roamed over her. Her black ringlets danced on her shoulder as her head moved to take in the elaborate carvings.

She turned and looked quizzical.

"What?"

"I'm just soaking up the beauty and majesty." I bowed. She melted me as the corners of her eyes squinted slightly. Her lips pulled up in a smile. The gap in her front teeth accented her beauty.

I leaned in and whispered, "You get hotter by the day, just saying."

She lingered on me a moment then took Cat's arm and crossed the street. I was lost in my reverie but quickly recovered. What the hell were we getting ourselves into?

And then I sensed it. I had noticed him a few moments ago but had paid no attention. Cargo pants, a snug army-green T. A telephoto lens. I turned, he was five feet away, taking photos of Arin and Cat. He noticed me and snapped a close-up of my face.

"What are you doing?" I closed the gap. "Who are you with?"

He began walking away. I was reaching for him when

Buck grabbed my arm and shook his head. "It's legal, nothing you can do."

Buck took his own phone in hand. "Hey, buddy."

The photographer turned to Buck. Buck snapped a photo. "I'll be watching out for you."

"As if," the man answered.

"As if what?"

"As if I give a fuck." He slid the camera strap over his shoulder and headed north on Tenth.

"Paparazzi or Nazi?" I said. Buck shrugged his shoulders.

We caught up with Cat and Arin and entered the City Hall Courtyard on Thirteenth Street. The carousel, water ice, and Philly soft pretzel vendors had eager customers lined up. We emerged on Fifteenth. There was no Fourteenth Street. It was called Broad Street, its south side butting up against City Hall and continuing on the other side, heading north, a boulevard that runs some twelve miles. Underneath us was the subway, the intersection of the east–west and north–south junctions. Tens of thousands of young festival-goers would emerge from this vast subterranean world to be greeted by an angry mob.

I watched Arin try to stifle a yawn. I put my hand on her shoulder as we crossed Fifteenth into Love Park. The pop-up beer garden was getting ready to open for the day. Kiosks lined the perimeter, and artists, hoping for a Labor Day weekend surge, had their wares on display. The city would be boot them out Saturday afternoon to be replaced by three thousand white supremacists.

Cat stopped cold. Her head swiveled, taking in the details.

"Buck, this is a nightmare. With Love Park filled with white supremacists, this place is a natural bottleneck." She surveyed the area some more. "Hundreds of people per minute could cross through to the Festival. Cut this off, and you have a narrow, V-shaped path, an invitation for confrontation. The judge must have been nuts to allow this here."

"I'm sure they will address it at the task force meeting." Buck and Cat drifted into the plaza, stopping briefly in front of the LOVE sculpture. The L sat atop the V, the O laid on its side over the E, a bit off-kilter, like love itself. As usual, a long line of people waited their turn to take selfies.

Buck tilted his head upward. "Love. Good luck with that."

Cat gave a fist-bump to his shoulder.

"Come on, soldier. We never give up on love." She scanned the surrounds. "Or preparation," she added. She pointed to the kids dodging the water that shot up from the ground, screaming in delight as the cool spray played over and under them. "We're here for them."

We continued down the Parkway, Swann Fountain just in front of us, its multiple streams of water dancing high, the art museum visible in the distance. I eyed the café across from the Cathedral Basilica of Saints Peter and Paul, where I had served as an altar boy occasionally.

"I'm starving," I said, pointing to Sister Cities Park and Café.

No one objected, so we crossed to this little oasis; brightly colored Adirondack chairs dotted the grounds, kids splashing around in a pond, and sculptures, both serious and fanciful. Tables with a rainbow of colored umbrellas invited us to sit down. Cat stopped cold in front of a bench, one of dozens along the Parkway. Her body went rigid and shook. Her hands flew to her face as she pivoted and walked away. Buck caught up with her and gently put his hands on her shoulders.

"I got you, Nine. I got you."

Cat stood, face covered, for a minute or more. Her hands dropped in slow motion, head lifting to take in Buck, then turning to see Arin and me standing two feet off her shoulder.

"I slept there for three weeks," she said, pointing to the bench. "I wasn't thinking about it until now. It sent my mind back to Iraq."

"The explosion?" Arin asked.

"No." Cat's right arm trembled. "The time I watched Sally Jenkins's face get blown off."

Cat insisted she was OK but the tension in her jaw told another story. She rolled her shoulders, took deep, slow breaths, and then walked into the café and ordered a tuna panini.

We took our food to an outside table. Buck had ordered a cheese steak and the smell of fried onions was driving me crazy. Clouds were forming overhead. Cat took a few slow breaths through her nose. "The humidity is climbing."

"It's supposed to rain tonight, remnants from hurricane Ida. New York and New England have flood warnings," Buck said.

Arin yawned.

"Don't do that to me," I said, struggling to suppress a yawn of my own. I couldn't believe Arin and I had just returned from Scotland hours ago. I bit into my Italian hoagie, olive oil running down my hand, and I felt a small surge of energy as the spices and meats and cheeses collided in my mouth.

Cat was still clearly struggling to shake off the traumatic memory.

"Arin, distract me. Tell me more about Martin and Frederick in Ireland." She was staring at her food, having a hard time making eye contact.

Arin laid her sandwich on the tray and took a sip of her ginger beer.

"Try to imagine what Frederick Douglass was thinking, experiencing." Arin took another sip and continued. "He was twenty-seven years old. Welts on his back from the whip. He's only had a few years of freedom, and not the freedom we take for granted. Douglass knows that if the bounty hunters found him, he would cease to exist. He had a first-class ticket on the ship across the Atlantic, but the wealthy whites in first class raised hell, threatened to throw him overboard. They forced him to stay in steerage. Martin Fahey had assured him he would be welcomed in Ireland, if not on the ship that took him there."

Arin paused. Cat had hardly touched her tuna panini. Her head lifted. She moved her hand close to Arin.

"Please, I need to know more."

"Me too," Buck chimed in. "I can't believe I need a Jamaican princess to teach me American history."

"I'm not sure any princess could teach you anything." Arin tapped Buck's skull with her knuckles. "It's pretty thick."

"Set me up with one of your fine Jamaican friends and we'll find out."

"I love my country, can't do that to my people." Arin covered her mouth as she laughed.

The three of us had spent a lot of time together during Covid. Arin and Buck had become best buds. He would take a bullet for Arin. We all would for each other.

Cat watched the exchange. She broke off a chunk of bread from her sandwich and rolled it into a ball as a long sigh escaped her. I recognized that sound of loneliness. I knew she roamed in the world of the needy; of moments that few could comprehend. It wasn't just that her eyes had seen things that no one should; I sensed that her soul had shattered in places she was uncertain could be repaired. She carried the burden of other lives. Cat had taken the oath to "protect from enemies, both foreign and domestic." She had almost died fighting the foreign. Now the domestic had become the greater threat.

The George Floyd protests took place all around the Parkway. How would I explain George Floyd to Frederick Douglass? I'd be embarrassed. "Good sir, we had a Black president, but we seem to be stuck. And three thousand people will arrive in a few days who hate you simply because you are Black.

I felt something touch my shoulder.

"You look worse than me," Cat said.

I had met Cat only a few hours ago, so I didn't really know her. But I knew the rollercoaster ride of ancestral memory. You had zero control. The memories came and went as they pleased, sometimes so real that you couldn't separate them from your own reality.

"You are writing everything down?" I laid my hoagie on the paper plate.

"Yeah, Dr. Garcia stressed that." Cat drank some of her iced coffee. "It's like PTSD therapy. I keep a journal. Every time, you know, I write it down, kind of training the brain to remember that it's an event from the past. Otherwise, my nervous system thinks it's happening in real time."

Cat reached back to her ponytail and removed the band, her black hair falling free.

"I like it like that," Arin commented.

"Thanks. Hey, we cut you off. Tell us more."

"OK, but then it's your turn. We need to hear every detail from your memories."

I felt a few drops of rain. That was it. No more. Arin wiped a drop from her forehead.

"Douglass was only supposed to be in Ireland for a few days to promote his book. He remained for four months. It was life changing." Arin lifted her cell phone. "I want you all to hear his words. He wrote this as he was about to depart for Scotland. It's a letter to William Lloyd Garrison, his friend and mentor. Garrison was the leading U.S. abolitionist of his time. Douglass wrote it on New Year's Day, 1846."

Buck was listening as intently as Cat. I always joked that he reminded me of Wesley Snipes as the character Blade. He's assured me I'm a twin of Ronald McDonald. Today, he was less an action hero and more a university student, Arin his professor.

Arin found what she was looking for and read out the passage: "'I can truly say, I have spent some of the happiest moments of my life since landing in this country. I seem to have undergone a transformation. I live a new life. The warm and generous cooperation extended to me by the friends of my despised race, the prompt and liberal manner with which the press has rendered me its aid, the glorious enthusiasm with which thousands have flocked to hear the cruel wrongs of my down-trodden and long-enslaved fellow countrymen portrayed, the deep sympathy for the slave, and the strong abhorrence of the slaveholder everywhere evinced—the cordiality with which members and ministers of various religious bodies, and of various shades of religious opinion, have embraced me and lent me their aid—the kind hospitality constantly proffered to me by persons of the highest rank in society—the spirit of freedom that seems to animate all with whom I come in contact—and the entire absence of everything that looked like prejudice against me on account of the color of my skin—contrasted so strongly with my long and bitter experience in the United States, that I look with wonder and amazement on the transition.'"

Arin lowered the phone. "He closed the letter with one of the most moving testimonials of transformation in history." She recited from memory:

"'Instead of the bright blue sky of America, I am covered with the soft grey fog of the Emerald Isle. I breathe, and lo! the chattel becomes a man.'"

Cat was biting her lip. A tear rolled over her cheek and dropped to the table.

"What's up?" asked Buck.

Cat wiped her cheek with her sleeve. Her lips trembled as she tried to find the words.

"My great-great-grandfather was a big part of his journey.

I'm so proud to be from him. And now these racist assholes want to come to Philly and chant their hate."

"Some shit don't change, Cat." Buck had more defeat in his voice than I had witnessed before.

The sun was shining from the south, but clouds were gathering north of the city. A soft summer shower or a storm?

"Come on, Grandpa Fahey. Tell me what to do." She beckoned to the heavens.

We all followed her upward gaze, a communal moment of quiet, perhaps each of us having a silent conversation with a lost loved one.

Buck's phone buzzed. He read the screen then stood.

"The forecast has changed. Heavy wind and rain a little later. They have moved the task force meeting up." He took out his ID pack and slid the lanyard over his head, his photo and credentials visible in the clear plastic pocket. "Let's go."

CHAPTER 6

WEDNESDAY, SEPTEMBER 1, 2021.
EAKINS OVAL, PHILADELPHIA

The police had set up a large white event tent in front of the George Washington statue at Eakins Oval, the temporary control center for law enforcement and Homeland Security on the grounds of the Festival. A security perimeter of fences and a half dozen police kept those without credentials from entering. Deputy Commissioner Cruz intercepted us.

"Wait here for a few minutes. You're not cleared for this discussion. I'll signal you when it's OK to come in."

Buck and Cat had their hands on their hips and shook their heads simultaneously. Warriors hate to be sidelined.

"Cat, re-enact what you saw," I said. "Where was the guy standing when he pointed his fingers?"

We followed her to the far side of the Washington statue, facing the Philadelphia Museum of Art and the Rocky Steps that Sylvester Stalone's character made famous. The main stage for the Festival blocked a view of the steps. It was huge, miraculous. It didn't exist a few days ago. Massive columns of lights and sound systems appeared by virtue of engineers and muscle and hundreds of thousands of dollars.

Cat stepped forward.

"He was lined up about here, middle of the statue." Cat raised her arms, index fingers extended, pointing to the corners of the museum. She froze in place, closed her eyes, and began lowering her left arm. She twisted her body slowly so that her left arm pointed south-west, slightly behind her. Her right arm lowered until it was pointing, not at the museum, but to the north-west.

"Shit." She dropped her arms. "Buck, you need to get us in that meeting, now."

Buck led the four of us around the statue. Approximately fifteen people were in the tent. Cruz noted us and put his hand up for us to wait. Cat ignored him, strutted, shoulders back, chest out. Heads turned toward her.

"I told you to wait." Cruz was on his feet and pointed his finger an inch from Buck's chest. He took a quick glance at Commissioner Thompson. I saw her slight nod. "Detective McCoy, this better be important."

Cat eyed someone in the tent and signaled for him to come over. Blue suit, brown shoes, white shirt, no tie, trimmed brown beard, and styled hair. He looked like a movie star about to shoot a Rolex commercial.

"This is my boss, Scott Morrison," Cat said. "Best damned operator I ever worked with. Scott heads security for the museum."

Scott did not look happy to see us. Cat paid no attention.

"Is the video of Boland and Walsh available?"

Morrison leaned close to her, but I could still hear his words.

"This is the big leagues. Don't fuck this up, Cat."

As he walked to the table with the computers he said, "Ladies and Gentlemen, Marine Captain Cat Fahey, believes she has some intel for us. It has been my experience in the field that when she talks it's always advisable to listen. Sorry for the intrusion."

"Listen up, everyone." Commissioner Thompson stood, removing her hat. "The Pentagon has recalled Captain Fahey to active duty. I just want to set the record straight."

I noted the look of surprise from Morrison. He sat in front of his computer and brought the video onto the screen.

"The security camera is on the south side, midway up the steps. You will see Walsh with his back to us, looking across the street to Boland."

The video advanced. As Cat had described, Boland found his spot in front of the Washington statue and raised his arms, index fingers seeming to point to the corners of the art museum. Walsh gave a thumbs-up as Boland's arms dropped to his sides.

"OK," Morrison said, "what do you think we are looking at?"

Cat walked hurriedly around the table and stood next to the TV, dragging me with her.

"Key," she said, putting me on the spot in front of this elite group of security professionals. My throat dried. I felt a bit dizzy. But they looked at me as they had looked at Cat. With hope.

"They were marking a spot on the corners of the museum where they could create havoc. After all of the mass shootings in this country, it won't take much to send sixty thousand people stampeding toward the exit. How many will die?" I shrugged my shoulders, tried to clear my head. "But I have a feeling that Captain Fahey has a different idea."

"Please rerun the video," Cat requested. Morrison complied. I watched Cat closely and saw the expression on her face as it advanced.

"Slow it down by fifty percent." Cat copied the movement on the screen, arms rising, fingers extended, pausing at the top of the movement and then a quicker descent, left arm back, finger now pointing toward the skateboard park across the street. Her right arm moved at a diagonal, now running toward Pennsylvania Avenue. Her arms dropped in front of her. She followed the movement on the screen as Boland's fingers pointed down to his feet. Walsh copied him, then Walsh did a thumbs-up. None of us but Cat had seen that quick change of direction. "Two index fingers, side by side, pointing down. It's the call sign of the UAB, the United Aryan Brotherhood." Cat stared at the frozen screen for a moment. "The two fingers down signifies burning the system to the ground. It also makes the number 11, as in 9/11."

"We all know this," Agent Williams responded.

Cat stood quietly then looked downward. I followed her gaze: just grass and dirt to me. Something else was there to her, though.

"We are sitting on top of a freight train tunnel that starts by the river and exits about a quarter mile away on Pennsylvania Avenue."

A blonde woman with the initials DHS emblazoned on her jacket stood.

"Captain Fahey, there will be no trains during the Festival."

"When was the last time you checked the tunnel?"

The DHS agent lifted her clipboard.

"Yesterday. It's due for inspection tomorrow. The police will lock it down until after the Festival." She stood quietly, then nodded to agents Williams and Di Stefano. They lifted their phones. "We have a team running security checks inside the museum. They will head to the tunnel. Commissioner Thompson, can you direct your K-9 squad to have a look?"

The people in the tent were in various states of disrepair; a few staring into the distance, some leaning into each other, conferring, while others punched keys on their computers.

The safety of sixty thousand festival-goers and the life of one Vice President rested on their shoulders. Some thirty minutes had passed. All of them were now taking calls, making calls, texting. The four of us watched their faces, looking for any sign that something might have changed.

"Good job, Nine," Buck said. Arin and I nodded our agreement. Her face relaxed a bit, making room for a momentary blush on her cheeks.

I caught a shift in Agent Di Stefano's body language. His right elbow was dropped to his knee, phone to his ear, left hand rubbing his forehead. He stood.

"Attention, please. Three known white supremacists just entered Love Park. They are taking photos and videos. A scouting party."

"That's not unexpected," said Commissioner Thompson.

The blonde DHS Agent answered her phone, all eyes on her. Cat read the look. So did I.

She disconnected, pressed some buttons, and said to Di Stefano, "Just sent you an email. Put the image on the screen. What you are about to see wasn't there when we examined the tunnel yesterday. We need to know how and when this happened."

A moment later, we saw swastikas spray-painted on the tunnel wall, the outline of a cross. There, where a head might be on a crucifix, was a photo of the Vice President of the United States, one bullet hole in the middle of her forehead.

No one made a sound, the image too horrific not to stare. I filled the void.

"It's too easy. The bad guys are toying with you. They are playing a game," I said.

"And you are, again?" Agent Williams asked. I had wondered if he would start up.

"You know who I am. All of you do. I don't have your skills, Agent Williams …" I let that linger for a moment. "And you don't have mine or Captain Fahey's."

Cat wobbled next to me. I put my arm around her shoulder to steady her. Buck rushed over with a chair and we settled her into it. Her eyes were fixed nowhere, seemingly vacant, and then they closed as she leaned forward, her arms on her thighs. She began to tilt to her left. Buck kept her from falling. She grunted, then threw her arms over her head protectively.

Finally, her body relaxed. Cat tried to shake it off and pulled in some deep breaths.

"Well, that's embarrassing. Now you all think I'm a PTSD nut-job."

The blonde Homeland Security agent stood.

"Just the opposite. We are lucky to have you here. You identified Boland and Walsh and led us to the tunnel." She examined her colleagues. "I understand if someone is skeptical, but Captain Fahey is on a roll and we're rolling with her. Clear?"

All heads turned to the DHS agent. I caught sight of Williams and the astonished look on his face. He slowly rotated toward Cat, then back to the DHS Agent. The thin line of his lips was replaced with his mouth opening, lips parted, not quite a smile, more of a "What the hell" look on his face. He caught my stare and gave me a quick, subtle nod. A convert, perhaps?

"Please, Captain, tell us what you witnessed in your ancestral memory just now. Maybe it will help us," the DHS agent requested.

They leaned in, all of them, even Williams.

Cat gave them an overview of the story: Martin Fahey, Frederick Douglass, and Daniel O'Connell. They looked mesmerized, their attention complete, spellbound by this woman, her *Semper Fi* necklace dangling from her neck.

"What I just now experienced was unclear." Cat winced. "All I could tell was that Martin was on the ground, being kicked by several men. Then I heard a man say, 'We gonna kill us that n—.'" Cat paused. "The N-word. 'May as well kill some Irish scum while we're at it.'"

A booming thunderclap caused all of us to jump. Rain pelted the tent The DHS agent recovered to answer her phone.

"Explosive residue was found, but no explosives, no prints, no tracks, nothing." Rain hit the roof of the tent, making it hard to hear. "It's just a little rain, folks. We're not supposed to get much. Let's get back to our offices and stay on this. I want a video conference call at seven: police, FBI, Secret Service."

The DHS agent came over to us—blonde hair, braided into a ponytail, black jeans, charcoal-grey polo under a DHS windbreaker. And a huge smile.

"I'm Special Agent in Charge, Noreen Casey. Hello, Dr. Murphy."

Arin gave her a fist-bump.

"Key," the special agent continued, "when we are on the other side of this, I want to grab a Guinness and hear the parts of the story that aren't on TV." She placed her attention on Cat. "It's an honor, Captain. I've heard all about you from Agent Di Stefano." She looked out at the darkening sky. "I think you all should rest up tonight."

She peered over her shoulder to see Buck talking to Deputy Commissioner Cruz.

"I'll call Detective Mc Coy in the morning to give you an update."

We stood quietly as the DHS Agent walked away, only to be replaced by FBI Agent Di Stefano.

"I need a few minutes of your time. Let's wait for Buck."

The rain had stopped and the tent was quickly emptying. Di Stefano took a call and I arranged five chairs in a circle. I caught Buck's eye and made a gesture for him to join us. We sat, Buck grabbing a chair next to me a minute later.

Di Stefano took a seat and looked squarely at Cat.

"My fiancée served under you."

Cat's eyes widened in surprise.

"Maria Villanueva," the agent revealed. "She frequently tells me I wouldn't have her as a fiancée if it weren't for you. You saved her life. Thanks, Captain."

Cat let out a deep breath and I suspected she exhaled the memory of whatever battle that was. One of way too many.

"And all of that drama earlier with you and Williams?" I asked.

"He's one of the best you'll ever meet, but he's wound up too tight. I'll keep him on good behavior." Di Stefano brushed his hands together several times as if removing some dirt. "I'm hoping that we can dispense with formalities. I'm Joe. Baptized Giuseppe, but what kid in America would use that name? All good with first names?"

We nodded in unison.

"Everyone on the task force is part of a bureaucracy. We take orders, even when every instinct tells us they are wrong. That includes you, Buck. You three," he said, pointing at Cat, Arin, and me, "are the only ones outside of the box. I need you to *stay* out of the box. Do not accept any group-think at these meetings. Everyone here is trying their hardest, but we can overlook things because of bureaucratic thinking. We need your skills."

"Hold on, Joe," Cat objected. "We've got no authority."

"You have a lot more than you think. The Secretary of Homeland Security made that clear. You have a direct connection to me, twenty-four seven. All of you."

"I…" My hands went to my knees. I looked through the open flap, the bronze statue of Washington on his horse, the Native American in repose, looking over the land, his eyes meeting mine, it seemed. "I'm missing something. You have the full resources of Homeland Security at your fingertips. I mean, maybe we get lucky and pick up something you missed, but come on, Joe, there is nothing you can't throw at

…" My eyes forced shut. I looked around the now empty tent, then directly at Di Stefano. "OK, got it, there is a traitor in your midst. Am I right?"

Everyone shuffled noisily in their seat, breath held.

"I'm in the bureaucracy. I cannot confirm or deny. And you won't like what I tell you next," Di Stefano stated.

"I've grown used to not liking what comes next." I slid forward and felt my shoulders tighten, the thought of the blade nearing my throat.

Di Stefano looked me dead in the eye. I met his gaze as I felt a headache coming on.

"The dark money coming into right-wing extremist groups is unlike anything we've ever seen," Di Stefano started. "Someone, plural, possibly a nation state or states, has been running disinformation campaigns. They rile up the right, the left, and minority groups. They sow division and fear. I'm not telling you anything you haven't heard in the news. I am telling you it is vast, extremely well-funded, and designed to tear this country apart. And it's succeeding."

Di Stefano turned to Buck.

"Buck, you're in narcotics. What are you seeing?"

"It's a nightmare. The increase in drug traffic is off the charts."

"What else is off the charts here in Philly?"

Buck didn't need long for that answer.

"Gun violence. Homicides."

"How many candidates are in the Police Academy right now?"

Buck shook his head, folded his arms.

"Zero. And we are down about seven hundred officers." He slapped his legs. "No one wants to be a cop anymore."

"And you think that's coincidental? You think that's just because of the Defund the Police movement?"

"I'd argue it's the reaction to police brutality. George Floyd," Arin said with passion.

"That's true, Arin. And then, slowly, meticulously, those situations are manipulated to create chaos. Why do you think there's a new video showing police brutality every other day? Some of it's organic: dumb racist cops doing something stupid. The others are intentional. How many cops and vets were involved in the Capitol Riots? Their ranks are growing." A sudden gust of wind blew through the tent. Di Stefano paused, peered out of the tent, clouds gathering. "For every person horrified by those videos, there is an equal or greater number cheering them on," he concluded.

"You are right," said Cat. "I don't like what you are telling us."

"It gets worse. Who benefits? Drug cartels? Gun manufacturers? They are just pawns being moved around the board. Covid happens and they get us fighting over a mask and a vaccine. Brilliant. The pandemic is just one more event for them to manipulate. The January Six Capitol attack, same thing. The goal is chaos."

"Sow chaos," Cat said, "then promise that your candidate, your party, will save you from the very chaos they helped create. It's the autocratic playbook, taught to us in officer training school, so we know the signs in other countries. Now it's in our own country."

Di Stefano acknowledged Cat's statement with a nod.

"Let me be clear," he continued. "To start a fire, you need kindling. There is more kindling on the right. If it were on the left, they would use the left. All the higher power cares about is starting the fire." Di Stefano looked around the empty tent. Another gust of wind blew one of the flaps open, Cat's hair caught by the breeze.

"Our country is on the precipice. The social fabric is tearing. They are looking for a moment, an event horizon, to push it fully over the edge. This Saturday may be the event." Di Stefano splayed his fingers, and they were pointed at us. "We need to make certain that it's not."

I scanned the faces sitting in our little circle. No one moved, eyes cast to the ground. I pictured the statue of George Washington hovering over us just outside the tent.

"Who are they?" Arin broke the silence. "China, Russia?"

"I'm just a bureaucrat." The FBI agent shrugged. "I cannot confirm or deny. I can tell you that a name has surfaced that may interest you."

It was Arin and me he was talking to.

"Rabbit."

CHAPTER 7

I was out of my chair, walking in circles, neurons in my brain racing and colliding, trying to piece together what I had just heard. Arin's hands had covered her face. Buck had stood, looking at me. Cat was clueless, and it showed.

"How did you associate that name with us?" I asked.

"Do you think we would have allowed you anywhere near this tent if we hadn't put a microscope up your ..." Di Stefano looked at Buck. "Fact is you had Rabbit in your file about the drug bust two years ago. You also mentioned him in relation to what happened to Key and Arin in Jamaica."

Di Stefano leaned back in his chair, a study in calmness in the face of chaos.

"Take me through it."

Arin's breathing had grown heavy. She wore the humiliation of what had happened on her face.

"I can't do this. You talk." She hurried to the other side of the tent.

I wanted to comfort her, but I focused on Di Stefano instead.

"We were on a press tour following our event in Dublin. Jamaica was the last stop, just a few days before Christmas. Arin was, and remains, Jamaica's favorite daughter. There were TV cameras and people everywhere. When we exited the airport terminal, they shot me. Flesh wound." My mind spun with the images, the fear that the attack was meant for Arin. "An hour later I received a text that read, 'If we wanted you dead, you'd be dead.'"

I took my chair and spun it so that the back of it faced Agent Di Stefano. I sat, my arms folded over the back of the chair. The tent darkened, the sun hiding behind a cloud. Rain pattered on the canvas roof and then stopped as abruptly as it came.

"I read the text to the crowd and the international press at an event for us in Kingston. I intentionally said to the TV audience and the thousands of Jamaicans in the park, that Arin and I were going to find these people and kick their ass. I got the response I thought I would get. The text came a second later saying 'Good luck,' followed by …" I caught Buck's eye; he knew what was coming next and offered a slight nod. "'You wouldn't want Arin ending up like Tanya.'"

"Holy shit," Cat let out. "Your sister Tanya?" she asked Buck.

Buck nodded, everything about him tight, knotted. He was tough as nails until someone mentioned his sister. Tanya was my best friend, my little sister. Dead from an overdose. Whoever sent that message was part of the drug ring that got her addicted and laced some deadly fentanyl into the heroin. We had busted the underlings, but as usual the top of the food chain was so well hidden and impenetrable that we were left without closure. But we learned one name. One very well hidden and protected name: Rabbit.

"You undoubtedly know that Arin and her family are very

wealthy and her brother Joseph runs the businesses," I said to Di Stefano.

"Of course," he acknowledged.

"Arin's mom, Joyce Murphy, said something inadvertently that alarmed Arin. We had confronted her brother and mother. Joseph had hired someone to steal the cover of the *Book of Kells* from us. He finally admitted that he contacted someone who controlled the Caribbean underworld, meaning Toronto to Jamaica and all points between, including Queens. The name he gave was Rabbit."

Cat studied me. "It gets worse, doesn't it?"

I didn't answer directly.

"It turns out that Joyce was the one who had me shot."

"What the fuck?" Cat's gaze traveled from me to Arin.

"She said it was supposed to be a near miss or just a nick. She did it to make us heroes. The media would forget us in a week, she said, but not if we were near martyrs." I licked my lips, my throat parched. "She had arranged it with Rabbit, or, more likely, his people. And when she arrived home that night, when she got out of the car, she was shot too, a flesh wound to her thigh. A text came in on her phone, the same words: 'If we wanted you dead, you'd be dead.'"

Buck was standing behind me, his hands on my shoulders. Cat was immobile, her eyes open but vacant. She snapped out of it, took one look at Arin, and started to her. I grabbed her arm and shook my head.

"Give her a minute. She'll be OK."

Di Stefano leaned back in his chair, expression neutral, as if he heard this kind of crazy stuff daily, and he likely did.

"How did they make contact?" Di Stefano asked.

"Text. It's encrypted," Buck answered. "We've tried to break it every which way. They've never seen him, never spoken to him, and we can't find a trace." Buck sat in the empty chair behind me. The wind had picked up. "It's your turn, Joe."

"Twice," he responded. "His name has surfaced twice. Someone got sloppy. In both cases it referenced him and wire transfers. Agent Williams is trying to run it down, but nothing yet. Just be aware that his name might surface in this mess that we are in."

"I hope so," Buck said, tapping the metal seat of his folding chair, "I owe him a bullet."

Scott Morrison, Director of Security at the museum, rushed into the tent. He gave a slight wave to Agent Di Stefano.

"Cat, I want you to come to the tunnel, get your take on something."

Cat gestured to the three of us.

"The Detective can come," Morrison responded. "He has military experience."

"No can do, Scott. It's all of us or nothing," Cat answered.

"Bullshit, let's go." Morrison started.

"There's a problem. I've been ordered not to let any of them out of my sight. All or nothing, as Cat said." Buck, hands on his hips, his "Don't mess with me" demeanor as clear as a digital billboard.

"Whatever. Agent Di Stefano, you should join us."

"I have to get back. Fill me in at the task force meeting."

"You'll want to see this first-hand." Morrison took off briskly, aiming toward the crosswalk that would take us to the skateboard park and the train tunnel. Traffic was zooming by; motorcycles, engines gunning. Cars and double-decker tourist buses, the brave travelers risking a downpour. In two days, the road would be closed for the Made in the USA Festival.

Buck took Cat by the arm.

"You like this guy Morrison?"

"He's a prick most of the time. I don't think he even knows it. He got me the job, got me off the streets. So yeah, I love him when I'm not thinking of kicking him in the balls. He's a great operator, Buck. A lone wolf, pain in the ass, security genius."

We took the stairway into the skateboard park, past graffitied cantilever walls and a dozen young people in various states of flight and free-fall.

Morrison stopped at a gate, the tunnel just ten feet ahead, an officer on guard. He wore tactical gear, with an M4 slung over his chest. He fist-bumped Buck and glanced at our ID tags. A generator buzzed at the entrance; long cords ran from it, high intensity lamps lighting the graffiti-covered walls and arched ceilings. We passed two forensic officers examining the area around them. The smell of human piss, animal droppings, and other matter that rotted, combined in a pungent attack on my sense of smell. We walked for about two hundred yards toward the sound of voices a hundred feet ahead.

FBI agents huddled in front of the swastikas.

The scene was surreal—the photo of the VP, bullet hole dead center forehead.

"That's an actual bullet hole. We've examined the residue," one agent informed Di Stefano.

"A little farther." Morrison moved on. He stopped thirty yards beyond the swastikas. There was no direct light, just the glow from the tableau. He took a flashlight from his back pocket and ran the light over what was now clearly a door jamb. No hinges were visible. No door knob.

"There's a three-inch-thick metal door on the other side of this. This side swings out, the metal door swings in." He pointed the light to the ground. "We found scuff marks from the opening of this door, same on the inside. No fingerprints, no footprints, nothing. The tunnel on the other side runs under the steps and into the museum. It's unused. It's only the second time I've been down here."

"What was its purpose?" Buck asked.

"The blueprints say emergency exit. Almost no one knows it's here." Morrison put the flashlight in his back pocket. "Think on it." Morrison headed back the way we came, still talking. "It's likely they came in through the museum somehow. I have it secured on the other side. We set a camera and motion detectors on it."

"That's it? You brought us down here to see a door frame," I hollered to him.

He stopped but didn't turn.

"I didn't bring you down for anything. I brought Cat down. She'll figure out why. Give her a minute."

We looked at each other in the ghostly light. Agent Di Stefano shook his head, bewildered as us, I assumed, and headed back toward the swastikas. I reached my hand to his shoulder and tilted my head toward Cat.

"You should stay for this."

Cat leaned against the wall, put one foot up behind her, her knee jutted forward, her hand tapping it. She dropped her leg and stood ramrod straight.

"Buck, do you remember the team of operators that called themselves the Dead Center Squad?"

"Not ringing a bell."

"There were maybe three, five, guys. They were a kill squad. Whoever their target was, they would put a bullet through their photo, dead center, just like with the VP. And they never left a trace."

The chill that ran through me had nothing to do with the cold air of the underground tunnel.

CHAPTER 8

"We are securing the area for the night. Start making your way out." A police officer waved his flashlight, the tunnel walls bouncing with the light.

"Give us five," Di Stefano said.

"Sorry, sir, I was told to clear the tunnel."

Buck stepped over to the cop and showed his badge, said a few words I couldn't hear. The young officer took a step back. Buck opened the flashlight on his phone and aimed it at the door jamb.

We stood close in the dark tunnel, the light from Buck's phone making the five of us look ghoulish. It seems that whoever put the crucifix in the tunnel came through these doors.

"What are you thinking, Joe?" I asked.

"Between us," Di Stefano asked.

"Between us," I affirmed.

"I'm thinking of wringing Morrison's neck. This breach should have been reported to me immediately." Di Stefano turned to the police officer. "Tell your superior to bring lights here, now. This is an FBI Crime Scene."

Di Stefano looked at his phone. "Let's go. I have zero connection. Secret Service will shit a brick when they hear about this."

I was glad to get home. I needed time to think and process the day. I needed food. And a cold beer. Arin looked wrung out. I yawned and rubbed my temples. The sky was getting darker; lightning pulsed white against the sky. I called in a delivery order to a great Italian place close to home.

I sat alone in the kitchen. Cat, Buck and Arin went to freshen up before dinner. I frequently cleared my mind by thinking about anything other than the problem at hand. Sitting at the island counter, I let my eyes roam the space: white cabinets, black marble countertops, brushed nickel appliances with accents of red. My eyes landed on an array of photos. It was my mother's shrine to me; a photo journal of my various stages of supposed genius as a kid. Blue Ribbons dangled on my chest in every photo. I had been the Archdiocese of Philadelphia math champ in fifth grade, beating the high school wiz kids. I was the All-State Chess Champ in seventh and eighth grade. Every onset of brilliance was short lived. It flamed out in one to three years. I didn't mind it as a kid, something exciting always replaced it. It wasn't until my teens that I realized that I was a freak of nature and often the butt of jokes.

Dr. Garcia had informed me that the mutated gene created these 'genius' episodes, culminating in my ancestral memories. I could do with a dose of genius right now.

· · ·

I put the food out, an Italian feast of antipasti, salad, pasta, grilled branzino, and saltimbocca. Buck set the table and Arin opened a Chardonnay and a Barolo. I opened a beer.

"I need to start with an ice-cold."

"I'll take a little if you don't mind." Cat tilted her glass. "The red wine looks good after this."

Arin poured some white. Buck poured red. Arin lifted her glass.

"If the world is going to hell on Saturday, we may as well prepare in style. And big-up, Cat. You were amazing today."

It was great to see Arin come back to life after the gut check from earlier. She'd made strides with her mother, but it had been hard for them to see each other during the lockdowns. They still had repairing to do.

Di Stefano told us he would report the Dead Center Squad to Homeland Security. Cat didn't know the individuals; she had only heard of them. Buck said hundreds of little military squads gave themselves names, just for the hell of it. Nothing official, nothing written.

I let the first sip of beer hit the back of my dry throat and savored the relief. I opened the aluminum foil covering the branzino. Steam billowed and the scent of grilled fish made me happy to dig in.

Food was passed. Forks got busy.

"Are things as bad as Di Stefano made them sound?" I asked Buck.

"He gave you the rosy version." Buck wiped his face with his napkin as some juices from the chicken ran down his chin. "I'm on the task force with the DEA, FBI, and ATF. Alcohol, Tobacco, and Firearms, Arin."

"I'm familiar," Arin responded.

Buck spooned some pasta onto his plate.

"We have seen a dramatic change in distribution over the past eighteen months. Guns used to be an amateur free-for-all. We'd see two, maybe five at a time. Now it's more like the arms deals you see in the movies. Twenty-five, one hundred guns at a time. Mostly heading to Black and Hispanic gangs." Buck took a stab of pasta, let it play in his mouth for a moment, then followed it with some wine. "There had been peaceful coexistence. Then trouble started. Rumors, provocations, all deliberate to get them fighting, killing. In other words, a disinformation campaign designed to sow chaos."

"Same thing Di Stefano was talking about." Cat put her fork down. "We saw it in Iraq among Shia and Sunni communities that had lived peacefully together. Peace doesn't make money."

Buck sipped some wine, swallowed, then shook his head. "A few months ago, a Black minister, a Hispanic minister, and a white Catholic priest started an inter-faith group to intervene, bring them together. The Black minister was shot in the church parking lot. The Hispanic minister was knifed to death walking his dog at night, and the priest disappeared, abducted." Buck pushed his food around his plate. "Want to know the kicker?'

"Witnesses identified the attacker as white?" Arin waited for Buck's response.

"You heard about it in the news or just a guess?" Buck asked Arin.

"Educated guess." Arin swirled the Chardonnay in her glass. "Get Black and Hispanic folk killing themselves and each other, sit back and enjoy the show." She sipped her wine. "Divide and conquer. It's the oldest story. Only now it travels at the speed of a tweet."

"Wait a minute. Are you seriously saying this is all part of a right-wing plot?" They looked at me as if I was a slow learner. I was beginning to wonder.

"Of course," Buck answered. "But the money, the cyber disinformation, possibly even the command structure, might come from Moscow or Beijing. That's what Di Stefano was pointing to."

"And the threat against the Vice President?"

"Secret Service will do everything to get her to cancel," Arin said while scooping tiramisu from the container. "But once she sees the photo with the bullet through her head, she'll never cancel."

I tried to steal a bite of tiramisu from her plate but she batted my fork away. Instead, she lifted a helping on her fork and fed it to me. The inviting aroma of vanilla and coffee lingered. I licked my lips and she fed me one more bite.

"Why?" I asked. "Why won't she cancel?"

"She's a politician. She'll want it on every channel. Remember what my mother said? Being a near martyr will make you a legend. Too much truth in that."

"I don't want to be a martyr," Cat stated. "Frederick Douglass said that to Martin." Cat rubbed her eyes with her thumb and forefinger, pushed herself off the stool, grabbed her wine and drained the glass in a gulp. She left the kitchen. A few moments passed and the sound of her harmonica filled the house. This time, it sounded country-ish, like something you'd hear on a truck commercial. It was urgent, like a train heading right at you. Then it stopped abruptly, notes dangling mid-air.

Cat returned, took her seat, and continued as if she had never left the table.

"'I don't want to be a martyr. God willing never, but at least not yet, Martin. For a martyr to cause change, they must slay him when he has reached the mountaintop. I have barely ascended the base. As you have insisted, we will go to England and Ireland, and from there I will resume my climb.'"

Cat's hands went upward, as if to the mountaintop, while Arin soaked up the revelations.

"'Then we shall go, Frederick, for you'll never plough a field by turning it over in your mind.'" Her voice had softened.

I thought of my own struggle to reconcile my bizarre ancestral memories, though a bit of envy crept into my veins. I longed for new adventures with Aedan.

"That memory has repeated a few times. I see nothing. Just hear those words." Cat ran her fingers through her hair.

I noticed for the first time that she had dimples when she frowned, and her green eyes oddly brightened. Her lips pulled to the right when she experienced stress.

"I know there's something." Cat tapped her head. "Some clue, a freaking warning buried in here somewhere. How the hell do I get it to come out, Key?"

"It either will or it won't, Cat. Either way, your skills got us here so far. And I won't be of any help unless I get some sleep."

"Me too," Arin added.

Cat put her hand on Arin's.

"It's strange. I've spent so much time watching videos of you and Key, feel like I've known you a long time."

Cat removed her hand from Arin's.

"Tell me one more story about Frederick before you go," she said, barely above a whisper.

Arin seemed to consider for a moment, her head tilted toward the ceiling, as if the inspiration would beam down to her.

"Douglass had become fast friends with an Irish priest, Theobald Mathew, known as 'The Apostle of Temperance.' Mathew had converted tens of thousands of Irish to give up drinking and take a sobriety pledge. Douglass was fervently against alcohol. He had seen first-hand the slaveholders ply his people into drunken submission."

I saw a look of anger flash across Buck's face: Tanya, her addiction, her death, and the rip in the fabric of his spirit.

"Same shit," Buck's eyes lost focus, "different century. I deal with it every day."

Buck has been shifting, slipping, losing his grip. And Cat? How did she not just say, 'I'm done, I've given enough'?

I took Buck by the shoulder and pulled him close.

"We do this. Right?"

"Do what?" Buck leaned over the table and helped himself to some roasted peppers and eggplant.

"We think out of the box and stay out of the box. You taught me that. I don't know how often you've said, 'I gotcha, Key,'" I whispered to my closest friend. "Just saying: I gotcha, Buck." I gave his arm a little squeeze. His right hand was below the table, only visible to me. He gave me the finger and a smile. All felt right with the world. For a moment anyway.

There was a large roasted maitake mushroom lying on the antipasti plate. I felt compelled to stab it with my fork. I wasn't hungry; I just wanted to mush something around.

"Di Stefano is afraid the FBI will miss something," I said. "He dropped the name Rabbit, knowing it would rattle me. So, I'm playing out of the box."

I checked the time on my phone: 4:20 p.m. on the east coast, 9:20 in Ireland. I sent a text that read *URGENT*, knowing Collins would call me in a few minutes on an encrypted line.

"I just sent a text to Padraig Collins," I told Cat. "Do you know that name?"

"The rich guy from Ireland? Of course. He was instrumental in helping you find the treasure. I have the recording of the press conference you did at Trinity, watched it over twenty times. What do you want from him?"

"He has resources you can't even imagine, some of the best hackers on the planet. Collins is one of the least conventional thinkers anywhere. He's the definition of thinking out of the box."

My phone rattled. I lifted it to my ear, knowing to expect a few seconds of electronic noise.

"Key," came the Derry accent. "I was hoping you would connect, lad. What's the update?"

I put the phone on speaker.

"I'm here with Arin, Buck, and Marine Captain Cat Fahey. We n—"

"Take me off speaker," Collins said, sounding pissed.

"What?" I walked to the living room.

"Never put me on the phone with someone I don't know. You should know better."

"We have a problem bigger than your paranoia, Padraig. The Vice President needs your help. She just doesn't know it. Not yet."

"All I know is the little Buck told me."

I recounted that the VP was closing out the first night of the Festival, and the threat to her life. Plus, the swastikas and her photo with the bullet hole.

"Do you know the name Martin Fahey? He was a nine-teenth-century abolitionist."

"Fahey, the one that accompanied Frederick Douglass to Ireland? What's that have to do with anything?"

"Buck told you that he was with someone that has the gene. She is Martin Fahey's great-great-granddaughter. Her memories are of him." I paused, knowing that I was about to blow his mind. "Accompanying Douglass in Ireland."

"Jaysus, that's fantastic."

"Just like Aedan with me, she believes he's trying to warn her about something to do with the VP."

The line went quiet. I thought I had lost the connection. Then I heard him breathe and I could sense the electric charge of his brain assimilating the information and trying to understand it.

"Put me on speaker."

I walked back to the kitchen and laid the phone on the table. The light from the phone refracted through a cut crystal pitcher from Ireland, creating a rainbow of color in the glass.

At my parents' house in Philadelphia you are never far from Ireland.

"You're on, Padraig."

"Captain Fahey, my apologies. I have a rule never to talk on speaker when there is someone I don't know."

"It's a smart rule, Mr. Collins."

"Please, call me Padraig."

"Only if you call me Cat."

Collins let a small laugh escape.

"Are you aware of the Frederick Douglass walking tour in Dublin? Martin Fahey is mentioned in the tour. I want to hear all about your experience. But that's not why you called. Key, what do you need?"

"I need your hacker team to find Rabbit."

"We tried, two years ago."

"The FBI said his name has surfaced twice, associated with wire transfers. Write these names down. Patrick Boland and Lewis Walsh. They are white-collar white supremacists. Cat spotted them here doing reconnaissance. That's all I have."

"It's not much, lad."

"That never stopped you before."

The line went quiet. Finally, Cat looked up at me.

"Padraig?"

"If Rabbit's to be found, we'll find him. And I'll skin the fecker."

"I don't think so, Padraig." Buck drummed his fingers on the table. "I have a bullet with his name on it."

"I bet you do, Buck. I bet you do."

———

Collins laid his phone on the desk in his study and crossed to the window overlooking the Irish Sea. A sliver of a September moon lit the water below. A trace of information, that's all that Key offered, yet the hunt excited him. He glimpsed his face in the reflection. He liked to think he didn't look a day over fifty-five. He had the physique of a fit forty-year-old, not the sixty-three-year-old he was. But there were more and more days when he felt the indignities of age. He was happy for the shot of adrenaline that aroused his muscles and brain.

Padraig Collins lived for the chase. He understood the shadows. He was their creature. His team would penetrate the dark realm, find the cretins that threatened the VP and shine a light up their arse. An unstable America made for a dangerous world. An unstable world was bad for business. Helping save the Vice President of the United States was good for business. Collins smiled inwardly, imagining the White House ceremony, a grateful nation recognizing his contribution. Not bad for a rough-and-tumble kid from Derry. But there was not much time. In Collins's mind, there was only ever one question to ask: Who benefits from the chaos? And from there, follow the money.

CHAPTER 9

Arin hadn't heard me enter the room. I sat on our bed and noticed the bathroom door was slightly ajar. I could see her looking into the mirror, steam evaporating on the glass. She was staring, frozen, perhaps not seeing herself. She glimpsed me in the reflection; her eyes did not leave mine. Her dark curls, moist, covered the back of her neck while her silk robe lay open and revealing—her radiant beauty, dulled by what I took as sadness.

She left the bathroom, pulled back the covers on the bed, and climbed under them. I lie next to her, her back to me.

"Do you want to talk?"

She answered with silence. There have been times in the past when the memories of her mother's betrayal had surfaced, and the only balm had been time and space. I brushed the hair off her neck and offered a massage, her shoulders and neck loosening at the touch. I fought off the jetlag for a few minutes more, my mind begging for sleep. I laid my hand on her shoulder, her back rising and falling with deep breaths and the sound of a stifled sob. She brushed my fingers with hers. Her breathing slowed. Her body relaxed. I gently kissed the back of her neck. It was but hours ago that I held her as we viewed the craggy rocks and gentle swell of the water between Iona and Mull. I imagined pulling a boat into the water then helping Arin aboard. I tugged the oars, swiftly gliding into the unknown.

I floated on the surface of sleep. It was not rest, just roiling, bobbing up and down, feeling weary in this poor excuse for slumber. I was surprised to see Aedan and Siobhan sitting in the bow of the boat, facing me. My muscles strained as I pulled the oars into the swift waters of the River Boyne, sweating as I tried to forward the boat upriver, seeming to go nowhere. Aedan pointed to a cove with an embankment and said to me, "Best you get out here; you'll never get the hang of it."

I sat up, startled, as I always did with this recurring dream. I hated it. I hated the emptiness of it. Arin rustled. I could never get back to sleep after the dream, so I slipped quietly out of bed. Thankfully, Buck had set up the coffee. I pushed the start button. The clock read 5:32, dark outside, perhaps an hour before sunrise. I took my phone off sleep mode and was greeted by a dozen texts from my mom.

Are you OK?

Worried sick, call.

It was 10:32 a.m. in Ireland. I called.

"What are you so worried about?" I asked when my mother answered.

"Are ye serious?" The concerned-mother strain was in her voice. "Turn on the news. Philly is damn near underwater from the hurricane, um, uh, Ida."

"I'll have a look outside first. Sun's not up yet." I went to the front door, expecting to see Noah's Ark slip by. Nothing. It had rained for sure, but nothing had happened here. I turned on the porch light. "It must have hit somewhere else. I just rolled out of bed. Gonna grab a coffee and turn on the TV. I'll call you back."

"Get back to Ireland as soon as you can." It was my dad's voice. "We miss Arin."

"Thanks, Dad. I love you too." I missed them. Arin missed them. Although we talked to them frequently over video chat, Mom and Arin had their own private chats. They both spoke Irish, deepening their relationship.

As I poured my coffee, I felt Arin's arms slip around my waist, and her chin nuzzle my back. I stood still for a moment, enjoying her welcoming embrace, and reached for another cup.

"Let's go back to bed," she said, her hand caressing my bottom.

"OK, but first let's turn on the news." I told her what my mother had said.

"Get yourself a cup." She reached out and took my coffee with a sleepy smile. I poured another cup; the aroma alone was awakening my brain. We went to the living room. Arin found the remote. The screen came to life as helicopter searchlights roamed the hellish scene below them.

"Oh my God." Arin's hands covered her face. We could barely see the roofs of cars.

A chopper flew over Manayunk, just a few miles away. Main Street ran parallel to the Schuylkill River. Cars were floating down the road, some being pulled across lots and into the ferocious river. I could hear a helicopter zooming over the house, heading west. A moment later, it was on TV. Its lights followed the river and the submerged bike and running trail seven blocks away.

Arin put down her coffee.

"No way the Festival will happen. We have to see this, let's go."

We tried to be quiet. Cat was sleeping just down the hall, Buck on the third floor. We changed quickly.

"Bring your ID in case we need it." I slid mine over my head and headed out, texting my parents: *Looks like the damage is all along the Schuylkill River, nothing near the house.*

We jogged west on Delancey. There was barely a sign that it had even rained until we reached Twenty-Third Street. The sun was rising; it looked like any other morning. Then the noise reached us, the sound of water rushing, having its way with this slice of the city. Sirens pierced the air in surround sound. Lights were on in most of the apartments and condos down this end. I assumed the horrified occupants were staring in disbelief.

We stopped at Schuylkill Park at Twenty-Fifth Street. Water was slowly rising over the park, mud pushing forward in waves, like lava sliding down the volcano, taking every inch. Playground swings jostled on their chains, inches above the torrent. One end of a seesaw jutted in the air while the other was lost in the swamp. The underground parking lots of office and apartment buildings were submerged. Cars lost to Ida. I wondered how many lost lives would be attributed to this freak storm that started in Louisiana and stretched to Philly and perhaps beyond.

Arin and I walked north a few blocks; mud, water, and debris were rolling down Twenty-Fifth. Arin pointed to a skateboard, wheels up toward the sky, racing down the street until it rammed the top of a fire hydrant. We headed east until we reached Rittenhouse Square. Again, there was no sign of Ida. The benches were dry, a different world than what we witnessed a few blocks away. We sat.

Helicopters make their way around the city. Drones fly low, zigzagging like insects on the hunt.

"The Festival starts in two days. The VP will be here. No way. I'm sure they will cancel it."

"Probably," Arin said without much conviction. "Key." Her eyes continued to look away at the skyline or a drone. "Last night, I wasn't thinking about my mother."

"OK."

She bit her lip. Usually not a good sign. I waited.

"I need to go to Jamaica when this is over."

"Arin, what's going on? You go to Jamaica whenever you want." Arin had her elbows resting on her thighs, her head bobbing, her eyes darting everywhere, landing on the golden doodle pulling on his leash to get to her. My heart raced. "Arin?"

Her eyes shot upward to a drone about fifty feet above, its lights blinking.

"I've been asked to meet with top political leaders," she said to her hands rather than to me.

"And?"

"They want me to run for Prime Minister."

It shouldn't have been a shock to me. But it was. She had told me two years ago that her mother had been grooming her all her life for this. Arin had said no.

"Your mother has renewed her campaign to convince you?"

"It has nothing to do with my mother," she snapped.

I ran a thumb over my forehead, thinking somehow it might keep my heart from pounding so hard. A shard of light broke through the trees, casting leafy shadows on Arin.

"I'm sorry, Key." She reached her hand to me. "I'm off balance right now. Everything is." Arin stood and began walking toward Walnut Street, leaving me on the bench. I stood as she turned and walked back to me. "I keep thinking how little control I have over events. Covid response, hurricane response." She pointed toward the river. "Education, bettering people's lives. We've largely been sidelined by the pandemic for over a year. But not the Prime Minister. He does something. He acts and makes a difference. I need to give it some thought."

"Why now, right in the middle of this VP thing?"

"It's because we are in the middle of the VP thing. I haven't seen you look this excited in over a year."

"What do you mean?" I took a step back.

"When Agent Di Stefano said the name Rabbit yesterday, I felt kicked in the gut. But you, you were lit up. Your mind was on the hunt, ready for action. That's exactly how I felt the moment Cat said the name Frederick Douglass. I felt alive."

Arin reached her palm to my face. The warmth of her skin to mine.

"Seven hundred thousand people have died from Covid in this country alone. It's mind-numbing. It could have been you. Or me. Regardless, a little piece of us has died, atrophied, like muscles unused. We've become numb. All of us." Her arms motioned widely. "I saw you wake up yesterday. I felt myself wake up. I see Cat, fighting her way back, trying to reclaim her life. And I wonder. I just wonder."

The sun was stronger now, illuminating Arin. A glow. "When do we go to Jamaica?"

Her eyes clouded over and I felt my stomach drop.

"You don't want me to go," I said. My heart was freaking out. The words from my recurring dream rushed in: *Best you get out here, you'll never get the hang of it.*

"It's not like that. You are the love of my life. If you're there, I will look for every hint of how you feel. I'll read and analyze every minute bit of your body language." She placed her hands on my chest. "I need to consider this without any influence. I won't go until this is over with the VP. When I come back, we'll discuss it. I won't decide without you. But I need to know, if I say yes to running, will you be with me?"

"Why are you asking me that question? You know the answer."

Arin laid her head on my chest. I felt a tear fall on my hand. And her fingers grip my coat.

"Because I need to hear you say it."

I pulled her tight, then tighter. I wanted to feel her body, soul, dreams, and fears meld into me. And mine into her.

"Yes."

We held the embrace. And the truth of what Arin said. I *had* woken up. I hadn't realized that some part of me had fallen into the void. I missed Aedan. I missed the thrill, the unknown, the primordial connection.

Arin leaned her head back to look up at me. "How are we going to help Cat with her memories?"

I let my eyes roam over the park. At least a dozen dogs were leading their owners through the square, babies in carriages pushed by parents checking their phones. All seemingly oblivious to the destruction just a few blocks west.

"I don't know. Two things accelerated mine: the formula Dr. Garcia gave me and the trauma caused by you and my parents being kidnapped. God knows Cat's had plenty of trauma, and I don't know if taking the formula is a good idea for someone with PTSD. Guess we can ask Dr. Garcia?"

"Moot point on the formula. The Vice President arrives in two days, if they don't cancel. Not enough time for the formula to activate."

"Then you are the formula."

"What? What do you mean?" Arin took my hand and led me back to the bench. "How am I the formula?"

"You just told me that you came to life when you learned she has the memories from her great-great-grandfather and Douglass. You need to bring them to life for Cat. It might stimulate something."

The theme song to the movie *Blade* sounded in my pocket —Buck's ringtone.

I pressed the button. "What's up?"

"Where are you?"

"Have you seen what's going on?"

"My phone hasn't stopped. It woke me up." Buck went

silent. "Holy shit. I just put the TV on. People are kayaking on the Vine Street Expressway."

"Yeah, and it's a mess over at the river."

"Listen, Cat sat up for a while and put a dent in the whiskey supply. I hear her rustling around upstairs. I have to go to headquarters, so I need you back here with her. Are you far away?"

"No, around the corner at Rittenhouse."

Arin pulled the phone close and put it on speaker.

"Is the Festival canceled?"

"They are assessing the area, seeing if there's damage. There's a ton of pressure not to cancel. That's why I have to go. I won't be gone long."

"Go. We'll be there in three," Arin said and hit the "end" button.

Arin opened the front door as Cat came down the steps from the bedroom. She stopped midway.

"Thanks for letting me stay here for a few days. By the way, your home is gorgeous."

"It's all his mom's doing." Arin hooked her thumb in my direction.

I rarely give it a thought anymore, but I looked at the design with fresh eyes. The bones of a nineteenth-century home, modernized. A floating staircase, charcoal wood floor, Post-Impressionist paintings of Irish landscapes, and my favorite photo: mom onstage, backing up Van Morrison on violin.

Cat didn't look hungover; in fact, she looked excited.

"What?" She tilted her body. "Why are you looking at me like that? Ahhh, Buck told you I was a bad girl last night, right?"

"Damn, Cat, I forgot you're a mind reader," I answered.

"I metabolize whiskey like other people metabolize water.

Six shots is my limit. I only had five, so maybe I should have one for breakfast." She laughed and made her way down to the landing.

"I'm guessing you haven't heard the news. How 'bout I make breakfast and Arin shows you what's going on a few blocks away."

Cat shot a look at me and then at the door; her hand went to her ever present harmonica in her pocket.

"What is it?"

"Flooding, all along the river." Arin took Cat by the arm and led her into the living room.

I opened the fridge, took out eggs, butter, the left-over roasted veggies, and the grated Pecorino cheese. I cracked six eggs into a bowl, added a tablespoon of water, and began the whisking action that my father taught me. He was the omelet king of the house. All in the wrist, small, fast movements, letting the air and water work their way into the viscous fabric of the eggs. Go too far and you get meringue; not far enough and the eggs are dense, flavorless. He told me you couldn't say "whisk fifteen beats," or "for thirty seconds." Didn't work that way. You couldn't account for wrist strength or motion in a recipe.

It was in the crevices, the cracks, the tiny fissures that eggs and life bubbled up.

He told me to find the nuances, my own rhythm. So I whisked.

CHAPTER 10

All six Dobermanns sat astride, their tails wagged feverishly. Two panted loudly, still recovering from their dash through the property, the morning ritual. None barked. That was forbidden. But the strain of anticipation was palpable. It was the same every morning their master was on site.

At the sound of the door, they sat on their haunches, their hardened muscular bodies at attention, elite sentinels always at the ready. Li Chen stood in front of them for the inspection. He nodded and began his run. Three took off in front of him, three behind, for the punishing race through the jungle terrain, up hills, over rocks and roots and winding paths. The dogs in front were never more than five feet from their master. Two of the dogs behind kept a tight formation, side by side at seven feet; the final dog stayed at an almost precise twenty feet. Chen increased his speed as he encountered the final hill. The dogs broke free at the clap of his hands, racing each other on the final three hundred yards of sweat and muscle and joy.

As they returned to the compound, the lead dogs stopped in front of the pull-up bar; the rear dogs took a position on the opposite side and waited patiently for their master to complete his twenty pull-ups and fifty push-ups. When finished, Chen clapped, and the dogs turned to their waiting meal. He looked at his watch: 6:30 a.m.

The carriage house door opened. A thirty-something-year-old stepped onto the porch. He looked more like someone in a reggae band than the computer genius that he was. If Li Chen had a friend, Yvonne Lewis would be it.

But no one called him Yvonne, or Lewis. Just E. They had been together since sixth grade. Chen was frequently beat on and called all sorts of Chinese slurs. E was feared back then and quickly dispensed with Chen's tormentors. Chen returned the loyalty and eventually made E a rich man. Terrence Diamond was E's closest friend, bonded by their love of computer code. They were a package deal.

"Boss, yuh must see dis. Philly underwater."

Chen took the three steps to the porch in one movement and followed E to the computer monitors; each one fed scenes from different parts of Philadelphia, some from the air, some from the ground, all devastating.

"What are they saying?" Chen couldn't take his eyes off the flooding river, the vast number of cars underwater, and the expressway that cut below the roadways, now a canal.

"Hurricane Ida only s'posed to bring a lickle rain in di city, but it hit hard pon the river in the north," E answered.

"The Festival area?"

Diamond was sitting next to E. The computer whiz tapped the screen with the eraser end of a pencil.

"The TV stations have drones in the air. I'm trying to get into their feeds, maybe five more minutes." He continued typing commands on the keyboard.

"E, anything you're picking up from the police?"

E shook his head, his long bulky dreadlocks moving with each twist.

"No, the sun just up a short time." The three of them looked toward the large window facing the wraparound porch. The morning sun bounced off the dark wood, the thick varnish playing the role of a mirror, sending fragments of light onto the side of the house, a luminous dance of colors in contrast to the dark, muddy waters of Philadelphia.

Li Chen fed this information into his brain. The data was too sparse to arrive at any conclusions. He stood mesmerized by the chaos on the screen. It appeared inevitable that they would cancel the Festival and the VP would move on to another event.

"I'm in," Diamond announced. "There's only about five minutes of drone video so far. I'm going to rewind and let it run."

Chen took up position behind Diamond. He had studied aerials of the city and was trying to get his bearings—the clock on the video ticked away; one minute, two, three. The rear of the art museum came into view at precisely minute four.

"Forward the video slowly." The drone hovered over the river and the flooded roadways that allowed traffic in and out of the city. The only thing moving was mud and water.

Diamond tapped some keys and allowed the video to speed up. The drone didn't move, but the timer did. The footage caught up to the feed in real time. Finally, the drone moved east, closing in on the rear of the museum; the Festival grounds sat on the other side, not yet visible. The drone operator paused the drone, giving a view of the bulging river just a stone's throw west of the museum.

"Bumboclaat son of a bitch, move the fucking thing." Li Chen screamed Jamaican curses at the operator sitting nearly two thousand miles away. After what seemed like twenty minutes but was less than two, the drone began a slow movement east, over the west façade of the art museum, and a slight movement due west, centering over the raging water and the expressway on the other side. At this angle, the Festival grounds would remain out of view. Li Chen's patience and calm were practiced responses, but the frustration was building, and his people sensed it. The outcome was rarely good.

"Find that fucking operator so I can fly there and personally strangle the piece of shit."

It was as if the operator heard him. The drone changed course and moved east by north-east. The steps made famous by the movie Rocky came into view. Then the back of the main stage, then the front, all intact. Soon the entire Benjamin Franklin Parkway, the Festival's grounds, were looking a little the worse for wear. People wearing yellow vests examined the mini-city, its construction almost complete.

Terrence Diamond sat to the left of E. He had a Master's in computer science from McGill University in Canada. His family was from Mandeville, Jamaica, poor as goat-shit. He had won a full scholarship because he aced some bullshit coding contest that the Canadian government sponsored. Computer coding was less difficult than remembering to brush his teeth.

His challenge, his passion, was memorizing the collected works of Shakespeare, then, using one or two lines from the master, he created something new on the spot: a song, poetry, a motivational speech to the Dobermanns. Li Chen put up with him because he walked the tightrope of genius.

"The damage seems to be concentrated at the river. They spent too much money on building the Festival grounds. The show will go on."

Li Chen exhaled. Then both men turned to see something extremely rare. Li Chen's smile.

CHAPTER 11

Thursday, September 2, 2021.
Delancey Place, Philadelphia

"Key, that looks fantastic." Cat fussed over the roasted veg omelet and the sourdough rolls I had heated. "I'm famished."

We dug into the food. Cat broke a roll in half, spooned some eggs onto the bread, sprinkled some cheese, and let out a "hmmm" as she bit in. Not bad for a guy just learning to cook. She washed it down with a sip of coffee. I gave her a moment to enjoy her meal before I started.

"Arin will take you to Ireland in your mind at the time Douglass was there with Martin. I'm hoping it will stimulate your memory. Your job is to relax, Cat. If you see or feel anything, just pause and explore it."

Arin opened her laptop.

"I have something for you to watch," she said, turning the screen toward Cat. "The first is a video collage of photos from that period in Dublin."

Cat lifted a napkin from the table and wiped the corners of her mouth. She looked at the screen and rubbed her head.

"Hold on. You want me to relax? Give me a minute." Cat left the table. Seconds later, the sound of harmonica wafted. This time it was Arin who looked surprised.

"She's playing Bob Marley's 'Redemption Song.'" Arin closed her eyes and gently swayed with the music.

Marley was in the blood of Jamaicans the way Dylan and Springsteen affected the American psyche. I heard Arin softly humming the song, A moment later, Cat returned and took her seat.

"I know, it's weird, right? Just a little thing I do. It doesn't just help me relax; it makes me happy. I'd be nervous before a mission, play for a minute then helmet up and go. With a smile. I don't mess with the formula."

"Good, you shouldn't mess with it. Ready?" Arin had a look at the screen.

Cat offered Arin a fist-bump, then Arin hit play. 1840s Dublin passed by in photo after black-and-white photo. I watched her eyes as she studied the screen: a squint, a few blinks, mostly nothing.

"This is a recent video of the Frederick Douglass Walking Tour in Dublin." Arin maneuvered her mouse and clicked on it. A new video occupied the screen. "This is City Hall, where Douglass gave his first speech."

Arin let the video run without sound. The columned façade stood stately, regal, a testament to eighteenth-century British wealth. The view of the rotunda revealed the vaulted ceiling, the marble, the gold, the statuary. I watched as Cat absently scratched her cheek and adjusted in her chair. She leaned in an inch or two, shook her head, her fingers tightening into her palm, then flexing.

Arin advanced the video to the Mansion House, where Frederick Douglass and Martin Fahey had dined with the Lord Mayor of Dublin. I caught a slight tic of her mouth as she placed her fingers on the screen.

"It feels familiar. Nothing more. Maybe it will come to me later."

Arin acknowledged Cat with a quick smile. I got the coffee pot while Arin forwarded the video to the next location. I topped off everyone's cup and heard Cat gasp.

"This is Daniel O'Connell's house," Arin stated. The camera panned over Merrion Square Park, the canopy of tall oaks and evergreens shading the paths. It lingered a moment on "The Victims" sculpture, dedicated to those who suffered the famine. The gorgeous Georgian architecture for which Merrion Square is known was displayed as the camera showed off the colorful doors in blues, golds, greens, and yellows. Finally, the camera focused on number 58, a plaque commemorating the property as the Dublin home of "The Liberator."

Cat had closed her eyes. She sat still—no blinking, no slight movement of fingers or face—like a painting.

"He's been there." Cat opened her eyes. "It's a loop. He goes up the steps, then he's at the bottom, goes up, repeat."

"He? You mean Douglass?" Arin asked.

"No." Cat put the coffee to her lips, took a small sip. "Martin, he's alone." Her eyes shut again. "It's urgent; he's frightened. I think he's been inside." Cat looked at Arin then me. "How did you deal with this? It's frustrating."

"True," I admitted. "It was only when my parents were kidnapped that the details about the treasure came to me. There's an important difference."

Her body turned toward me and she scanned my face. I assumed that her finely tuned skill of reading people was at work.

"I was looking for a hidden treasure," I continued, "one we knew had existed and had good reason to believe was in Ireland. It wouldn't have mattered if it took four more hours or four more days to figure it out; my parents would have been OK. Aedan, my ancestor, didn't reach across centuries from the grave and tell me anything. It felt like that sometimes, but everything I experienced came through an actual memory of his."

"Not sure I get the point." Cat shrugged.

"It's not possible for Frederick or Martin to warn you about what will happen," Arin said. "What is possible is that you might learn something that stimulates a correlation or an insight."

I pointed to the computer screen. "You have seen this video. It's in your memory now. Right?"

"Yes," Cat responded.

"The Ancestral Memory gene contains an exact copy of your memory. If you were my ancestor and I inherited your memories," I pointed to the screen again, "this is what I would see. I'd be passive. Just like watching a movie, I can't alter its outcome. I can only learn from it."

Cat put her fingers on the screen, a look of confusion on her face.

"I believe you're experiencing the memories now, days before the VP arrives, because something is lurking in your subconscious, and you fervently hope it might be relevant." I put my hand on hers and tapped it. "I hope you're right."

Cat looked to Arin on her left then me on her right. Her attention landed on a photo of me, mid-air, intercepting a football. Penn State. The play that sent us to the Championship. I was a junior. Heady stuff.

"Guys, I've studied everything I can get my hands on about the Ancestral Memory gene." Cat interrupted my gridiron recollections. "Key, you've been a prodigy in many different arenas. The skills come and go. Right?"

"Yeah."

"Me?" Cat touched her hand to her head and ran her fingers through her dark hair. "I'm a single-skill freak. Have been since I can remember. These powers come from the gene.

The scientific literature states, 'The gene stimulates new neural pathways.' Eventually, it morphs into memories."

"True," I said, wondering where this was going.

"Until now, the researchers believed that we were passive viewers."

"What do you mean, 'until now'?" Arin beat me to the question.

Cat rubbed her temples. Her lips pulled left then right, a little weird, like she was signaling something in her mind.

"Arin, your voice just went up an octave; your right hand was closed, relaxed, then your fingers pointed toward me. Your desire to understand what I meant shot out of you like fireworks. I not only saw it, I felt it. Yet it all happened in less than a second. At the same moment, Key, you tensed; you pulled back into the chair a quarter inch. You were surprised that there was information that you didn't yet know about the gene."

"Cat, where are you going with this?" I tried to calm myself.

She dropped her head into her hands.

"I hate this skill sometimes. It's too much, too much information coming in," she said, barely above a whisper. She sat up straight. "But it's what makes me Nine."

She turned in her chair, her attention on me.

"When I spoke with Dr. Garcia, I told her about my skill, how it's ruled, sometimes ruined, my life. She told me you, Key, are the lucky one."

I was aware of my surprise, my head lifting, my eyes widening. Arin stood and stepped behind me, her hands on my shoulders, now watching Cat from behind me.

"She said that your multiple skills made you well rounded, ready to receive a variety of information. You have multiple nerve endings, so to say. I have one. And it's been rubbed raw."

Cat looked at me as if all of this made complete sense. But there was a look in her eyes, a revelation.

"What else did she tell you?" I asked.

A calmness spread across Cat's being. Her green eyes took on new life.

"People with one skill, so intense that it's like an exposed nerve, the researchers think it opens a unique neural pathway. Dr. Garcia believes it's possible that Martin can tell me something."

Arin's hands tightened on my shoulders. My brain was more scrambled than the eggs we had just eaten. I needed to talk to Dr. Garcia.

"Key, a minute ago you said that I hoped for a correlation. There already is one."

"What correlation?"

"There was a civil war brewing then, and there is a civil war brewing now. There were powerful, wealthy people who wanted to keep slavery alive, to the point of secession from the Union. It's the same thing happening now, just more dangerous. There wasn't cyber warfare then, or AK's by the thousands on the streets."

Cat stood and walked around the island, her eyes sweeping over my mother's archeology photos. She stopped in front of a photo of the missing cover of the *Book of Kells*, the treasure Arin and I found.

"With Arin's help, you found the treasure and helped move Northern Ireland and the Republic one step closer to unity." She started to leave the room but stopped. "That means I have the best team in the world to help me," she said, and pointed to Arin and me. "And by the way, fuck reality, I never much cared for it. I prefer to create my own. And now I'm going to go have a nice little chat with Grandpa Fahey, see what he can tell me."

CHAPTER 12

L i Chen was a master of living two lives: one for public consumption, the other locked behind layers—a rose, the outer petals carefully constructed, the inner core almost impossible to find. His freshly pressed shirt and suit were laid out for him. His black shoes were polished to perfection. He would look the part for the newspaper and TV reporters who would await him for the ground-breaking ceremony. Today was for the public side.

Negotiations between the Jamaican government and a Chinese resort development company eager to invest in the island nation had broken down. At the urging of the Chinese, the Jamaican government handed the development contract over to Chen's company, Infrastructure Strategies Group. Today he would stand next to his Chinese counterpart, ribbons would be cut, and ceremonial shovels would break the soil for a five-star luxury resort in Port Antonio. Unlike its more famous neighbors to the west, Ocho Rios, Montego Bay, and Negril, Port Antonio had few resort properties despite being the most beautiful part of Jamaica. The new resort would provide a needed boost to the local economy and give Jamaica post-Covid bragging rights to the tourism world.

Chen was lauded as the hero who saved the day. No one in Jamaica, except Li Chen, knew the outcome was planned in a Beijing conference room long before the negotiations began.

Walking from the main house to the carriage house, Chen crossed under a papaya tree on his left and a mango tree on his right. Terrence Diamond and E did not bother to look up. No other employees were permitted to enter the carriage house. Two Dobermanns stood guard on the porch to make sure of it.

"News?"

"No, sir," E answered.

Chen stared at Diamond. Diamond was preoccupied with whatever was on his screen. Although sometimes Chen wanted to smack him when he recited his nonsense mash-ups, Chen began to think of Diamond's words as his good-luck charm. Today he couldn't leave without one. E noticed him standing there, slapped Diamond on the shoulder, and gestured toward their boss.

Diamond began bobbing his head, rolling and swaying while his thoughts formed around the words of The Bard. He began, like a poet at a reading:

> "To die, to sleep, to sleep, perchance to dream.
> For in that sleep of death what dreams may come
> when God might deliver you as the prodigal son
> We dream, we scheme, part saint, mostly sinner
> Taste every drop before our life's winter
> For in that sleep of death what dreams may come
> How long will they kill our prophets
> yet claim they love the Son."

Chen never knew what they meant, and he didn't care. It was a ritual, plain and simple, and it helped him think. He took in a deep breath and left the house. The Dobermanns didn't move, and their tails didn't wag in affection.

The Range Rover arrived and one of his security detail opened the rear door for him. The driver pressed the button, the rear hatch opened and two Dobermanns jumped in.

The custom-built Range Rover handled the bumpy mountain road as they drove through Moore Town, past Saint Paul's Church, where a thin, elderly man in a white shirt and black tie gingerly held a bouquet, his lips moving, a prayer perhaps, or a declaration of love to the spouse who lay under the dirt.

Fifteen minutes later, the car turned onto a recently cleared road. The driver pulled up to a white event tent, Jamaican and Chinese flags anchored at each corner.

Chen waited for his door to be opened by the two local women wearing identical dresses of green, yellow, and black, the colors of the Jamaican flag. They placed a lei of the national flower, *lignum vitae*, a startling lavender-blue, over his head, then escorted him into the tent. He was first greeted by the Prime Minister and then the Chinese Ambassador. Beyond the tent was a red ribbon attached to posts on either side that were anchored to the ground ten feet away from a thirty-foot-high cliff. The plan called for a dramatic stairway to the white sand beach below, plus two glass elevators to ferry the wealthy resort-goers to the beach and back again.

The TV reporters and news photographers positioned themselves near the ribbon. The sun was climbing, gathering its strength, lifting the morning dew from the ground. Humidity; the odor of ocean and plant life permeating, rising. The female journalists checked their make-up in hand-held mirrors; the men looked underarm for stains.

Chen nodded to his counterpart, Mr. Xi Liang, who talked with the Jamaican Minister of Tourism. She was long-winded.

And beautiful; Xi Liang had a weak spot for beautiful women.

The Prime Minister's Press Secretary, also on hand for the event, gathered everyone and handed the commemorative shovels to Xi Liang, the Minister of Tourism, and Chen. She escorted the group to the ribbon, where the Prime Minister and the Ambassador made statements and used the ceremonial scissors. The shovels broke the ground; poses were made for the press, and hands were shaken. Chen hated this part, the public part. He preferred the murky water where electric eels hid, only to stick their head out when it was time to strike.

Four motorcycle police led the caravan that would shuttle Jamaican and Chinese dignitaries to the Trident Castle Hotel just ten minutes away, where the Jamaican government was hosting a luncheon. Ian Fleming wrote his James Bond books but a short distance from here. The filmmakers shot many of the Bond movies nearby.

Chen sat in the back of his Range Rover, waiting for a response to his text to E. As the car rolled along the palm-lined road, he wished he loved this place. He didn't understand why people held places in such affection and with such dedication. It was just a place. He did love the fact that it was his, though. His domain. Li Chen was born in Jamaica, from a long line of Chinese ancestors. The original émigrés landed there as indentured servants in the 1800s. Chen spoke Mandarin at home, English at school, Jamaican Patois everywhere else. His parents owned a chain of grocery stores around the small island nation. They were not in the super-wealthy class, but money was never a problem for Li's family. Like other families of means, they sent their children to other countries for their education, most often to Canada or England. Li's father, though, had insisted that he go to China. China was fast becoming a global superpower, and it was time, he had said, for the Chen family to make a place for themselves.

Chen's phone vibrated. A thumbs-up icon. It meant they had not canceled the Festival; the Vice President of the United States would arrive in Philadelphia as planned.

Chen waited at the entrance of the Trident for Xi Liang. As they entered the beautiful boutique resort, painted the whitest of white, the sun almost blinding in its reflection, Chen leaned toward Liang and whispered, "It's on." They turned to the press and, hand in hand, raised their arms together, celebrating the success of their negotiations.

Chen and Liang were handed champagne flutes then escorted into the ballroom, to be greeted with cheers. The Prime Minister and the Ambassador toasted their accomplishments, each heaping praise on their current great relationship and how it was only the beginning. Chen thought that was hard to imagine: the Chinese already owned much of the island.

As the lame speeches ended and the mingling began, Chen and Liang stepped into a private room. Liang spoke quietly.

"There will be three incidents on Friday. One will appear to come from Antifa. Saturday, the grand finale. By Sunday, America will be in turmoil."

"They make it easy," Chen replied. He almost thought of Liang as a friend. He wanted to, but it was his nature to think of everyone and everything as a simple tool to use as needed. Xi Liang had taught him this.

At eighteen, Chen had arrived in a strange land. His ancestors had mixed with Black Jamaicans. His dark skin and Asian facial features didn't turn a single head in Jamaica, but the students at Shanghai Jiao Tong University did not know what to make of him, a Black man with a Chinese name and features, and fluent in their language. He became one of the most popular kids on campus; his fellow students were curious about him and Jamaica. Reggae and Marley. Rum and ganja.

Li possessed an agile and curious mind and had sailed through his economics, agriculture, finance, and Chinese history studies. He felt unshackled from the mental constraints of small-island parochialism. He was hungry to be Chinese, hungry to eat from the fast-expanding feast of Chinese money and power. Beijing took notice.

China was investing billions in Africa, but its appetite for expansion into the Americas was also part of a strategic plan. It would soon be time to play in the backyard of the United States. Chen was offered a full scholarship for an MBA, a gift from the People's Republic to their friends in Jamaica. Jamaica was the largest English-speaking country in the Caribbean.

After receiving his MBA, Li spent a year training to be an asset, a sophisticated businessman who could clear the path for all manner of Chinese business interests throughout the Americas. And if the power of money was not enough to persuade a decision maker, then other methods could be deployed, as long as it could never be tied to Beijing.

Chen had learned how to build business networks, shell companies, and create offshore accounts. He was free to expand his income in either dark or legitimate enterprises. They made it clear to him: those enterprises were there to serve China's needs.

Legitimate enterprises were boring to him, except as opportunities to wash money or front his expanding syndicate: drugs, human trafficking, hacking.

Following his year of training in China, he was sent to Africa for hands-on experience in real-world economics, what critics called "economic colonialism." He returned to Jamaica a wealthy man and negotiated major deals between Jamaica and China. Roads, bridges, and bribes increased his wealth and influence. Xi Liang was and remained his handler.

"The money will be wired, as usual, once the task is complete." Liang smiled.

"And your portion will be set aside. You should be able to buy an island before long." Chen raised his champagne flute. "And fill it with all the beautiful women you long for."

Chen thought about Saturday and a chill ran through him —if something went wrong, if the FBI and CIA found a way to him, if Beijing decided to bury any possible trail to them ... Chen knew he was expendable. Everyone was. Understanding that was what kept him alive. He wondered if his corpulent handler also remembered that lesson.

CHAPTER 13

Thursday, September 2, 2021.
Delancey Place, Philadelphia

Cat Fahey stood in the study that belonged to Key's mother, Megan Murphy. Its unique oval shape made it inviting, calming, like being held in the palms of a trusted loved one. Natural light streamed through the bow-shaped windows while the stained glass sent a cascade of colors to romp through the small room.

Cat was mesmerized by the stained-glass artwork that displayed a woman's back. An Irish queen, perhaps—regal, strong, long hair flowing over her forest-green cloak, surveying the lands of her realm. Cat moved about the room reverentially. This was a sacred space to her. Key, his story, his actions, every word from every interview had been committed to her memory. He was hope. He was proof that ancestral memory could be used for good. Though the memories might drive one mad, having them was not a curse of madness.

Cat stood beside the desk and studied the wall of photos, her fingers gently touching one of them, a teenage Key and his parents at Trinity College Library, the home of the *Book of Kells*. Her eyes fell on another photo. Key appeared to be around five, and Buck looked to be twelve. Key stood next to Tanya, Tanya's mother's arm draped over their shoulders, her smile radiant. Buck's father had his arm over Key's dad's shoulder. Buck stood between Key's parents. They were an extended family, if not by blood then by grace.

Cat felt the familiar chasm open, threatening to swallow her whole. Everything. She would give everything, anything, to have been in that photo, surrounded by love. But the acrid taste of a rotten marriage burned her throat, the putrid memory of a child witnessing the opposite of love that defined and defiled her parents. Her father was a sword master of the tongue, cutting deep into the marrow of any dream, any wish, anything that brought light. Her mother, hollowed by time and ten thousand indignities, a pile of unfulfilled possibility. And there stood Cat. A child. She was able to see the world in ways that few could, answering questions before they were asked, so great was her ability to read the all-but-invisible tells that humans made.

Her hand brushed the photo, sending an unwelcome charge through her; this Black family and white family, dedicated to each other, would have been loathed by her racist father. Whatever she loved, her father hated. Whatever he hated, she then loved.

Her sixteenth birthday washed over her. She tried to stuff it back in its corner, but it insisted. Two neighbor boys, friends, walked her to the movies, where they would meet up with others to celebrate her birthday. She felt the tingling, the magnetic or electrical disruption of her cells that sometimes preceded the actions of others. She smelled the boys' intentions. They usually cut through the alley, but Cat turned from it.

"Where you going? This is our short-cut."

"I don't want to go that way." She had walked away, but one of the boys stepped in front of her.

Cat recalled choking back the fear, keeping a smile, wanting to move. The boy put his arms around her waist and lifted her to the alley entry.

"I just want to be the first one to kiss you on your sixteenth birthday."

She pushed herself away from him.

"That's not all you want. Stop it."

"What? That's all, one kiss."

She pointed to the other boy.

"He has a hard-on, and so do you."

"Then it's your lucky day."

He pushed her against the wall.

It was easy, as if she could read his mind. She had laughed.

"It's not me you want to fuck," she said, pointing to the other boy. "It's him."

She sensed the monster rage in him, the fist about to form, the pain he wanted to release by transferring it to her. She was on him before he could move, driving her fist into his nose. He was crumpled, bloody. The other boy was motionless, stunned. She ran home to tell her mother, shaking, frightened by her rage. The words flew out of her mouth, her mother looking over Cat's shoulder.

"Oh, Christ." She turned to see her father. His hand already nearing her face.

"You fucking slut." The impact of his slap sent her to the floor. He stood over her. "Those boys must have been desperate."

Cat tried to shut it down before it broke her any further, as it still did after all these years. A shard of golden light crossed her eyes and she looked up to see the Irish queen, sunlight brightening the room. She sat in the leather chair and forced deep breaths into her lungs, slowly exhaling, the shadows in the recesses of her mind taking shape, human form, moving, breathing …

"I find the air agreeable, Martin."

We strolled along the River Liffey, the sky bright and almost cloudless, most days a rare sight. Carriages rolled by, the odor of horse, a common and constant reminder of the city.

"Dublin is beautiful this time of year, Frederick, and, my friend, you seem content in her."

Frederick stopped walking. He took his time, nodding to passers-by and exchanging a few words with well-wishers.

"I am content. But I am also troubled." Frederick ran his fingers over his thick and rebellious hair.

"Why? What troubles you?"

"My naiveté troubles me," Frederick answered.

A group of boys ran by us on the street, kicking a ball. They were dirty and scrawny but laughing as they tried to best each other. Frederick watched then continued.

"I did not know that white people lived in such deprivation. I assumed that all European whites lived like you. The poverty here is among the worst I've witnessed."

"Even on the plantation?"

"Yes. To work the fields, we had to be fed. Look around you. These are your people." Douglass turned with his hands in the air. "Many of them look like they haven't had a meal in weeks."

I must measure my words. I was entrusted as his host and guide, needing to keep his mind focused on the great abolitionist cause. He was a man of passion and compassion, perhaps taking on every great cause and diluting our overarching purpose.

"There are rumors that there is a blight of the potato crop. The starving are streaming into the city for crust or coin."

I watched this great ambassador of emancipation stare out over the city, the spires reaching to the heavens, the starving reaching for salvation.

"I am not a freeman, Martin. Another human being claims to own me, but I have declared myself free. I kneel before no man. Yet my stomach is not empty. If it were, perhaps I would not be so lofty. Perhaps I would bow, for hunger is a cruel master."

Cat grew aware of a sound, a door, movement. A voice moving through the house reached her. Buck.

"The Festival has not been canceled. The VP will be here," she heard him say.

Cat let herself have a moment in the room. The photo of Key, a young teen, already taller than his parents, standing in front of a banner at Trinity College that read, *"The Book of Kells."*

Cat walked into the kitchen, all eyes on her.

"Come tell us about it." I patted the stool next to me, then swept crumbs from the island counter into my hand and dropped them on my plate.

"Tell us about what?" Buck asked. He sat on his stool, crossed his arms and yawned.

"A memory has become vivid, complete, no longer just fragments," I explained to Buck. "So, Cat, what did Martin tell you?"

Cat started toward me, but her phone rang before she could sit. She read the screen.

"It's my boss," she announced.

I wasn't sure if she meant Scott Morrison or the Pentagon.

"Hey, Scott." She listened for a moment. "No problem, but you know you get all of us." Cat disconnected.

"He was letting me know that the Festival is a go. He needs me to come over and walk through our security measures." Cat looked like a boxer who had won the round, excited but still beat-up; wariness in her eyes, yet bouncing on her toes. "Can you believe the timing?"

"You can tell us on the way," I assured her.

"Just give me ten. I'm not sure a shower will help ..." Cat pointed to herself "... but a girl's gotta try."

We all headed to our rooms to freshen up. Arin was the last down, the three of us waiting in the foyer. I looked at her T-shirt, laughed, and shook my head.

"Really?"

It held a self-portrait of Vincent Van Gogh, a covid mask dangling from his lone ear.

CHAPTER 14

There were only a few cars on the road but the city was crawling with gawkers on foot, camera phones in hand, jaws agape, much like Arin and me a few hours ago. Even with two rivers, major flooding was not a thing in Philly until now. Buck took Eighteenth Street and turned left on the outer band of the Benjamin Franklin Parkway. He slowed so we could get a better view of the Festival grounds. It looked like it did yesterday: summer in the city, stages rising, grass shimmering in the sunlight, workers building a town within the city.

Buck drove to the north side of the museum, rode up the hill, and parked. A guard gave him a thumbs-up after a glance at his badge. The museum sat elevated like the Acropolis, Grecian columns summoning the ancients. The famous steps in front were the gateway to downtown, the glorious view of the Parkway—trees, the flags of every nation, skyscrapers, and William Penn standing on his pedestal atop City Hall. The rear of the museum was the gateway to one of the largest urban park systems in the U.S. A staircase led to the back lawn, azalea gardens, sculptures and fountains, Boat House Row, angry floodwaters washing over much of it.

The west entrance door flew open. Scott Morrison looked toward Cat and waved his hand for her to follow. He moved quickly up a path to a gazebo, one of my favorite places in the city. Arin and I come up at least once a week after running the Schuylkill Trail. The sunsets here were unrivaled. The view today nearly knocked the wind out of me.

I could see the raging waters. What I couldn't see were the riverbanks. From this viewpoint, the river had spread across Kelly and MLK Drives. I watched the roof of a VW Beetle veer toward Boat House Row. How would the city cope when sixty thousand people poured into it in less than forty-eight hours? How would they keep those people safe from three thousand white supremacists?

"Fireworks," Scott Morrison pointed to the lawn, approximately two hundred yards long. "They start setting up in a few minutes. They parked the trucks over by Lemon Hill, out of range of the flood. Cat, I need you to take charge of security here."

"I don't mean to butt in, but Cat is active-duty military. Can she even work for you?" I wanted to see Morrison's reaction.

Morrison's eyes narrowed; his neck pulled back. His eyes scanned me, then canceled me with complete disregard. He turned to leave.

"He's right, Scott," Buck said. "Plus, her talents are better served elsewhere."

Morrison walked to within three inches of Cat.

"Agent Di Stefano is your liaison. Until he tells me otherwise, you still work for me. Or did I miss the memo where you are now the head of security?"

"No." Cat kept her eyes on his.

"No, what?"

"No, Scott."

"No, what?"

"No, Sir." Cat's voice strained on that response.

"And in case you don't fully understand, the Vice President will walk into that building in two days." He pointed to the museum. "I need to ensure that she walks out in one piece."

Morrison then rounded on me.

"I've read all about you, both of you. You let your best friend die," he said to me. "And you," he said, his finger almost jabbing Buck, "you let your kid sister die."

I expected Buck to pull out his gun and empty it into Morrison at the mention of Tanya.

"Frankly, I don't want either of you anywhere near the VP." Morrison gritted his teeth like he was hoping for a fight.

Cat gripped Morrison's shirt. "I got this."

Morrison looked at her hand, his jaw tightening.

"Get your hand off me."

Cat tightened her grip.

"Best you walk away. Now. Sir."

Morrison grabbed her by the wrist.

"Get your ass down there."

Cat's face was relaxed, calm, unnervingly so. She looked Morrison in the face.

"If you ever talk to me like that again I'll rip your throat out," she said, barely above a whisper.

Morrison backed away. He pulled his blue linen sports jacket by the collar, straightening it, then turned toward the museum, the heels of his brown leather shoes striking the pavement like a performer in *Riverdance*.

"I don't like it," I said, looking at the raging water as it pushed east to meet the Delaware River. "That was a performance. You know him, Cat. Do you agree?"

"Yeah, but I'm not sure why. All Scott ever cared about was the success of the mission. Something's changed. I could see it in his eyes."

We turned at the sound of a semi as it rounded the fountain below and stopped at the bottom of the lawn.

"It seemed like he was trying to piss you guys off," Arin offered.

"He accomplished his goal if that's the case." Buck's arms were folded over his chest.

"He's an idiot, Buck," Arin said.

"No, he's not. I agree with Key and Cat. He got under my skin on purpose." Buck unfolded his arms. "What's his game?"

"We're getting special treatment from DHS, FBI, and the Police Commissioner. Maybe he resents us?" Arin pointed to her Van Gogh shirt. "Or he just didn't like my shirt."

Cat allowed a small laugh.

"Probably nothing. Sometimes Scott's just wired tight. You watch. He'll switch to Zen mode soon, the lone-wolf operator. He's like that, all eggshells to start, and then you can't ruffle him." She pointed toward the truck carrying the fireworks. "I need to get down there."

Buck's phone rang as we were halfway down the lawn. Arin followed Cat, and I stayed with Buck. He stopped cold.

"What?" I asked as soon as he disconnected.

"That was Deputy Commissioner Cruz." Buck shook his head and absently adjusted his cred pack, pulling on the lanyard. "Fifty of the white supremacist group were gathered in Love Park. They just split up, groups of ten, clearly advance teams. One of the groups is heading this way. Cruz wants Cat to get eyes on them."

"What about Morrison?"

"Cruz is calling him now. A squad car will be here in two minutes to assist with security until Cat gets back."

The task force tent at Eakins Oval was still in place. The Festival grounds were fenced off. No one entered without the proper ID.

Buck had been updated by text: five men had taken the northern perimeter, five the southern. We watched as best we could, but trees blocked the sightlines. And then they appeared: five on each side of the Festival fence, heading our way, geared up, paramilitary, American Flag scarves covering their faces, helmets or boogie hats on their heads.

"I don't get it. Do these guys think they're soldiers?" Arin asked. "Most of them look so out of shape they couldn't pass a fitness test for picknies."

"For what?" Cat looked perplexed.

"Sorry, 'pickney' means children in Jamaican."

"That sounds about right ... but really dangerous children." Cat pivoted between the group to the north to the ones on the south side.

"Don't let their looks fool you. A bunch of them are ex-military," Buck added as we watched them march toward us. "The ones in good shape, recently out of jail, hardcore haters."

Buck was right. The closer they came, the more disciplined they appeared.

The northern group stood parallel to the tent. One of them stepped to the fence. He put up two fingers, like a peace sign, then pointed his fingers toward his eyes. I've seen enough movies and TV to know it was the military sign for "Eyes on me." He put his hand up, then split his fingers like the Vulcan greeting on *Star Trek*.

Cat turned to Buck.

"You see what I'm seeing?"

"It's the military sign for the number nine," Buck instructed. "Except that the thumb stays on the palm. In Cat's unit, they moved their thumb up and down. It was the sign for Captain Fahey: Nine."

"Why don't they just do this." Arin held up four fingers on one hand, five on the other.

"One hand has to be on the trigger," Buck answered.

Cat walked toward the man. We followed.

"So, the rumors are true," the masked man stated. "The living legend Nine is here, in the flesh."

Cat was three feet away from him, separated by the four-foot-tall cyclone fence. The man pulled his bandana down and moved to within an inch of the fence. Cat stood silently and examined him. His head seemed small for his body, his face pock-marked, a goatee protruded from his chin, about three inches long.

"Dit?"

"It's been a while, Captain. You look good, despite the hearsay that you've been living on park benches."

He was around six, maybe six-one—reasonably good shape. Buck slid past me and stood close to Cat.

"What happened to you, man? Why are you part of this?" Cat's voice seemed to catch a little.

"What happened to me is exactly what I signed up for. Training." The man she called Dit smiled. "The Marines trained me. I fought in their bullshit war and now I'm here to do my patriotic duty. There's a lot of us, Nine. There's room for you."

"And for him?" I watched her tilt her head to Buck.

He looked straight at Buck.

"Well, hell yeah. We always need someone to cook up some fried chicken." He leaned a little closer to Buck, reading off his credential pack. "Buck McCoy. I remember that name from Iraq. Detective McCoy, how does it feel to have a white man's last name? Maybe it was from your grandpappy's owner?"

I didn't know how he did it, but Buck gave him nothing—not taking the bait. Cat flexed her fingers, fists forming. Arin flew between Cat and Buck, pushing them aside, and slapped the man over the fence, smacking against his ear. Hard.

"What the fuck, bitch?" The man teetered back a few steps, hand on his ear, rubbing it. "Damn good thing for you there's a fence between us."

"There's a gate right there." Arin pointed thirty feet to her right. "But I see you and the boys have been to the costume shop; maybe you don't want to soil your pretend-soldier outfits."

His four comrades still had their faces covered, but their body language was loud and clear, muscles tightened, flexed, ready.

Arin started for the gate. I grabbed hold of her arm but she shook me off and trotted. The security guard opened it for her. The guard wore her pistol, Muslim headwear, her eyes alive, her phone ready to capture the moment. The five militiamen didn't move. Arin hurried toward them. I did not doubt that she could hold her own against any one of them, but not five. I ran after her, and Buck and Cat followed us out.

Arin stood two inches from Dit, his jaw jutting out, the black goatee extended upward as his head tilted back.

"What you got for me," Arin said.

We had been training daily. I'd been teaching Arin Krav Maga, and she'd been teaching me Jiu-Jitsu. By moving so close to Dit, it gave him no room to maneuver. One of Dit's four men instinctively moved in on his prey. Arin expected it, had trained for it.

Her right leg had moved back for stability. She leaned away, separated from Dit by an almost precise five inches, while her right hand deflected the other man's punch, his fist landing on the edge of Dit's chin. Before the man could change his kinetic direction and pull his arm back, Arin wrapped her left arm around his and tugged him tight to her body, while her right elbow delivered three consecutive blows to his head.

Arin released him and he stumbled back. Dit and the others moved toward her, and Buck stepped beside her, his badge and gun prominent. No mistaking who was now in charge.

"Get outta here," Buck ordered.

"It's public property. We'll leave when I say we'll leave," Dit countered.

Buck pointed to the guy that Arin had elbowed, his hands on his knees, blood falling to the ground.

"I'm about to arrest him for assault."

"Fuck you," Dit replied. "We've got work to do. Let's go." He turned to lead his small cadre toward the large abstract sculpture that bordered Twenty-Fourth Street.

"Dit, I'm serious. I thought you were a patriot," Cat said.

"And I thought you were a patriot. Time is running out, Cat. You'll need to pick sides."

"What are you talking about? You think your little band of wannabees will win a war or something?" Her hands were up, almost pleading.

Dit stopped twenty feet away and turned to Cat. "January Six was a dress rehearsal, Cat. You have no idea."

He turned again, his guys in front of him, his back to us. I recoiled at what I saw next. On the back of the necks of all five was a tattoo.

A crucifix made of swastikas.

We stood there staring. Transfixed. Beneath us was the train tunnel … a crucifix, swastikas, a photo of the VP, a bullet hole through her forehead. I grabbed my phone from my back pocket and took photos of their necks until they were out of view. Dit must have sensed it. His middle finger shot up as he continued toward Fairmount.

I walked toward them and hollered Dit's name. They stopped, Dit turned to me, then looked to see Buck, Cat and Arin thirty-five feet or so away from me. I held my hands out to the side, palms open.

"Can we talk for a minute?"

Dit looked at his crew, then walked over to me, keeping an arm's length distance.

"My name's Key."

"I know who you are, what do you want?" His American flag bandana hung around his neck, his eyes searched my face.

"I'm trying to understand why, why you wear swastikas." I tried to keep my voice non-judgmental, despite my urge to punch him.

Dit turned his head in the direction where Arin stood and nodded toward her. "That's your girl?"

"My woman, yes."

"Don't give me that politically correct woke bullshit." He shook his head and tugged a bit on his goatee. "Your girl is Black. Don't matter how much white she got in her. Therefore, you'll never understand."

"Understand what?"

"I don't hate Blacks. Hell, I don't even hate Jews, long as they are in Israel where they belong. God gave them their country. He gave the Blacks an entire fucking continent. And he gave us America."

My arms lifted, my palms up in question.

"Stop." Dit put a hand up. "I know what you're going to say. And yeah, the Indians got a raw deal. I feel bad for them. But it was God's plan. All they had to do was be obedient to the white man. That's all any of em need to do."

I felt my fists forming but I relaxed them and leaned in a little. "You don't really expect anyone to do that, right?"

Dit removed his boogie hat, had a slow look around, as if

he was taking a moment to find the right words to educate the ignorant idiot he was addressing.

"Ya see, you all got it wrong. This ain't a race war, it's a religious war, Key. It's the Crusades, clearing the Holy Land for the men God created it for. But you as a white man have lost your way, you got confused. Repent, before it's too late."

He put his hat on, gave me a knowing, even kindly look. The look that said he'd hate to kill a white man, *but buddy, that's your choice*. Dit turned back to join his crew.

"Hey Dit."

He stopped and looked.

"I'm impressed."

"By what?"

"How you got the swastika cross with the VP's photo into the train tunnel. Bullet hole through her forehead. Masterful touch."

The look of confusion that spread across his face confirmed what I suspected; while he was playing us, someone else was playing him.

I trotted over to the crew. Arin put her arm through mine.

"What was that about," she asked

Before I could answer I noticed Cat was wobbly, her eyes closed, head tilted upward. Arin must have seen this as well. She moved next to her, prepared to catch her if she started to fall. Cat began narrating and Arin hit record on her phone.

… I pause at the bottom of the steps, thrilled that I have been invited into the home of the great man. To have a home on Merrion Square was the stuff of wealth, of power, reserved for the British and Anglo-Irish aristocracy. To have the leader of Irish Catholic emancipation as a neighbor must be a thorn in the arse of the gentry, and I allow myself a moment of pleasure at the thought.

The doorman greets me and shows me to the office. Daniel O'Connell is leaning on his desk, arms folded. He looks up at the interruption, and Frederick turns in his chair to see me.

"Our young friend has told me of your great work in America." *He extends his hand across the desk and I reach out to meet it.*

"It is an honor, Sir."

"The honor is mine, Martin. Please, have a seat. Frederick was just giving me his thoughts on religion and abolition."

"Martin is well versed," *Frederick replies.* "We share the opinion that Christianity ought to be the natural ally of abolition, yet in many quarters in America, they use it as a weapon to perpetuate slavery."

"And you are surprised?" *O'Connell looks at Frederick like a father might at a naïve son.*

"No, but I am angry and disappointed that they use the words of the Almighty as a whip against my people."

"As you should be. Frederick, do you know why I am feared by the powerful?" *O'Connell's ample brows rise.* "Because I understand that they use religion to divide and conquer. They fan the flames of Protestant hate against us, yet I have never used my voice against Protestants. I have never said that Catholics or Irish are better than any others. I simply say that we have the God-given right to live our lives with dignity, as do all oppressed. The thing the powerful fear the most is equality. With equality, there is no royalty or monarchy, no gentry, no God-given superiority. Race and religion are always used as weapons of division."

On the wall behind O'Connell hangs a portrait of him addressing a massive crowd at Tara, the ancient ritual site of Irish kings, some million people hungry for his words.

"But I have been told that many a visitor to this very office is turned from your door if you learn they support slavery."

O'Connell laughs, his cheeks shaking a bit.

"And that will be true till the day I die. And if one of them shows up at my grave to pay me their respects, I will ask my guardian angel to take a wing and swat them away. But I will never *argue that they should be considered a lesser human than you and I."*

O'Connell coughs and wipes perspiration from his brow. He leans even closer. His head twitches slightly, a little spittle escaping down one side of his face.

"Your book is selling well. There are no empty seats at your lectures. Your stature is growing. Word of you is not only spreading in the Americas but in Europe as well. The fruits of American slavery are money and power, and much of that money flows to other corners of the earth. Leaders denounce the idea of slavery, but if a pound enters their pocket, well, you know better than me, they talk, but that is all."

"I sense a warning." Frederick and I wait for his response. The great man leans back in his chair, his chest rising. I expect his voice to bellow, but he whispers.

"I have been told that you are in danger."

CHAPTER 15

A helicopter swooped overhead and lowered near the task force tent. We watched three people run under the wash of the rotors, DHS emblazoned on their windbreakers. They raced into the tent as the chopper made its ascent.

Cat emerged from her moments with Martin Fahey and cursed the interruption.

Arin took her by the hand.

"Don't stress. Don't overthink it. If something is there, you'll find it. *Everyting irie …* means everything is good."

"Sorry, Arin. Right now, nothing is good."

Cat was right. Nothing good about any of this. The sky above was bright, but a wall of dark clouds was pressing in. Remnants of the hurricane? How bloody fitting.

Agent Di Stefano stepped out of the tent and waved us over. He held his smartphone out; a video played of Arin confronting Dit, avoiding the blow from his comrade, three rapid elbow strikes to his head.

"You've been busy, Dr. Murphy. Over twelve hundred views in the first five minutes."

Arin took her phone from her pocket. She viewed a text that had just come in and started laughing.

"What?" I asked. "Read it."

Arin was blushing. "This is from a Jamaican friend; she forwarded it from Twitter: *Yuh see our yardie girl smack dat eediat. Next time shi put har foot up fi him battyhole. No mess wid a Jamaican woman.*

Arin returned her phone to her pocket. "Jamaicans will party all night over this. We don't need much excuse."

The female guard at the gate had her eyes buried in her phone, likely watching the video she posted go viral. I held my phone to Di Stefano, the Nazi tattoo image enlarged.

"They all wore this."

"I know," Di Stefano nodded. His attention shifted to Arin, but he said nothing.

"What's up, Joe?" Her voice was tight. "Tell me."

The FBI Agent diverted his eyes and gazed over the city, seeming to land on the Comcast Center building a short distance away.

"There are several threats, some brutal." Di Stefano held up his phone. "Most of the comments cheer you on, Arin, but several are violent. Sick. Probably nonsense, but your face has been known all over the world. Same with you, Key."

Di Stefano stared me down, mano a mano.

"Get off the streets. All of you." He turned to Buck. "You got this?"

Buck gave a slight tilt of the head.

"The house is a mini fortress. Key is licensed to carry, and so is Cat," he answered.

"Unless you have some updates, I need to get back in there." Di Stefano's thumb pointed to the tent over his shoulder.

"The leader of that crew served in Iraq. Cat knows him," Buck said.

"Todd Falcone. Nickname is Dit." Cat looked up at the towering statue of General George Washington, seemingly in motion, his horse in step, his cloak whipping in the wind, charging forward to create a nation. "Dit was a corporal, and a traitor as far as I'm concerned."

"I talked to him, after the confrontation," I said.

"And?" Di Stefano asked.

"Despite the nazi crucifixes on their necks, he was completely unaware about the one in the tunnel."

"How the hell does he know about the tunnel, we haven't released that info." The five o'clock shadow on Di Stefano's face seemed to darken.

"I told him that it was a brilliant move on his part. He had no idea what I was talking about Joe."

Di Stefano shook his head. "That wasn't supposed to be shared. It's my fault. I told you to think out of the box. You did. I need to think about what this means."

"It means he's getting played," I answered.

"I guess you're right." Di Stefano looked at Buck." Get these people off the streets, please. Think on all of this. Call me if got something."

Di Stefano headed back into the tent, the four of us headed toward the museum.

"How did he get that name?" Arin asked.

"He was always saying 'ya going to eatdit,' 'ya going to finishdit,' 'can I have some of dit.' Everyone just started calling him Dit." Cat shot her arms to the side, fingers splayed. "He was a good Marine. Now he wants a civil war. I mean, what the … what happened?"

"He was never a good Marine. He joined to get trained for his civil war." Buck sneered, and started walking toward the art museum steps. "My grandfather killed Nazis, and now they proudly parade around the country with their swastikas.

They're all trained up, courtesy of the U.S. government and taxpayers."

"Buck," Cat called out.

Buck stopped cold, immobile.

"And when their bullets fly, remember who they're aiming at first." Buck touched his black skin, and my heart broke.

People ran the Rocky Steps as if it was a normal day, even though the river was still wreaking havoc a few hundred yards away. Access to the steps would close tomorrow. By ten in the morning, the Secret Service would own every inch, every step, every crevice. And it would stay that way until the VP departed.

Buck took the steps swiftly.

"Buck." Arin hurried toward him. He either didn't hear her, or he ignored her. I sped up, Cat at my side. We made it to the top, a little breathless. Arin looped her arm in Buck's, buddy to buddy. I noted the contrast of her lighter skin to his dark. Arin had once confided that it was difficult living between the two worlds, often mistaken for Italian or Hispanic. But once people identified her as Black, she became the "other" to some of them.

She knew that if the bullets started flying, the bad guys wouldn't be confused.

Buck didn't pause. He didn't acknowledge Arin's presence and she didn't press it. She kept pace. She kept the faith —a bond of shared hurt and indignities.

We walked around the north wing of the museum to the rear, where the car was parked. I caught Buck's eye and moved a few feet away for a quiet exchange with him.

"What?" He glared.

"Fuck you, you know what. You owe me three dollars for last night's dinner. You think I forgot. You try to distract me with all this militia, Nazi stuff. No way." I put my hand out and rubbed my fingers together.

He laughed like I hoped he would. His chest expanded

then relaxed; a sigh, a quiet one. One a brother would hear.

"I don't know if I can keep doing this."

"Doing what, being a detective? Or being an asshole?" I gave him my best wise-guy look.

I tried to hold in my laughter. He threw me into a head-lock and pretended to pummel my stomach. I finally stepped away.

"Offer is good whenever you're ready."

Arin, Buck, and I had talked for the past year about him taking over as the director of the Foundation, which in part was named after his sister: the Tanya McCoy and Mack Murphy Children's Foundation.

"Arin is going to Jamaica to meet with the leaders of her party," I continued. "They want her to run for Prime Minister."

"And she's considering it this time?" Buck glanced at Arin and Cat talking by the car like foxhole buddies.

I nodded.

"She told me this morning." I shuffled my feet a few inches closer to Buck. "The election's not for four years, but they would want her there getting ready."

"I see the look in your eyes. What's wrong?"

"She doesn't want me to go with her: no outside influence, evaluate on her own terms." I felt the little butterflies-in-the-stomach thing. My face felt flush.

"I don't like it. It's not like Arin."

"Are you kidding? It's just like Arin. She's homesick, rest-less. I fell in love with a wild thing. The best way to lose her is to fence her in. Covid did that, fenced her in. She needs some-thing. Something big, or all her energy will fold inward." I put my hand on Buck's shoulder. "And it will choke us."

The museum's sculpture garden sat one hundred feet across the road. My favorite sculpture dominated the top of a hill: an almost ten-foot-tall three-way plug. It always made me smile, the ordinary made extraordinary.

A text hit my phone. *In 2 minutes. URGENT.* I held it for Buck to see. "It's Collins."

Buck gave me a nod.

We stood quietly, waiting. There was a pungent smell, earth and humans, the river a cauldron, stirring and dispersing its odors.

The phone rang.

"Is Buck with you?"

"Yes."

"Anyone else?" Collins asked.

"Cat and Arin are nearby if we need them."

"Put me on speaker."

"Done."

"I have nothing on Rabbit yet. Boland and Walsh, we found one of their communication channels buried in the Dark Web. You have a big problem, Buck. There will be kidnappings today in four states, children of the chairperson of the boards of elections. Punishment for certifying the election."

"When?" Buck asked.

"In the next thirty minutes. You could already be too late. One of them is the Philadelphia Elections Commissioner, happening in a place called East Falls."

"Shit." Buck took my arm and hustled me toward his car.

"I'll send you the details. And Buck, keep my name out of this."

East Falls was just ten minutes away, but it may as well have been an hour. Kelly Drive was flooded, and traffic was a mess. Buck turned his siren on and enabled the strobe lights to flash on the front of his vehicle. Arin and Cat sat in the back. Buck sped across Kelly Drive and turned left onto Pennsylvania Avenue. He handed me his phone.

"Call Cruz, give him the details. Get the other locations to him."

Buck turned onto Ridge Avenue and blared his way to Tilden Street in East Falls, an upscale Philly neighborhood. Two cruisers, lights flashing, blocked the small, tree-lined street. Buck pulled up behind them and hopped out.

"Stay here," he ordered.

We stood outside the car, waiting, watching, as were neighbors. Two black SUVs stopped behind us. Four FBI agents rushed into the house. A few minutes later Buck stood on the front steps and waved us over.

"No kidnapping. But wait till you see this." Buck walked us through the house and opened the rear door to a backyard. There stood a wooden crucifix covered in swastikas. A photo of a man was mounted on it, a bullet hole through his forehead. Attached to the apex of the wooden cross was a note written on cardboard: "You could have stopped the steal, there is a price for being a coward and a traitor."

"I assume that's the election commissioner?"

"Yeah, it turns out the family hadn't discovered it yet. They were surprised by the police at their door. The officers moved the family upstairs while they had a look around."

Buck was about to say something else but got interrupted.

"Detective Mc Coy, I'm Special Agent Chang." The young woman held a smart tablet. "I have Agent Di Stefano on here. He wants a word."

She held the device so that he could see all of us. He gave a tilt of his head.

"I understand you called this in. Care to enlighten me?"

"We got a tip," Buck answered.

"Elaborate." Di Stefano waited.

"When I see you. What's the status at the other locations?"

"Kidnappings in Arizona, Wisconsin, and Georgia. Begs the question, why not Philly?" Di Stefano paused.

"It's simple," I answered while I stared at the crucifix. "It's the same people who placed the VP's photo in the tunnel. They're letting you know that they can pull off coordinated efforts right under your nose."

Di Stefano nodded. "OK, but that doesn't explain why they didn't take the kid."

"Confusion, diversion," Cat answered. "They've got you spinning your wheels trying to figure this out instead of focusing on the VP."

"Boland and Walsh," Buck said. He leaned in closer to the device. "They are smack in the middle of this. You need to find them."

Di Stefano looked away from the camera for a moment, the deep lines in his forehead revealed his tension. "I need you back at the tent."

Di Stefano disappeared from the screen.

The police had cordoned off Eakins Oval to traffic, but onlookers were out in mass. Buck held his badge out of the window and waited for the officer to move the barrier.

Di Stefano was standing at the far end of the tent with DHS Agent Noreen Casey and Cat's boss, Scott Morrison. Their voices were low, but their expressions were loud. Di Stefano's right hand kept flexing into a fist, Casey's glare withering. It was Morrison who seemed unaffected, relaxed. I assumed Di Stefano was confronting Morrison about the door from the museum into the train tunnel.

Morrison finished his conversation and hurried past us for the exit. Cat's body tightened, her face a bit red. Morrison gave not a nod or a wink, as if he had never met her. Then he stopped suddenly, turned slowly, and walked back to us.

He stared at Cat, his head nodding ever so slightly.

"I screwed up. I didn't follow protocol with the tunnel thing." He glanced over at Di Stefano then brought his attention back to all of us. "I'm used to having operational control,

I'm not much of a team player," he said contritely. "Been a bit of an ass lately. Sorry, Captain."

Cat looked to the ground, ran her fingers through her hair, cocked her head to the right while taking Morrison in. "You're all right, Scott. Let's just do our best for the VP."

I watched Morrison, his gait not so self-assured and commanding, as he disappeared on the other side of the colossal main stage.

DHS Agent Casey waved us over to her. She stood in front of a computer screen. The viral video of Arin humiliating the tattoo-wearing Nazi was running on repeat. Di Stefano joined us.

"I understand you know this guy." The DHS Agent pointed to Dit.

"I thought I did," Cat answered. "But yeah. I know him a little."

"We've been watching him for a few years. He steps close to the line but never over, knows his way around the law. Dit's a hardcore hater, a true believer. He sat out January Six, but we have evidence that he was an organizer. A lot of the elite of that world sit out the battles. They concentrate on getting ready for the war."

"Which raises the question, who tipped you off about the kidnappings?" Di Stefano asked.

"Who tipped us is unimportant," Buck answered. "The two guys that Cat saw around the art museum, Boland and Walsh, are the organizers of today's events." Buck had a look at the screen; my eyes followed his. The video of Arin's elbow striking that white supremacist repeated and repeated. Buck grinned. Some justice in a day that had held little.

The FBI and DHS Agents exchanged looks.

"We're on first names, right? Please call me Noreen." She nervously rubbed her right hand over her left forearm. "I didn't want to say it in front of everyone yesterday, but I have tested positive for the Ancestral Memory gene. Joe knows about it. I have been getting glimpses: real, so freaking real. Sometimes they stop me in my tracks. Key, I know that's how it started for you, right?"

"Yes, a sword swinging close to me."

"A hand reaching down," Cat answered, fingers tapping the side of her leg.

"So, when you look at what's happening now, with this shitshow, what do you see?" Casey asked.

Noreen Casey seemed happy to be talking to us. I've experienced this many times from people who have the gene. They get excited, reverential sometimes, like I'm the Pope of Ancestral Memory. But it was Noreen that had power, real power. As Buck said, I'm just the "memory whisperer."

"What do you see, Noreen?" I asked in return. I was genuinely curious. They had everything, every resource. They understood the patterns, penetrated the data points, made connections, tapped phones, hacked accounts, and planted undercover agents inside every possible terrorist group. But for some reason, DHS Agent Casey wanted our opinion.

"I see all the reports that my underlings and overlords want me to see. I'm not sure I'm seeing the truth." Agent Casey looked me in the soul. She did the same with Cat. As if the ancestral gene gave us clairvoyant powers. It didn't. I was more confused now than I was two hours ago. But I did have an opinion.

"What I see is a chess game in which your opponent is reeling you in just before they declare checkmate. We were being played."

"There won't be any problem for the VP on Saturday? Is that what you're saying," Di Stefano asked.

"I have no clue. It's your job to figure that out. Follow me." I walked out of the tent, around the grand Eakins statue, facing the main stage and the Rocky Steps. "We agreed that

Boland and Walsh stood on those steps, in front of the security cameras, likely knowing that Cat was aware of them. These guys are pros. They purposely chose that spot."

I looked at the ground beneath me, pointing my index and forefinger downward. "They knew you would find the crucifix in the tunnel. Then fifty of their soldiers show up today, dressed in battle gear, the Nazi crucifix on their necks. Not very subtle."

"Their action today against the election commissioners was coordinated in four states," Noreen stated. "No fingerprints. No evidence. That's extremely difficult to pull off and the media is all over it. It's a terror campaign." Agent Casey pointed to the stage. "The Vice President will stand there in two days. Conclusions?"

I observed the tourists gathered in front of the Rocky statue taking selfies. Others played out the Sylvester Stallone ritual, racing to the top of the steps, fists pumping. "Their game is about misdirection, confusion, and chaos. They want Homeland Security distracted and the public in fear."

"Something's on your mind, Key." Buck gave me a little push on the shoulder. "Just say it."

"I don't think they will try to kill the VP. They know the weight of the government would descend on them in full force. But they will create an incident that sends sixty thousand people running for the gates, and many could die in the crush. The VP will be rushed into hiding. Fear and chaos. That's their goal."

"I disagree." All eyes turned to Cat. "I think they will try to kill her."

"Why do you think that?" Arin's voice strained at the question.

Cat's right arm was rising, her hand extended as if to grasp something. "*'They are coming to kill you, Frederick,'* we just don't know how."

CHAPTER 16

THURSDAY, SEPTEMBER 2, 2021.
MOORE TOWN, JAMAICA

The car carrying Li Chen easily maneuvered up the mountain road, past the pastel walls of St. Paul's Anglican Church, which sat in contrast to the jungle-like surroundings. The faded yellows and pinks and blues were but a burst of color on a mountain lane that was lonely in the sameness of jungle green.

One mile from the church, on a road that didn't exist on a map, sat a two-story estate home, a relic from the colonial days, beautiful by any standard. On its fifty acres were fruit trees, vegetable gardens, sheep, goats, hens, and roosters. A greenhouse the size of two tennis courts, occupied by hundreds of strains of marijuana plants, looked more like a science lab than a ganja hothouse.

Dobermanns roamed the fenced perimeter, weaving between palm, mango, and banana trees. Motion-detector cameras sat camouflaged in trees, and a team of armed men sat bored in guardhouses that dotted the facility. The higher altitude provided cooler air, and the massive palm trees gave shelter from the sun.

A large carriage house sat twenty yards off the residence. A smaller version of the main house, its cedar roof provided cover over its white-columned porch. It felt like a place where dark rum and Cuban cigars would be enjoyed by men in Panama hats.

Li Chen had returned from the event in Port Antonio. He shed his suit for white linen pants, sandals, and a navy-blue bamboo T-shirt that hugged his lean, muscular body.

He summoned Diamond and E to the hothouse, amongst rows of cannabis plants. This was not a commercial hothouse but a scientific research facility. It was home to just two employees who had finished their work for the day—one a master grower, the other a genetic scientist and expert in genetically modified medicinal plants.

The eastern half of the facility was dedicated to genetically enhancing the effects of THC. In plain English, it was to make it more potent and therefore more valuable. The western side was for genetically engineered medical marijuana. That was where the fortune would be made.

Chen did not enjoy ganja. It made him paranoid and rendered his decision-making prowess useless. He did not mind Diamond or E using it; it seemed to focus them and increase their ability to analyze data. He watched as they lit and smoked the potent herb. They walked together in silence, past the rows of plants grown from ancient seeds and those from CRISPR gene-editing technology.

The news from Philadelphia had been good. The Made in the USA Festival would go on. The VP would attend. The presence of fifty Nazi lunatics on the streets today was a stroke of genius.

He laughed at the thought of Arin Murphy clobbering the face of that white supremacist, a barely useful idiot. The views and shares had crossed twenty-five thousand last he looked. She was gorgeous. So was her brother, Joseph. Though he had hated Joseph since high school, he still wouldn't mind fucking him. Or her. Or both at the same time. That would be delicious. He knew that she was considering a run for Prime Minister. Let's see if she survives the weekend, he thought; that would be an excellent test of her worthiness.

"Let your plans be dark and impenetrable as night, and when you move, fall like a thunderbolt," Chen said aloud, quoting Sun Tzu from *The Art of War*.

Neither Diamond nor E paid much attention. They were used to their boss reciting random quotes. Chen stopped at one plant; the outline of the leaf was gold, the interior a dense green, one of the more promising of the modified strains. He stared at the cannabis, but his mind was sweeping over the details of the weekend.

"Did Rabbit communicate with Boland and Walsh as discussed?"

"Yeh, boss," E answered. "Just like you say."

Chen switched his attention to Diamond.

"Do one for me."

Diamond looked pleased to be asked and gave a ganja-induced smile, his head bobbing and swaying as he conjured the words of Shakespeare and summoned his own muse.

"So good night, good night! Parting is such sweet sorrow,
Thus we'll smoke more weed when we meet tomorrow
When fate shall bring us together again
We'll roll a joint and embrace as friends
God bless this herb and all its visions
Though I eat too much and make bad decisions
So let us think and speak with wit and grace
And make the most of life's fleeting pace."

Diamond inhaled deeply, holding the ganja in his lungs and a slight smile on his lips.

CHAPTER 17

Thursday, September 2, 2021.
Delancey Place

Buck turned onto Delancey Place and hit the brakes. Our house was in sight. Like most homes on this block, my parents' house was historically certified. Today it looked more like a circus. Twenty yards ahead sat TV trucks, and reporters waiting on the street and sidewalks. I was hoping Buck would back up, but it was too late. Cars had pulled up behind us.

"No, no, no, no, no." I turned in my seat to see Cat in a panic. "I can't go near reporters. Can't happen." She was shaking.

"Arin, they're here for you. Buck, take Cat through the back. We'll keep this short." Arin got out, I followed. She took my arm and we walked down the sidewalk toward the house. The press saw us and lined up for the ambush while Buck drove down the street and around the corner.

Reporters shouted questions while we were still twenty feet away.

"Hold on. First, back up, do not block the steps. We might

need to get away from you, fast." That got a chuckle, but they complied. "This will be short. I know you are here for me and not Dr. Murphy, but she'll be on stand-by." They looked at me like I was nuts and began hollering questions at Arin.

"One at a time," Arin held her hand up and then pointed to one reporter.

"Dr. Murphy, why did you strike that man today?"

Arin seemed to consider the question; she rubbed her hands together for a moment, then regarded the reporter. "I assume you saw the video. He tried to punch me. It was self-defense."

"Witnesses report that you were behind a low fence when you suddenly slapped a man. Then you hurried through the gate, where the confrontation continued. Who did you slap, and why?"

Arin shook her head and grimaced. "That was a mistake. I shouldn't have slapped him."

I watched the reporters as they stared in amazement at this admission. "No, I should have punched his lights out."

"It's been a long day, everyone." I took Arin by the arm and started toward the steps.

"Key, Dr. Murphy, you've been seen at the Eakins Oval security tent yesterday and today conferring with the FBI and DHS. What's your role?"

I was not expecting that question. There was no good answer. If I said nothing, it would fuel speculation. "We have no role, to speak of. As you know, Arin is an anthropologist who specializes in how people of different ethnicities interact with each other."

Arin picked up on the theme and jumped in. "There will be young people of every shade here. I was honored to answer some questions, you know, more of a sensitivity training on how to best handle any potential conflict."

We headed up the steps and I unlocked the door. A

reporter's voice rang out. "Have you checked the tweets? There are dozens of death threats. What's your response?"

The unmistakable joy of little voices spilled up Delancey Place. A group of around twelve five-year-old's, daycare I guessed, crossed over Eighteenth Street ten yards away, teachers in tow. Arin and I watched them for a moment, their laughter a welcome boost.

I turned back to the reporter, but my attention was captured by someone over her shoulder, across the street. A hooded figure, tactical sunglasses, American flag bandana covering his face. He raised two fingers, pointed them to his eyes, then slowly lowered them, pointing downward. *Burn it to the ground.*

I regained my composure, thanked the reporters, and then hurried into the house. We hustled into the kitchen.

"There was a guy across the street just now, masked, sunglasses, hoodie. Gave me the two-finger United Aryan Brotherhood sign."

Buck and Cat got off the kitchen stools as I ranted.

Buck took me by the arm.

"Key and I will make certain the security systems are operating. Arin, take Cat to the basement, check the doors, make sure everything is secure."

"We'll meet you there in a few minutes," I added.

Buck opened the door to a closet off the foyer where a smart tablet sat on a shelf. It controlled the closed-circuit security system. Buck tapped in a few commands and five thumbnail video feeds occupied the screen. He selected one, the second-floor camera that focused on the steps into the house and the surrounding sidewalk. It showed the news teams packing up, no doubt frustrated by the brevity of our impromptu conference.

"Where was he?" Buck asked.

"Sidewalk, across the street." I pointed to the thumbnails. "Here."

The thumbnail grew to fill the screen. "He's gone. Rewind it to where he enters."

Buck sped the rewind, and thirty seconds later we saw a hooded figure turn the corner at Eighteenth and Delancey. He leaned against the wall.

"Put the feeds side by side on the same timestamp."

Buck split the screen, one feed covering the front steps, the other with the man in it. He typed in the timestamp, and both videos were now in synch, on pause, Arin and me on the steps. The intruder wore a grey hoodie, sunglasses, an American flag bandana, and black pants.

"Go," I said. Buck pushed the start button. Two fingers rose to his eyes, then the fingers pointed downward. I watched myself turn from him, Arin and I walking into the house, the reporters still shouting. The man pushed off the wall, looked directly at the second-floor camera, and raised his middle finger. He then turned toward Eighteenth Street.

"Holy shit," Buck said, pausing the video. He pointed to the thick blue stripe running down the side of his pants. "Police issue."

I stared silently, leaned in close to have a better look at the stripe, the man, searching for any other clue. "We were meant to see that."

Buck leaned against the closet door jamb, arms folded.

"Have you cleaned and oiled your gun?"

I left Buck to his task and stepped into my mother's little sanctuary, where I had discovered family ghosts, truths, and revelations two years ago. I knew Buck would examine the videos: his detective impulse. If there was something to be divined, he would find it. I didn't know what it was like to have an actual brother; I did know what it was like to have someone so close that he felt like blood, *like* a brother. And a sister. Tanya and Buck ran in my veins. Arin, so different.

Buck and Tanya were like clay and water and sand; jokes and teasing, the vapors of childhood, cops and robbers, hide and seek, pirates and coves and treasure. Arin was air, breath itself. She was also fire, passion and probing, nothing that could be contained. Should not be contained.

I opened the drawer, hefted the leather-bound book with the Murphy coat of arms embossed on the cover, and laid it in front of me. I remembered so clearly. Two years ago, my mother had asked me to do three things before I said yes or no. I had learned from my parents only twenty-four hours before that I had the Ancestral gene. The memories I was experiencing were of Aedan. His uncle, the king of the Murphy Clan, had assigned him the task of protecting the holy project that we knew as the *Book of Kells*.

The first of the three things was to read the account. In these pages lay the words of my great grandfather, Eamon Murphy, about his encounter with Mack Murphy, whom I would later learn was Arin's great-great-grandfather. Mack and Eamon shared the family tree. Their ancestor Fergus Murphy was ripped from Ireland by Cromwell's henchmen and sent by prison ship to Jamaica to toil the fields for his English overlords. Fergus left behind a pregnant wife, from whom I eventually descended, and found a new wife in Jamaica, from whom Arin descended. Though our bloodlines traveled different paths over three hundred years, Mack Murphy's words joined the two of us in the grand adventure; through his clues, we found the treasure hidden by Aedan over twelve hundred years ago.

The second thing my mother requested was that I meet with Dr. Garcia, the genetic scientist who had discovered the Ancestral Memory gene.

The third: fly to Jamaica on zero notice, meet the Murphy family, examine the clues, and decide whether to search for

135

the treasure. Or not. Fate intervened. I took one look at Arin and the decision was made. It wasn't just her looks, despite the charge of electricity I felt when I saw the black curls ringing her face and the gap in her teeth that made her smile an addiction. It was the simultaneous and contradictory feeling that she was both safe harbor and riotous adventure. And that the gods of happiness said, "It's your turn, young man; don't be an asshole; go for it."

I did. And not a day went by that I didn't experience a moment of fear that I'd lose her. The gods of happiness tended to be a fickle lot.

I opened the book to my great grandfather's letter documenting his precious moments with Mack Murphy. My memories with Aedan played in my brain as if he were flesh and blood sitting across from me. My eyes closed and then came the words I heard him say two years ago, oft-repeated in my daydreams: "It's your turn to be a warrior, to be strong and complete the mission." He had told me, in the thrill of my imagination, that he would be my guide. How I wished he could guide me now. I felt his hand rest on my shoulder and a quiver of air brush my cheek. My eyes opened as Arin's lips met mine. She kept them there, a slight movement of her lower lip, her fingers caressing the back of my neck.

"Were you having a visit with Aedan?"

"And Mack and Eamon and Fergus."

"We need to help Cat continue her visits with Martin and Douglass. We are downstairs waiting for you." She turned to leave, but I took her hand and followed her to the basement.

This was my mother's professional realm; her archeology lab lay hidden behind sliding panels on which the Claddagh ring was painted in gold relief: two hands clasped, holding a heart, a royal crown resting above. My father had his office on the third floor. So strange to think that they had not been in the house in over two years. Though Arin and I had planned to visit them in Ireland from Scotland, Frederick Douglass and Martin Fahey had different plans for us.

A large whiteboard on the wall lent seriousness to the room. Buck hustled down the stairs as I set chairs for us and contemplated the empty board.

Cat had her hair down, dark and unbrushed, a bit of havoc. She stood and twisted it into a ponytail and wrapped a band around it. With a marker in hand she wrote the word "Rabbit," and enclosed it in a circle. She added a circle below it, then one to the left and another to the right, and all had intersecting points: a Venn diagram.

On the bottom left circle, Cat wrote "Feds;" on the right, she wrote "Key-Arin-Buck."

"I keep thinking about this mystery man." She pointed to the word Rabbit. "In fact, we don't know if it's a man, a woman, or a group. When we do threat assessments in the military, the first order of business is to understand who the players are. We are blind. We need to get un-blind. There is no way Di Stefano would bring up this name unless he believed that there was a connection."

Buck stood, grabbed a blue marker and wrote "Joseph and Joyce" in the intersecting circle on the right. I watched Arin bite her lip and shake her head at the reminder of her brother and mother's connection. In the non-intersecting section, he wrote "Tanya-Arin-Key." In the intersecting left circle, the one marked Feds, he wrote, "wire transfer."

"Put Boland and Walsh in there." I pointed to the Rabbit circle. "We don't know if they're connected with Rabbit, but my money says they are."

"Why? Elaborate." Arin said.

I took a marker in hand. "From the little we know, Rabbit makes things happen but doesn't get his hands dirty. He moves the money, gives the orders maybe." Under Boland and Walsh, I wrote "reconnaissance," "rally permit," "Nazi crucifix." "These two are responsible for the death threat against the VP."

"You certain about that?" Cat asked, tapping her chin with her knuckles.

"Collins found the plans for the Board of Elections threats in their chat room." I placed my fingers on Boland and Walsh's names. "Nazi crucifix at the Commissioners' homes, The VP's photo, Dit and his classy crew of Nazi tatted insurrectionists."

"What if someone else put it there, assuming that the Feds would dig?" Arin stated.

"To what purpose?"

"Your words to DHS an hour ago: it's a chess game, misdirection and confusion. We were being played," Buck answered. "It's possible that Rabbit or someone is pulling the strings on this."

There was a pitcher of ice water on the table courtesy of Arin. I filled a glass while trying to sort things out in my mind.

"Buck, call Di Stefano. He needs to give us more to work with."

Buck hesitated for a moment, staring at the Venn diagram. He dialed; the FBI Agent answered. Buck disconnected. "He's finishing a call; he'll connect in five."

Buck laid the phone in front of him. Cat tugged on her ponytail and shifted in her chair.

"This is bullshit. Give me the phone, Buck." Cat eyed it and was about to reach for it. Buck lifted it and dialed on speaker mode.

"What? I told you I'd call." Di Stefano said.

"Are you on with the President?" Cat hollered impatiently.

"Yes."

"Bullshit, a lowly FBI Agent doesn't get to talk to the President," Cat responded. Cat looked at the whiteboard, the Venn diagram. "Whoever you are on with, call them back."

Quiet. A lonely moment. The four of us sitting there. The line dead. Then not.

"What's up?"

Cat pointed to me.

"Joe, this is Key. You said Rabbit's name came up regarding wire transfers. We need more info."

"Why, what are you thinking?"

"If you want us to think out of the box, you need to give us more to go on."

Buck nodded his approval of my response.

"We intercepted two emails. One was around six months ago, the other around three. It only referenced that Rabbit sent wires. No amounts. The email recipients simply do not exist. Fake addresses were going to fake companies or individuals. Standard. However, I left this out. Two weeks ago, a gun shipment that ATF was following. They intercepted a conversation that said, 'If you miss the delivery date, Rabbit will wrap a rope around your balls, attach them to an anchor, and drop you into shark-infested waters. He paid. He wants them.'"

"Who was on the call?"

"That's way above your clearance, Key. I can tell you it was a mid-level member of the previous administration, well connected, known conspiracy-theory believer. And he's gone off the grid. We tracked the call he made to New York. Queens, to be exact. The phone he was calling was a burner." Agent Di Stefano cleared his throat. "Your turn. Who gave you the tip on Boland and Walsh?"

"That's way above your clearance, Special Agent, but I assume you've done a deep dive into their dark caves." Buck waited for an answer.

"Of course. But we haven't found the info that you did."

"That means we've earned our stripes, Joe," Cat said, eyeing the phone. "If you were to take a wild guess, where is the money coming from, and where is it landing?"

"Darndest thing, Captain. We think they are hiding it by transferring small amounts, three to four thousand at a time, into hundreds of accounts. Anything under five grand doesn't trip the alarm."

"Any other crumbs you can toss?" Cat asked.

"Sure." The FBI agent sighed. "Arin should get a good attorney. You're all over social media and TV for your elbow strikes to the head and saying that you should have put Dit's lights out."

"I meant it."

"You humiliated them, Arin. They don't play nice. I asked Deputy Commissioner Cruz to have a car out front and one in the back driveway. Arin, I mean this, do not leave the house by yourself. And the rest of you, do not leave the house without a gun." Di Stefano ended the call.

Arin doodled on her notepad, her brain working something out. Cat stood and arched her back.

"I just texted Padraig," I announced.

A moment later my phone rang.

"I have an update." I repeated what Di Stefano said about the mid-level man. "Does that give your team enough to work with? And Padraig, one other thing. They think the money is being transferred in transactions under five K, but to many accounts."

Padraig simply disconnected. I guessed it was enough for him to go on. I, on the other hand, felt like hitting a punching bag. Arin sat by my right shoulder, Buck off my left, Cat next to him, all looking listless. The basement had become our workout area: dumbbells, kettlebells, sparring gear. I needed to pump some blood and energy into my body. I got up and grabbed the thirty-five-pound dumbbells, did a rapid series of bicep curls until the burn came, the pain, then did ten more.

Buck's phone buzzed. He smiled—something I hadn't witnessed in a while. He handed me his phone. I put the weights down and read the text:

15 of us at McGillin's waiting to raise a glass to Arin. Take a short break from saving the world and get your ass over here.

It came from Malcolm, a good friend of Buck's and one of the best cops in the city. I read the text to Cat and Arin.

"Not a lot we can do until Padraig gets back to us. I'm hungry," I said.

Arin put her marker on the desk.

"Di Stefano said not to leave the house," she said.

I wondered how this debate was going to go. The Professor versus the Detective.

"No he didn't, he said for you not to leave alone and to take a gun." Buck had his shoulder holster over the back of his chair. He put it on over his white T, then slipped his arms into his short-sleeve button-down, the front left open. He straightened his badge over his belt.

"The cop posted in the alley, I'll have him give us a ride," Buck said.

Arin took the whiteboard marker and wrote, "the Vice President might die here on Saturday."

"Just a note to focus us when we return."

———

Padraig Collins leaned against his Mercedes and looked at his hands, hands that had killed people during the Troubles. Collins of the daylight kept those thoughts at a distance. Collins of the two a.m. nocturnal twisting and turning of ghosts and demons could not escape so easily. Collins of the day believed that Christ had died for his sins and that he was forgiven. In the ocean of sweat and dreams, the nocturnal

Collins felt the presence of evil, his own wickedness, and tried to reach the vapors of holiness that washed in to save him, wisps of the worthy saints tugging him to safety.

Like Collins himself, his patron saint Columba had killed, had caused turmoil. Columba was exiled to Iona, Scotland and began a ministry uniting the Scotti and the Picts. Columba had demanded of Collins that he must lead Ireland to unity in exchange for his salvation. That he be a peacemaker.

Fate had offered him an opportunity to extend his reach for salvation. The Vice President of the United States was at risk. If there was a country he loved almost as much as Ireland, it was the United States. Yet America, the land of hopes and dreams, was drowning in hatred and division.

Collins pushed off the Mercedes to view the Clontarf Castle Hotel. He turned back to the hedgerow that stood tall before him. An archway, subtle and almost invisible, was carved into the hedge. He passed through and dialed a code on his phone. The perimeter security door opened and he stepped into the courtyard of the carriage house.

He approached the Welcome sign and placed his eye directly over the optical scanner. The door opened and he walked through the entrance. Originally a carriage house for the castle, it was now the home of Collins's elite hacker team. His legitimate empire had offices throughout Ireland and Europe, but the Clontarf Team was his most precious asset, off the books, untraceable.

Collins entered, and Anwulika forced a smile. It pained Collins. She was a life force, one of the few humans who made him smile, laugh, and forgive her many indiscretions. Collins had attributed her slow but certain loss of spirit to the pandemic. But he now knew better.

"We need to talk."

Anwulika stood, six-foot, Nigerian proud.

"As you say, boss man."

Collins extended his hands to her, intimate. She took them. He was thirty years her senior. He loved her as a father, his daughter's distress weighing on him.

"You are troubled. What will help release your burden?"

Like him, Anwulika had killed. She had been gang-raped by a group of men, men who told her that good cock would teach her not to be a lesbian. One by one, she had tracked them, bled them out, steel against arteries. She claimed she delighted in the retribution. But Collins had watched her light dim, her happiness fade. He knew that the taking of life reduced the brightness of one's own spirit. It must. It was the natural consequence. You had only two choices: fade and become a monster, or confess and brighten your light.

"I am not troubled. You mistake my melancholy for burden." She squeezed his hand in affirmation.

Collins simply stared into her eyes. The bold, self-assured Anwulika was not in them. She tried to hold his gaze, but the gentle caring he showed caused a fissure, a small crack, a nakedness of emotion that she could not hide.

"I am not ashamed of what I did." She pulled her hands from his and stepped back. "I visit them every night," she spat, her voice rising. "I plunge my blade into their hearts and delight in removing them from the earth. It makes me happy."

"And yet you are unhappy. You are leaving me. I feel it."

Anwulika turned from him and slapped the wall.

"I live in this small dark place, day after day. It's my fucking prison, Padraig. I can't breathe. I can't touch the universe from in here. I must ..." Her hands shook. "I must also exist outside of here."

"And where, my dear Anwulika, would you like to go?"

"Antarctica."

"Really?"

"Yes, really." She seemed to grow taller, eyes partially closed. "I want to stand in the extreme, in a place few go. I want to feel the bottom of the earth and scream proudly; I am a Black woman, an African woman. I belong anywhere on earth. Anwulika belongs where Anwulika decides she belongs."

Collins looked up at his tall protégé as a calmness settled over her. She opened her eyes to his smile.

"Do it. Soon. But first, I need you to help me save another proud Black woman, one who has gone where none have gone before her. The Vice President of the United States."

CHAPTER 18

Thursday, September 2, 2021.
Midtown Village, Philadelphia

McGillin's Olde Ale House always took me by surprise, sitting at the end of Drury Lane, which locals called Dreary Lane. The Lane might have been ugly, but McGillin's was an invitation of color and Irish flags. The outdoor dining area was packed, hungry diners standing to the side, pints of beer in hand, waiting for a table to open. It was crazy that Philly woke up to a flood that very morning, and people were still kayaking on the expressway.

Buck reminded us to show our proof of vaccination; otherwise, there was no going inside. The bouncer examined our cards and then opened the door. It took a second for the crowd to look our way, and then it started.

"Arin, Arin," clap, clap, clap, repeat. Arin blushed at the attention.

Malcolm hollered out, "You a true Philly girl now," which prompted a round of "Philly, Philly, Philly" from the crowd.

Malcolm thrust beers into our hands, and the thirty or so indoor guests raised a cheer to Arin. Most of the crowd were cops I recognized. Arin was the show; everyone took selfies with her and posted them. No one seemed to recognize Cat. That was a good thing. She had enough craziness running through her mind and nervous system, but now she was slapping hands and raising her glass. Buck was introducing her to his friends. She needed this. Sometimes the only way to get a clear head is to toss back a few and forget that the world is teetering.

I felt drawn to the stairwell. The "Lit Brothers" sign remained over the landing. I had stood there with Buck the day my memories began in full-on living color. I had been overwhelmed and afraid, assuming I had lost my mind. Now the memories were just a normal part of my existence. Rarely anything new. And I longed for them. They tugged at me, wanted attention, but they offered no revelations anymore, like clips from a movie I'd seen a million times. I lived with the hope that Aedan would appear with a new adventure for me.

I leaned against the wall and watched the miracle that was Arin. She turned, saw me, and excused herself from the group peppering her with praise and questions.

"I'm beat, still jet lagging. You?" She covered her mouth and yawned.

"I'm standing here thinking about what a great Prime Minister you would be."

"Really?"

"Yea mon, if yuh wan it."

She was used to me butchering Jamaican accents. I worked hard at making it bad, which was easy for me.

I touched Arin's right shoulder and tilted my head as Cat approached. She had a beer in her left hand and a shot glass in her right. She walked over, all smiles, and stopped a foot from the stairwell. Cat's shot glass slipped from her hand, banging on the floor. The smell of whiskey filled the air.

"They were here." Cat tentatively placed her foot on the

landing, as if ghosts were waiting for her. She stood, silent, examining the walls, pocked and dented, the steps worn by a century of footfalls.

"Martin walked up the stairs first. He looked around. For threats, maybe?" Cat ran her right hand through her hair and stepped onto the stairwell. "Frederick followed." She stared up the steps for a long moment. "Is that possible?" she said to me.

Buck had joined us, side-stepping the puddle of whiskey and the shot glass on the floor.

"I know a little of the history," he said.

Cat looked hopeful.

"This place opened the year Lincoln became President. My father bought me my first beer here. He told me that abolitionists met upstairs. Meant nothing to me then, but there you have it, Cat. The bottom of American society gathered here back then: the Irish and the Blacks."

We followed Cat up the steps. The amount of memorabilia in this place made it a mini museum. Newspaper clippings dating back to the Civil War were mounted next to the front page of the *Philadelphia Inquirer*, portraying the 1974 Flyers' Stanley Cup victory.

Cat reached the second floor and let her eyes take in the gallery of photos. She walked as someone might in the Sistine Chapel, head craned, a sense of reverence in her steps. She moved to the end of the hall and entered a room. People sat in conversation, beers and wings and whiskey on their tables. Cat twirled a lock of her hair with her index finger as her eyes swept along the walls, seeing, I assumed, what others could not. We waited for her to relay what she was experiencing. She backed into the hallway, returning to us.

"Martin said to Douglass, 'You must convince Lincoln to allow Negro troops.'"

"Lincoln didn't allow it until after the Emancipation

Proclamation in 1863," Arin told us. "If I remember correctly, Douglass and others started their pressure campaign in 1862."

I thought about the intense debates that must have taken place here. The cliché: "If the walls could only speak." I wished they could.

"I can't believe it. I can't believe I'm walking where they walked." Cat wore a smile. She looked content. Not something I'd seen since meeting her yesterday.

We made our way down the steps and stood near the landing, away from the crowd. A young woman, cornrow braids, nose pierced, eyes simultaneously shy and excited, walked to us carrying a tray that held a bottle of amber liquid and four glasses. She cast her eyes to the floor, then excitedly at Arin.

"Dr. Murphy, mi take yuh class uh Jamaica."

She broke away from her West Indian dialect and handed us each a tumbler and poured. "This was sent to you by phone order. Compliments of Dit."

"What did you just say?" Cat's eyes widened; her mouth hung open.

"Some guy just called. Said you know him."

"Say his name again."

The waitress looked taken aback at Cat's demanding tone.

"Dit, something like that. He said to congratulate Arin for the video going viral. He said even more of his friends were going to show up Saturday as a result."

CHAPTER 19

FRIDAY, SEPTEMBER 3, 2021.
LONG BAY BEACH, JAMAICA

Li Chen stood on the cool sand, the crystal-clear water rolling close to his toes. His six Dobermanns sat behind him, unwavering attention on their master. It was a Friday morning ritual, catching the first touch of color in the sky, a light breeze off the water. The mile-long beach was home to coconut trees, royal palms, and red mangroves. The jasmine and vanilla odor of frangipani trees made its way to the shore. Chen drew the captivating aroma through his nose; memories aroused—mostly good ones.

Chen loved his barefoot runs. His father would take him to Jamaican beaches, each more challenging than the last, stopwatch in hand. He would cheer his son on, occasionally cursing him in Mandarin if he failed to put forth the effort. Chen ran track in high school, easily beating most of his opponents. Practicing on a track with sneakers was one thing. It was quite a different level of demand to increase and maintain speed on the ever shifting terrain of a beach. His muscled legs showed the results of a life of disciplined athleticism.

No one was crazy enough to get close to a man surrounded by six deadly dogs. Nonetheless, Chen's armed bodyguard stood to attention twenty feet away.

As the horizon began its daily dance of reds and blues and orange, playing soft light on the white sand, Chen turned west and assumed his starting position. The lead dogs trotted to the front and awaited his first step. Chen needed his mind clear and sharp. Nothing could go wrong in Philadelphia. He had amassed a small fortune, but it would be all for nothing if he didn't live to enjoy it.

————

Diamond and E turned to the sound of the door opening. Showered and alert, Chen looked at his watch.

"Are they ready?"

E nodded.

"Lawyers will send the documents at nine as you instructed."

CHAPTER 20

The coffee sucked. So did the yogurt and fruit. The bagels were tasteless. We had added nothing to the whiteboard. The last thing written there was the reminder from Arin: "The Vice President of the United States might die here on Saturday."

"A cop, an anthropologist, and two people with the Ancestral Memory Gene walk into an Irish pub."

Arin, Buck, and Cat stared at me listlessly.

"The bartender takes one look at them," I continued, "and says, 'For Guinness' sake, you look like you need a pint.' The four of them pat their pockets and shake their heads. 'We got nothing,' they say in unison."

I throw my hands out, like I'm waiting for applause.

"Was that supposed to be funny?"

Cat's head tilted, eyes narrowed, a look of confusion, like a cop interrogating a suspect. I think I'll abandon my stand-up comedy career.

"Look, DHS is all over this. Just 'cause we got nothing

doesn't mean they aren't about to knock some doors down." Buck, trying to reassure us; his face calm, his voice commanding. I knew him too well. I wasn't buying it.

His phone rang. "Mc Coy."

We unsuccessfully tried to hear what was being said. He disconnected.

"That was Cruz. The One Six lawyers just successfully expanded the rally. They will gather at Independence Hall at four tomorrow and march to Love Park at five. They will be at Love Park from six to ten." Buck lifted his coffee cup. "One less thing to worry about, I guess."

"You guess?" Arin asked.

"They won't be there when the festival-goers arrive in the morning. That's a good thing," Buck replied.

Cat shook her head. "Aw, man. The looney tunes will be there when the VP is speaking. I don't like it."

We were sitting at the table, around the whiteboard. All I could see, over and over, were the words "might die here on Saturday." That was tomorrow. The day after today. Thirty hours from now. Fireworks and the VP. The freaking Vice President of the United States, the only woman to attain that office. I was wrong. Cat was right. They were going to kill her.

I slammed my hand on the table. Everyone jumped back, startled.

"I'm sick of being toyed with. They never intended to have the rally at the original time. They had always planned to do this."

"What are you talking about?" Arin asked.

"Key's right," Cat added. "Draw all the resources and attention to one thing while executing another. The police would have already allocated resources for the original permit."

"Keep us off balance." Buck ran his finger around the rim of his cup.

"Engage people with what they expect; it is what they are able to discern and confirms their projections. It settles them into predictable patterns of response, occupying their minds while you wait for the extraordinary moment—that which they cannot anticipate." Cat said.

"*The Art of War*," Buck responded. "But they are doing the opposite. Normal would have been to keep the rally as is and then change something," Buck responded to Cat.

"No," I said emphatically. I planted my elbows on the desk, joined my hands together, and rested my forehead against them. Pieces of memory from our search for the treasure two years ago washed through my brain. I was a pawn in an elaborate chess game. Padraig Collins was the chess master. Unbeknownst to me, he was watching my every move and then jumped three steps ahead of me. I saw the dewy grass, smelled the upturned earth, felt the thrill of holding the missing pages from the *Book*, all the while sensing someone's presence.

"Homeland Security expected this move. They were waiting for it. If the One-Six lawyers didn't change their plans, that would have spooked the Feds. Now they have been lulled. What were your words, Cat? 'It settles them into predictable patterns of response?'"

Cat nodded.

"Just like the Capitol Riots. The authorities were lulled. It was the President's rally, after all. Permits had been secured, everything legit. The Commander-in-Chief told them to go to the Capitol Building. That's when a small cadre of conspirators moved the masses into action. Most people had no idea they were being used as part of a plan. All the leaders needed was an angry mob to orchestrate."

I stood and walked a few feet, the Claddagh ring inches away. I laid my fingers on the crown. "Cat, Dit is one of the leaders. But even he doesn't know the final outcome. He's moving his pawns while someone else is moving him. I need you to have eyes on Dit, see if you can read the situation."

Cat slowly lifted her eyes from the table to me; her shoulders pulled back; it was as if energy coursed down her arms to her fingers. Warrior ready. "Beats the hell out of sitting in a basement."

"Buck, call Di Stefano. We need to meet with him and the DHS agent."

Buck lifted his phone. Mine buzzed as he did.

"It's Collins. He'll call from an encrypted phone. Let's talk to him first."

Two minutes later I answered his call.

"I think we found him, lad. Everyone's with you?"

Padraig Collins's accent thickened when he was excited. He could be hard to understand.

"Yes," I answered.

"Put me on speaker."

"We're here."

"Write this down."

Buck already had pen and paper in hand.

"Andre Milo, born Andrej Milošević. Does the name Milošević mean anything to you?"

Cat shot a look at Buck. "Slobodan Milošević, the rat bastard murderer from Serbia, that's the only one I know."

"That's the one. Now you know why Andre shortened his name."

"I gather they are related somehow?" Buck asked.

"He's a nephew, born in the U.S. His parents were in the Yugoslavian diplomatic corps to the U.S. They moved back to Serbia when Andre was five. He became very close to his uncle, served as an aide when his uncle was President."

"What makes you think he's the guy?" Arin bridged her hands, elbows on the table. Cat had every synapse of her brain on warp speed, ready to devour the answer, her body damn near pressing through the table.

"It appears that our boyo was greatly influenced by his uncle. He believes in ethnic purity, ethnic cleansing, and Christian Nationalism. Andre assisted his uncle's attempted genocide against Muslims." Collins paused; the sound of paper being shuffled filled the void. "He's been working in the State Department for over twenty years. He turned down several opportunities to rise in the ranks. Andre is the ultimate mid-level operative. By choice."

"How certain are you that Milo's our guy?" I asked.

"Zero. But one hundred percent certain that he fits the description. So, before we chase our tails, you need to get me confirmation that he's the target." I could hear Collins breathing into the phone. "And by the way, he's disappeared, two, maybe three weeks."

The line went dead. The four of us sat quietly, then Arin turned to the whiteboard and pointed to her reminder that the VP might die tomorrow. Cat, Arin, and I turned to Buck. He lifted his phone and dialed FBI Agent Joe Di Stefano. "Joe. Andre Milo?"

Di Stefano replied immediately. "Yes."

Buck laid his phone on the table and nodded to us. I relayed the information to Collins by text: *Affirmative.*

Arin swept the phone from my hand. *Find him*, she texted to Collins, *maybe he'll lead us to Rabbit.*

Buck wanted to put a bullet in Rabbit. So did Arin.

Cat was staring at the panels hiding my mother's lab. She wasn't paying attention to the conversation. It's easy to drift off when your brain is sailing between ancestral memories and the present moment.

"I always meant to get a Claddagh ring." Cat leaned back in her chair and pointed to the wooden panels, the Claddagh ring painted in gold leaf on the wood.

"Monday, you and me, girls' day out. We'll each get a ring, have lunch, shake off the stench of Dit and Andre Milo," Arin said. "What do you think?"

Cat's eyes sparkled and a smile formed, rounding her cheeks. "I'd love to."

Her attention drifted back to the gold Claddagh. She gazed, her chest rising, her voice soft: sounds, words maybe. And then clear. I watched Arin turn on the audio recorder.

"Frederick, the great man sitting in front of you, The Liberator, that is him at the Hill of Tara." I point to the painting behind O'Connell. "Ireland had never witnessed a gathering so large. A million, it was reported. My mind cannot conceive the notion of one million strong. It is said, good Sir, that it took your carriage some two hours to make its way through the crowds."

O'Connell nods to me.

"At least two hours," he answers.

Frederick leans his elbows on O'Connell's desk.

"I believe you to be the greatest orator of all time, Sir, but how does your voice reach a million ears?"

O'Connell turns to the painting, runs his fingers over the artist's landscape, then turns to lay his palms over Frederick's.

"It took many hours. Most of the men and women spoke only Irish. Translators made their way through the crowd. But, young Frederick, the words were secondary. I was speaking to their dreams. Their hopes. They came that day to be healed. To commune with the downcast and the miserable. They came to stand among their ancient kings. They came to rise. To become men. And you will do the same for your people."

Frederick stands; their hands still grasped. I bear witness to two grand and indomitable souls; souls roaming in the void of space and time, seeking an anchor in the ethereal and material planes, the energy of angels, and the dirt and breath of soldiers.

"I must ask you. My time wanes. I have decried the whip, but I have never seen the welt."

Frederick stares into the eyes of his elder. The grand oak desk separates their bodies but not their spirit. Frederick removes his greatcoat and unbuttons his vest. He tugs his white shirt, chest, shoulders, and neck bared. He begins to turn, show his back, the scars of the whip, but O'Connell stretches his arm to him.

"You owe no man, no white man, that honor. But should you choose to, I swear that until my last breath I will decry slavery."

Two giants, needy for each other's witness, one emerging, one fading. Frederick turns. The sin of leather against skin. O'Connell, who I know has seen the worst, betrays a long exhale.

"You, young man, have thrown off the shackles, but they will try to put them on your people long after you are gone, just as they have with me. Tara was my greatest day. It was also the greatest threat to the authorities. They could no longer tolerate me. I am only recently out of prison."

O'Connell coughs and wipes the sweat from his brow. He leans even closer, his demeanor even more serious.

I sense a warning. Frederick and I wait for his response, fatigue plain in his eyes and sagging cheeks.

"I have been told that you are in danger. Rumors. Perhaps that is all. But there is a belief that assassins are crossing the ocean from America."

CHAPTER 21

C at's eyes were open, but she remained far away. She had narrated her experience, the trails of which clearly played in her mind. She seemed delighted by them. The shock of seeing through her ancestors' eyes had faded. Like me, she would crave them, mine them for detail, hope for revelations.

Humans were the only animal that hoped for hope, that had faith in faith, trusted in trust. The rest of the animal world lived in peaceful coexistence with nature until they were about to be eaten. Then everything changed.

I had been eaten, so to speak—many times. I was gifted with extraordinary talents. Then they went, just walked away. But the going had become ordinary, expected. The ancestral memories were part of living in a continuum of change. I learned to embrace it. Like visiting new countries: you took your photos, posted your moments. You moved on.

There were three things in my current life that I couldn't move on from. Arin. Then Buck. Then my parents. Buck would have disagreed with my priority list. He would have insisted my parents should be right after Arin. My parents would kindly remind me that their time on earth was limited and that Arin and Buck should be my world.

Them. My holy trinity, my cornerstones. They held me, I held them. I had hope in hope and faith in faith. We needed to be that for Cat. At that moment we were all she had.

And Buck. My heart told me he was hanging by a small and tenuous thread. His spirit was lonely. He was fighting hard to care about a world that disdained cops, a world that needed him but didn't know it. He used to revel in his successes in ridding the Philly streets of drugs and dealers. He laughed more, worried less. His revelry had faded. We were so close that when he got a cut, I bled. And so did Arin. She had become his little sister. His healer. Family.

My eyes lingered on her. If there were any possibility that there had been divine intervention in my life, she would be the radiant example, God yelling down from heaven, "Hey, asshole, what more do you need from me to believe?" And yet—sorry, God—too many people in Covid graves for me not to have my moments of doubt. Was it even possible not to doubt?

And yet here I sat, viewing this miraculous group gathered around the table, prepared to shake things up and kick some ass.

"Let's go."

"Where?" Arin shot a look at me. They all did.

"Call Di Stefano again. Put him on speaker."

Buck held the phone in his palm. Di Stefano answered on the first ring.

"Joe, it's Key. Do you have eyes on Dit?"

"Of course."

"Where is he?"

"New Jersey. Why?"

"Because I need to read him," Cat interjected.

The line went silent. All of us were having a staring match with the phone. Cat's body tensed, leaned forward.

"No. Too risky," Di Stefano answered.

"I'll call my police contacts in New Jersey, they'll know. We'll be on our way in ten minutes." Buck tapped his feet. We were met by silence.

"Go to the Cherry Hill Mall. Park near Macy's. Call me when you get there. Cat, just you and Buck. I don't want Arin on the streets. Key stays with her." The line went dead.

Buck scrolled something on his phone.

"Damn, no wonder they want Arin safely tucked in here. I just checked the number of views of your smackdown yesterday. I think you'll win the going viral award." Buck placed his phone on the table, took pen and paper in hand. "Can I have your autograph?"

Arin cocked her head and fluffed her hair. "You can take a selfie with me too if you like."

"Nah, I don't want to upstage you." Buck offered an exaggerated grin, then stood. "Let's go."

The three of us were on our feet. We looked at Cat, still sitting.

"Di Stefano said it's just me and you," Cat offered to Buck. We headed to the car.

Cat stayed in the chair a moment, then leaped up and clapped her hands. "OK then, give me five minutes. I'll meet you in the alley." She headed up the stairs.

We exited through the basement door to the alleyway where Buck had parked. Buck walked to the police car, giving him a heads-up, I assumed. He walked back to us as Cat came through the door. She was wearing cammie fatigues, a green T-shirt and a cap that had *USMC* emblazoned on the front.

"I don't know if we are going to see Dit, but if we do, I want him to see a Marine."

Buck saluted her. "Captain in the house."

I noticed for the first time that Arin was wearing a *Sergeant*

Pepper's Lonely Hearts Club T-shirt, black jeans, and white Converse sneakers. She looked hot. So did Cat in her combat fatigues. I felt drab. Not a very attractive T, wrinkled jeans, and beat-up sneakers. My clothes could blend in on the street, but at six-three and with reddish hair, I didn't blend in very well. Buck looked cool no matter what he wore. They looked ready for TV cameras. I looked ready to work in a community garden.

Arin asked Cat to sit in the back with her. Buck drove.

"Cat, your memory of being in O'Connell's house. It reminded me of something," Arin said.

"Tell me."

I listened as Buck drove past Restaurant Row, the sidewalk eateries full of an early lunch crowd. We headed for the Benjamin Franklin Bridge.

"O'Connell told them that Tara was his greatest day but that the authorities could no longer tolerate him. He had become a threat. O'Connell was organizing another large rally. This time in Clontarf, an area of Northside Dublin. It sits on the harbor."

I was looking over the back of my seat at Cat. She was staring out the window.

"Didn't some big battle happen there?" Cat asked.

"Long ago. As in 1014," I answered, surprised that I remembered. "Brian Boru was the King. The battle was between his troops and the Vikings. It was the Vikings that founded Dublin. They called it Dubh Linn. It means 'Black Pool', for the dark waters of the River Liffey. The Irish won the battle."

"Making Clontarf a very revered place," Arin added.

"O'Connell chose it for the symbolism, I assume." Cat glanced at me then at Arin. "Just like Dit and crew, starting at Independence Hall."

"Exactly. It was too powerful a symbol. The British Prime Minister ordered O'Connell's rally canceled the night before.

He had two warships and three thousand troops sitting in the harbor, ready to enforce his edict. Blood would have flowed in the streets."

Cat focused on Arin.

"What did O'Connell do?"

"The only thing he could do. He canceled the rally," Arin answered. "He was willing to give his own life, but he would not spill his countrymen's blood."

"Some politicians called him a coward for backing down," I added. "They believed that blood in the streets would backfire against the Brits, unite the Irish."

"Which is what the January Six insurrectionists hoped would be the outcome. They believed it would strengthen their cause. They likely have the same goal on Saturday." Arin sank a little farther in her seat.

Cat ran her fingers over the window, the air conditioner on. It was eighty-four and climbing. The blue columns of the bridge had a strobe-like effect as we passed by and descended into New Jersey. Washington crossing the Delaware River, surprising the British troops, turning the tide.

"Dit is moving his pawns. Someone is moving Dit. Andre Milo? Rabbit? Who is moving them?" Cat said as Buck stopped the car on the far edge of Macy's.

Buck didn't need to call Di Stefano. Twenty seconds after we parked, a van pulled parallel to Buck. An arm jutted out of the window, FBI ID held out for Buck to see.

"Get in," said a woman's voice.

We settled in as the van sped off. Buck's phone rang and he put it on speaker.

"Damn, Buck, I said just you and Cat."

"With all due respect, I don't answer to you. The Commissioner said I'm responsible for all three. End of story."

"OK, OK. You are going to a busy parking lot across the street from a small hotel. Fifty-five rooms, forty-seven men already there. They've booked out the entire place."

I had noted that the side of the FBI's van read "Garden State Catering," logo, phone number, the works. The seats were lumpy and uncomfortable, like they had borrowed it from a catering company twenty years ago and never returned it. The driver made a sharp left out of the parking lot. Our seats were glorified benches, and I slid into Arin.

"What are you seeing?" asked Buck.

"You tell me after you get there."

The line went dead. Di Stefano was not big on goodbyes.

The van pulled into the parking area of a Wawa. Most slots were taken, but a car pulled out, undoubtedly holding the space for the van, which backed in, the rear windows darkened but large. Prime viewing spot. The hotel was approximately thirty yards across the road, its parking lot almost full. Cat watched intently for about two minutes. Not a soul in sight.

"Dial Joe."

Buck did.

"Joe, you have eyes and ears inside?"

"Security cameras in the hallways. Surveillance devices in three rooms. The front desk covered."

"And?"

"Not a thing. They check in, go to their rooms, and don't come out—complete silence. There is food waiting for them. Water, soda, a few beers. What's your take?"

"My take is that you've got a big-ass problem. I'm sure you've figured it out."

"I want to hear it from you, Cat."

Cat turned to see the three of us and then looked across to the hotel. No movement. No one was looking out the windows. Parking lot full. Not a human in sight.

"They're all experienced operators, maintaining discipline.

They know you are listening and watching. That's a swat team over there."

Again, silence. Then the sound of a man inhaling, deep, sharp, and troubled.

"What're you going to do, Joe?"

"We ran every single one of them. No outstanding warrants. Right now, we have no cause to do anything but watch."

"Cell phones?" Buck asked.

"Radio silence," the FBI agent responded.

"Burners?"

"None that we can detect. It's like there's no one there. We see them in the halls. We have 360 surveillance on the building." Di Stefano cleared his throat. "No one's come out all day."

"Do you have someone on the inside?" Cat was focused, still, except for her jaw jutting in and out.

"No. It happened too fast for us to get set up correctly. Plus, it's a hand-picked crew. Even the clerk at the front desk is a sympathizer, giving fist-bumps as they check in."

"What's your play?" I asked.

"Hundreds of them are pouring into the city, spreading out, staying at different hotels and motels. But the guys you are looking at, they are the elite. We'll sit on them. I'll let you know if I need eyes on from you, Cat," Di Stefano answered.

"OK. Let me know where you can best use me," Cat said, still looking at the hotel.

"Hold on. Andre Milo? You clearly have a line on him. What do you know?" Di Stefano waited quietly for an answer.

"Not much yet," Buck answered. "But when we do, we expect a two-way street." Buck hit the off button.

Cat was squatting by the rear window—she lifted her binoculars for a final scan then sat next to Buck.

Arin turned to the driver.

"Take us back to the car, please."

The van backed out of the parking spot and headed down the road. All four of us were leaning forward, elbows on thighs—Arin next to me, Cat and Buck in the seats behind us. Arin was about to talk, but I shook my head and nodded toward the agents in the front. The van stopped next to Buck's car. We got out. The van rolled away.

Buck clicked the locks open and was about to get in.

"Hold up. Let's talk." Arin folded her hands in front of her.

"Why, is there a sale at Macy's?" It was good to see Buck cracking a joke.

We gathered around Arin, the sun growing stronger. I was sweating while Arin looked like it was a cool spring day.

"What's the one thing Di Stefano asked us to do?" Arin searched our faces.

"Think out of the box," I answered.

"And stay out of the box," Cat added.

"Resist the bureaucratic thinking. Di Stefano needs to play by the rules." Arin scanned our faces. "We don't."

"You all don't, but I do." Buck pointed to his badge. "Depends on what you have in mind."

A mischievous look spread across Arin's face.

"I'm all over the news, social media. It's time to use it."

"Doing what?" Cat asked.

"Holding a press conference."

"What? Where?" I had a hunch.

Arin pulled a band from her back pocket, grabbed her hair off her neck and pulled it into a ponytail, loose curls dangling free.

"In the parking lot of the hotel."

"What the ... Bad idea. The FBI is in the middle of surveillance." Buck shook his head. "I can't go anywhere near that."

"I don't want you to. Or Key. Just me, or me and Cat." Arin cocked her head toward Cat.

I could sense Cat calculating the situation. She started nodding.

"I love it. No way we can just let those assholes sit there playing us."

"You sure, Cat? You weren't happy about seeing the press yesterday." Buck kept his eyes on her.

Cat put her hands on her head.

"Some days, my head's on tight; some days, it's wobbly. It's on all good and tight today, soldier."

"OK. I need to call Di Stefano," Buck said.

"After we notify the press. Di Stefano will scream and holler, but

he's going to be happy that we got off our asses." Arin smiled and gave Cat and me our assignments. We started posting on social media and dialing the press.

CHAPTER 22

Friday, September 3, 2021.
Cherry Hill, New Jersey

W e stood outside the Wawa, a combination gas station and convenience store with sandwiches. Addictive sandwiches. First-place-you-stop-when-you-come-back-to-the-area sandwiches. I wasn't even hungry, but I ordered a tuna hoagie. Buck got the turkey. Cat and Arin abstained, not being true-blue Philly.

A woman threw the door open, iced tea in her right hand, phone against her ear in her left. Scrubs. She yanked her N95 down with her phone hand.

"Get him on oxygen. If we have to intubate, I'm pretty sure he's not going to make it."

We humans had hope in hope. But for how much longer? It occurred to me that Socrates likely asked the same question. Maybe we just went round and round.

Arin and Cat were making notes on their phones, prepping for the media. We waited for about ten minutes before the first TV van arrived at the hotel, then it was a convoy of TV, radio, and newspaper reporters, photographers in tow.

As planned, Buck stayed by the car in the Wawa parking lot across the street from the hotel. Cat, Arin, and I crossed to the awaiting cameras and microphones in the hotel parking lot. I remained about fifteen feet away as Cat and Arin took center stage. They faced the hotel, the press had their backs to it, the TV cameras were filming the façade as curtains parted in the windows, eyes looking out, bewildered faces.

The reporters jumped right in, but Arin silenced them, putting her hand up, examining them. They went quiet.

"My name is Doctor Arin Murphy." She nodded to Cat.

"I am Captain Cat Fahey. Tomorrow, some three thousand individuals will gather in front of Independence Hall. They will carry the American flag, as they did on January Six. We saw how they used it. They will likely wave the Nazi swastika. My forefathers and mothers spent their youths fighting Nazis, as did yours."

Cat spent a long moment staring into the cameras. Her hands were clasped behind her, shoulders back, chest out, feet shoulder-width. The reporters leaned in with cameras and microphones. People started to gather; the social media posts had alerted them.

"I fought for their right to march, protest, and voice even the most repulsive ideas. They have every right to be here." She waved her right index finger in the air. "But yesterday, a former Marine told me he joined the military to get trained to fight on American soil."

"He …" Cat raised her hands and shook her head. "… He told me that January Six was a dress rehearsal. He proclaimed that a new civil war was coming and that I would need to choose sides." Cat paused and glanced over her shoulder, a huge audience gathering behind her. Many of them were snapping photos and posting them.

"We had served together overseas," Cat continued, her voice growing louder. "I chose a side. I swore to protect the Constitution from enemies, both foreign and domestic. That was the man that Doctor Murphy slapped. He, and the men with him, had swastikas tattooed on their necks in the form of a crucifix. I hope that horrifies you as much as it horrifies me."

Cat gave a long pause. She scanned the windows of the hotel. The reporters craned to look where she was looking.

"This is the headquarters for their rally. The leaders are in there. He's in there. He is known as *Dit*. And he, all of them, hope that you are so ground down from the pandemic that you no longer care."

Police lights were now flashing all around me. Police cruisers, state and local, had pulled up along the road. So had cars. People craned their necks, listening to the news conference on radios and phones as they witnessed it live. I looked across the street in the Wawa parking lot to see if I could locate Buck. I knew he was there, but crowds had formed.

As Cat finished, Arin moved closer to the microphones.

"I am a Jamaican citizen." Arin let her accent hang strong. "But is it possible I love America as much or more than you? More than them?" She gestured to men peering from the hotel window on the second floor. "I can assure you that most Jamaicans do. People from all over the world look to you, the land of the free." Arin lifted her arm and motioned at the hotel behind her. "Come to Philadelphia tomorrow and stand in peaceful opposition. And if Dit wants to come out from behind the curtain and explain himself, I'm sure the press would love to hear from him."

Arin nodded toward the hotel. "If he's got the balls."

Two young women had pushed through the crowd, about three feet off my left shoulder. "She's amazing," one said, loud enough for me to hear. "She's that memory lady, with her boyfriend, what's his name?"

I had a quiet laugh and recalled that three days ago I had been on the island of Iona, recording an interview with the BBC. It had been my first time there in the flesh, although I had visited many times through Aedan's memories. The world could not get enough of my recollections of Aedan and Siobhan, a medieval fairy tale love story. They certainly could not get enough of me and Arin, especially Arin. She was all that: beautiful, radiantly intelligent, a brawler when need be, and a lover of humanity to her core. She was also part of a family worth over one billion dollars. She was just as comfortable addressing the UN, which she had done, as she was standing in this parking lot, facing the cameras and wondering aloud if Dit has any balls.

As Arin and Cat continued answering questions, I surveyed the scene around me. People were still pouring in, attempting to get a glance at Arin. The police were trying to keep people off the road and the traffic flowing. About fifty percent of the people had their masks under their chins, another twenty percent under their noses. Weary. I could see it. Feel it. Palpable. Kids in classrooms one day, learning online the next. Parents buried, grandparents lonely and afraid. It was as if we were all emerging from a two-year bar brawl.

My father got the virus in April. He got through OK, but the scars of feeling helpless cut deep in him and me. And much of the world. You'd think that might unite us. You'd think.

I turned my attention back to Arin and Cat. Cat was answering a question about being in the military. Then the reporter asked her something, and I felt my stomach get queasy.

"Captain Fahey, do you have the Ancestral Memory gene?"

We never got around to talking about how to handle that question.

"Yes."

"Do you experience memories?" The cameras rolled.

Cat smiled and nodded. "I do."

"That's exciting," the reporter said. "Can you tell us from who? Which ancestor?"

I watched Cat's face grow in contentment and Arin's in alarm, realizing what might happen.

"My great-great-grandfather, Martin Fahey."

"Have you witnessed anything of interest?"

Don't do it, Cat. I tried to will her not to go any further.

"You have no idea. He was a famous abolitionist; he did many things of interest."

A Black reporter raised his microphone at this.

"Please, Captain, tell us more."

Cat took a long look at the reporter. "I will. One day."

I noted a reporter looking at her phone, about one foot in front of Arin.

"Captain." She held her cell phone forward for Cat to see. "It says here that there was a Martin Fahey that accompanied Frederick Douglass to Ireland. Is that your ancestor?"

"Proudly, yes." Cat beamed.

"Have you seen Frederick Douglass in your memories?"

I noticed Arin had her hand on Cat's forearm. She gave an almost indiscernible squeeze. Cat cocked her head toward Arin. Arin gave a little shake of her head, so slight no one else would notice.

Once again, Cat scanned the hotel windows. She then turned to see the crowds that had gathered, then back to the reporter who had asked the question.

"On Saturday night, the first female Vice President will be in Philadelphia to celebrate America. I can only imagine that Frederick Douglass would be astounded and filled with pride to see a Black woman climb that stage. Unfortunately, he would likely not be surprised to see the men gathered there." Cat pointed to the hotel. "Let's get through this. I'll have a lot to tell you on the other side."

Arin took Cat's arm and together they walked toward me.

A smattering of applause began in the crowd, and then it got louder. Soon some jeering rang out.

Nearby, someone hollered, "Go back to Jamaica." And then it came, as I had feared—the N-word.

I felt my neck muscles bulge, a fist forming. I know Arin heard it. But she did the thing that haters despise. She ignored them. But Cat couldn't walk away so easy. She scanned the crowd to find the heckler. She wouldn't need to hear him shout the words, she could likely watch the twitch of his eyes, the anger in his jaw, and then she would get in his face. Buck had texted me that the FBI would take us to their Philly office and that he would meet us there. A Suburban pulled up and the rear door opened. Cat had found her mark; she was moving. Then her head tilted back and her body went limp.

"Arin," I said over the street noise. Arin moved to get under Cat's left arm, and we hustled her into the car.

———

Li Chen sat at the computer console watching the newsfeed of the press conference. Diamond and E stood behind him, bodies tense, muscles strained, awaiting the inevitable explosion.

Chen's fingers tapped the table. His eyes had closed. All things vanished, all but the parade of events that he planned. Arin and this other woman thought they were so clever. Flushing out the white supremacists. All they had done was create more chaos. Thousands of people would descend on the city, riled up, to oppose Dit and the others, just like he had seen in other American cities. Antifa would take the bait. He assumed that the police and the feds were in a panic, trying to decide how to respond with their already strained resources.

Chen pointed to the screen.

"I need to send them flowers and a thank-you note," he laughed.

CHAPTER 23

Friday, September 3, 2021.
Clontarf, Dublin

Her fingers flew effortlessly over the keyboard. If anyone was looking for an intruder, they would geotag the effort to a computer in Sudan. She was not in Sudan. She was in her cocoon. The place she had felt safe. Where she had experienced wonder, and healing, and blossoming. She had become wealthy, not just by Nigerian standards, but because she could buy a house, a million-dollar home, in cash. She had accomplished it from this room: this place that was an endless universe and a claustrophobic cave. But tonight, or today, or this morning, or whatever it said on the clock, she was the Captain of the *Starship Enterprise*, hurling deep into the dark corners of the web, chasing Andre Milo.

Anwulika was unaware that Dublin was shaking off the dust tonight, right now, an hour after sunset. It was the first Friday night that Dubliners could show a vaccine card and enter a restaurant. Where anyone, jabbed or not, could lift a pint outdoors and cheer "Sláinte!" and feel the old life enter their pores.

The goings-on in Dublin didn't matter. Her own dust had lifted. She had just watched two women, Arin Murphy and the Captain, gather in front of the cameras and take a stand. Arin and Key had been part of her life, though they didn't know it. She tried to focus on chasing Andre Milo, but she knew she needed one more, just one more hit.

She clicked rewind on the recording and laughed again as Arin said of Dit, "if he has the balls."

Padraig had asked her to help him save the life of the Vice President. She put her fingers on the screen.

"We got this, ladies. Anwulika is right here, gon' find this bastard."

Hours earlier, she had breached the State Department's human resource server. Andre Milo's request for extended leave sat there on a silver platter. He was approved to return to Serbia to assist his family. Like most of the world, he could not visit overseas family members, many of whom had suffered from Covid over the past two years. Anwulika understood it was a bullshit story, meant to cover the State's embarrassment while they tried to locate Milo. The FBI said that Milo had disappeared off the grid. That's all she needed to know.

"Andre, you are nowhere near Serbia. State, FBI, CIA, all would have found you by now," she said to her screen.

She returned to where she had first found reference to him, where she had found Walsh and Boland and the plan to terrorize the election officials. Anwulika did not need crumbs, plural; she required only a single digital speck. For three hours, she searched. Unrelenting. Like following the veins of a piece of wood full of termites: trails ending, veering, bending, until something crumbled.

She jumped up. Adrenaline forced her to, as did her aching back. But it was her desire that made her dance around her desk, arms gyrating over her head, a small victory lap.

"Milo, I told you that you could not hide from me."

She glanced at the screen, a green light flashing on a map: Astana, Kazakhstan.

Anwulika made a quick visit to the fridge and grabbed her homemade energy drink of kola nuts, ginseng, and ginger, an acquired taste. For her, it was a craving that would see her through the night. She pulled the chair out, sat, and commanded her keyboard to narrow in on the location, not surprised at what she found. She tapped in the name and opened the images: Khan Shatyr, a shopping mall shaped like a giant yurt. Somewhere in or around or under the mall sat a room with servers and computers. One or more of those computers had been dispersing dollars, funneled through hundreds of accounts.

Andre Milo either sat at one of those terminals or, more likely, gave the orders to a young hacker. Andre did not have to be in Kazakhstan to do it. He could be in Miami or Moscow. But his fingerprints were factually or figuratively all over the keyboard. Anwulika would use those fingerprints to find this traitor from the State Department. She had less than twenty-four hours to do it.

Anwulika allowed a moment of penguins and icebergs and unfathomable cold to fill her lungs and imagination. Her fingers were poised over the keys, a ballet of digits and speed about to be unleashed. She stretched her right hand out and displayed it in front of the screen.

"Waka, Andre. Here I come."

CHAPTER 24

FRIDAY, SEPTEMBER 3, 2021.
FBI HEADQUARTERS, PHILADELPHIA

FBI personnel stepped into the hall to watch us pass as we walked to the conference room. I wondered what they thought of our impromptu press conference. I assumed Agent Di Stefano was about to tell us.

Di Stefano was sitting at the end of the conference table; Buck sat next to him. Di Stefano looked up from his laptop.

"Do you know what the number-one trending hashtag is?"

Cat, Arin, and I just looked at him.

"*Hashtag, if he's got the balls.*" He punched in a few commands, and the monitor on the wall lit up. "Someone created this GIF."

It was Arin elbowing the guy in the head while Batman comic-style lettering read, "KABOW, BAM. IF HE'S GOT THE BALLS."

I laughed; Di Stefano didn't. He was one of those guys that could do his morning shave at eight and have a five o'clock shadow by ten. He lifted his chin to Buck.

"Joe was just showing me some of the right-wing message boards. Some real nasty death threats against Cat and Arin."

"Excellent," Cat said, earning a quizzical look from Di Stefano. "What? You wanted us to think out of the box. Is there a problem?"

"We don't know. They've maintained discipline inside the hotel. They're gathering but not talking. Passing written notes. But it's what's happening online that has us concerned. Not only the threats but the increase in the number of people coming to support the supremacists or oppose them."

"The Mayor has asked the Governor to send the National Guard." Buck set his coffee cup on the table. "Police are stretched to the limit. The flood, the Festival, and the supremacists' rally, any one of those is a huge stretch on resources by itself. Add the music VIPs and the Vice President." Buck shook his head and motioned for us to take a seat.

"The State Police are mobilizing three hundred additional troopers," Di Stefano added. "They will handle much of the security for the VIPs and maintain the highways, relieving some pressure on the police."

Cat had sat next to Di Stefano.

"Why are you telling us this? We're not in the need-to-know circle."

Di Stefano pushed his seat back a few inches from the table. He planted his hands on his knees and looked directly at Cat.

"I *am* in that circle, and I need to know every little thing that comes into your brain. I don't care if you think it's crazy. I don't care if you think it's Martin Fahey or ET telling you. I don't care if you believe that Yoda and Obi-Wan Kenobi visited you and revealed something. You are tuned into this somehow. It's what makes you Nine."

Di Stefano abruptly turned his attention to Arin, Buck and me, his face hard, a man running out of time.

"That goes for all of you. You learned about the terror threat on the election officials, and you somehow learned about Andre Milo. I don't have time to convince you to tell me how. If you have any info that can lead us to Milo or anyone else, you will give it to me immediately."

Di Stefano looked us in the eye, one at a time, as we nodded our assent.

"Did we upset anyone today in the Bureau? Homeland?" Arin asked.

The agent shook his head and laughed; his jet-black hair bounced off his forehead.

"Hell yeah."

"How about you, Joe? Did we piss you off?"

"I was counting on you, Arin. You shuffled the deck. Dit and his handlers were not expecting this. Well played."

"Joe, you are pissing me off right now," I said. I watched for his reaction but also kept Cat in my periphery. I was across the table from Arin, Buck off my right shoulder, Di Stefano next to him.

"Why is that?" Di Stefano asked.

I became aware of how quiet the conference room was. No noise from the hallways, no sound of traffic from the windows. Soundproof. I assumed recording devices were hidden somewhere. Maybe I had seen too many movies. I did a quick scan of the walls and ceiling.

"I don't expect you to share anything classified, but come on man, you don't care if it's Yoda or ET whispering in our ear? You give us nothing. How about *you* whisper a little something."

Agent Di Stefano looked straight ahead, past us. His left hand rested on the armrest, his right elbow on the conference table.

"The Russians launched a vaccine disinformation campaign using bots and trolls. What year did it begin?"

I looked at the others to see if anyone was going to

answer. I jumped in. "2020, I assume, after the pandemic started."

Joe waited to see if there were other answers. There weren't.

"2014. There was a small but growing anti-vax movement in the U.S. The Russians experimented. The bots were posting discussions in social media forums, and the trolls, real people, in this case working for Russia, began polite and thoughtful conversations about vaccines. Nothing incendiary. One parent to another. Something like, 'I don't want my child sitting next to someone not vaccinated.' 'I understand,' comes the answer from the other parent, a troll, 'but I'm very concerned about what I'm hearing about vaccines and autism.' 'Yeah,' responds the first parent, 'me too. But I still think the benefit outweighs the risk.'"

Joe placed both hands on the table. "All nice and reasonable and sowing doubt. Then …" he paused and looked around at us, tapped the table, drum-like, with his index finger, "an article appeared in an Indian medical journal saying that a study found a possible link between autism and vaccines."

"Let me guess," Cat said, "paid for in rubles?"

Di Stefano nodded.

"But this is the important part to understand. They didn't rush; they strung it out. First, an article in a French news-paper picked it up. Soon, a BBC medical correspondent was asked about it during a live broadcast. The Russians managed the campaign gingerly. When they saw it was taking root, they increased the bot and troll campaign in the U.S. The message: vaccines equal autism. By the time the article landed here, they no longer needed trolls. There was an army of American anti-vaxxers ready and waiting."

Di Stefano's phone buzzed. He looked at the text and put the phone aside.

"They perfected their tactics," Buck said. "They did it

again in the 2016 election, mostly using race to heighten tension and fear."

"And remember, they don't care who wins, Democrat or Republican. It means nothing to them. They want chaos, distraction, and disruption," Di Stefano added. "It was Khrushchev who said, 'We will destroy you from within.'"

"Your point is that the Russians are behind all of this?" Cat asked.

"Good question. Let's play it out just a little more. Who is the greatest industrial and technology copycat in the world?"

"China," Cat stated emphatically.

"Instead of investing in R&D and trying to catch up with us, they invest in industrial espionage and theft. Mostly cyber theft. To the tune of over one trillion dollars. They do the same thing when it comes to disinformation. They studied every move made by Russia, copied them, and improved where they could."

I threw my hands up.

"What are you trying to tell us?"

Agent Di Stefano looked like he had aged five years in the last ten minutes.

"We don't know who is running the show. Just as we think it's Russia, we see North Korea, Iran, and China playing the disinformation game. Are they copycatting or coordinating? We don't know."

"What *do* you know?" Arin asked, just above a whisper.

"The threat assessment for tomorrow is code red. Cat, I want you to do two things."

Cat nodded.

"Tell me."

"Go to the Festival grounds and do a security assessment, just as you would on a mission. My tactical commander will meet you there."

"I don't know if my boss will be happy to see me. I've been AWOL," Cat responded.

"Don't worry about Scott. He knows that the priority is you working with us." An edge to his voice, intentional or not.

"OK," Cat agreed. She moistened her lips with her tongue, head bobbing slightly. "Let's be honest, he's been an asshole the last few days."

"Can't comment." He lifted his phone as it buzzed with a text. "One more thing, Cat. Tomorrow, I want you on site two hours before the VP goes on. And as much as I'd like Arin and Key to lock down at home, I know I get all of you." He turned his attention to Arin. "Just do me a favor, Dr. Murphy."

Arin's shoulders lifted; her face and gestures reminded me of Robert De Niro when he said, 'Ya talking to *me*?'"

"Don't hit anyone."

"Can't promise." Arin smiled, getting up.

Cat and Buck stood as well.

"Give me a minute. I'll meet you in the hallway." I waited for them to leave. Buck's nose and lips pulled to the right. Translation: this better be good. Arin gave me a flick of her eyes and the tell of her left hand clenching. She hated being cut out of anything.

When the door closed, I turned to Di Stefano.

"Do you know who the traitor is?"

"You know I can't answer that."

"Joe, I didn't ask for names. I asked if you know."

"Why is that important to you?"

I stared at him, tapping my fingers in a drumbeat, waiting for an answer.

"We have our suspects. We are watching their every move." Di Stefano looked at his watch. "I have a task force meeting in five. Need to get ready."

I stood and reached for his hand, shook it, then walked to the door.

"Key, can I ask you a question?"

I looked back at him.

"Did you witness Padraig Collins kill a man? Rumor has it …" He turned in his chair, a little smirk on his lips.

I tried to keep my body, my face, neutral. I remained silent.

"Tell Collins that the efforts that he's making on our behalf will be met with gratitude from very powerful people."

The rise of my chest and the bite on my lip gave me away. Di Stefano smiled.

"I don't want you to think we are stupid."

Agent Di Stefano patted the chair next to him, where Cat had sat.

"And one other thing. If Cat loses her job, which I hope she does, she would be unemployed for three seconds. She belongs right here, Key."

As we exited the elevator, Cat walked to a quiet alcove in the Federal Building's lobby. She leaned her back against a marble column, government utilitarian, climbing from marble floors to the ceiling. A few plaques hung here and there. I guess it was all meant to say, "We don't spend your tax money on frills."

"Di Stefano's description of Russia manipulating the vaccine discussion in 2014 was a softball, a lesson in how they use misinformation and disinformation. He left something out. In that same year, Russia annexed Crimea."

Cat leaned her head to one side and brushed the hair off her neck.

"I was there, on loan to the Ukraine military."

"Why am I not surprised?" Arin said.

"When this is all done, Arin, maybe you can help me write my book," Cat said. Arin looked pleased.

"Why did Russia do it?" Cat continued. "The Ukrainians

had a revolution, ousting Putin's hand-picked puppet. Crimea was the warning shot: obey Mother Russia. The Ukrainians ignored them. It became clear that Russia would hack their election. The Ukrainian response? They switched almost overnight to paper ballots."

"No kidding, I didn't know that," Buck added.

"Ukraine reduced the number of entry points into their systems and beefed-up cyber security. But the Russians clobbered them anyway, hitting their power grids with a malware called NotPetya. It was the largest cyber-attack against a country. Intelligence experts believe Ukraine is a testing ground, Moscow preparing for their real goal."

"The U.S." Buck didn't make it sound like a question.

"Help me out, Cat. How does this relate to the VP?" I asked.

"Everything that's happened so far feels like a Russian operation," she answered.

"I hear a 'but' coming," Buck said.

"O'Connell told my great-great-grandfather and Frederick Douglass that assassins were on the way from America. The question is, who sent them, who paid, and who were they going to blame it on?"

"And?" I asked

"The Russians blamed the Ukrainian attack on rogue hackers. China has studied every move Russia has made. One of them is going to leave clues that point to the other. Both will deny, especially if the VP dies."

"And there's nothing we'd be able to do militarily. The U.S. won't risk a nuclear war." Buck finished his statement and walked toward the exit; our FBI escort was waiting to drive us.

"My money is on Russia," Cat said as we crossed the lobby. "I assume Homeland Security is all over this."

We walked silently for a few paces.

"Unless there are powerful people in our government who want it to happen," I said. "Andre Milo couldn't pull this off by himself."

CHAPTER 25

Friday, September 3, 2021.
Festival Site, Philadelphia

This mini-city was buzzing with vendors readying their booths, technicians testing sound, and medics preparing tents for the inevitable beer-induced sunstrokes and flying fists. Buck showed his badge and parked about thirty yards short of the Rocky statue.

Golf carts and hand trucks whisked beer, water, and sodas to dozens of vendors scattered along the Festival grounds. Stages were going up. Gigantic sound systems were blaring, "Testing one, two, three." There was jubilance in the air, despite the flood, the sun, and the hard work; this was proof of life.

Cat was on; her eyes swept the area.

"This is a Secret Service nightmare. There is no way to vet every vendor and their employees. Or pretty much anyone out here."

As we stepped onto the grass and began walking toward the Parkway, we heard a voice calling, "Captain Fahey!"

We turned to see a man in a black, FBI-emblazoned polo shirt and cap, hurrying toward us.

"I'm Special Agent Haddad. It's nice to meet you."

Cat looked him up and down.

"What makes you so special?"

Haddad looked at her quizzically.

"You said you're special; just wondering." Cat had a little smirk. "Just messing with you. How'd you know it was me?"

"You're kidding, right? Besides the fact that I am with the FBI, everyone in the world has seen your face today." He looked to Arin. "And yours, Dr. Murphy. And," he gestured to Cat, "you are wearing fatigues."

"Guess I'm subtle." She smiled. "Let's dispense with formalities. Call me Cat."

"Tony Haddad."

Introductions were made. Cat studied him for a moment.

"Lebanese, from Massachusetts, though not a strong Mass accent. Fluent in Arabic, can hear it in your English pronunciation. Forty, forty-two. I'm guessing spec-ops?"

"Agent Di Stefano warned me about your psychic abilities. I was Rangers, Urban Combat Specialist." He nodded to Buck. "I understand you were Rangers too. Good to have some soldiers with eyes on this. We are on a tight schedule. Follow me."

Agent Haddad began walking east. A forklift conveying a pallet of beer rolled past him.

"Let's start at the main entrance." Haddad pointed down the Parkway, the entry not yet visible due to trees, stages, and a Ferris wheel.

"One second," I said. "Since we are in front of the main stage, let's start here."

Haddad stopped and turned to me. "Sorry, Key, I was ordered to go through this assessment with Captain Fahey and Detective Mc Coy."

"*Sadiqni , eindama yaqul kay shyyan famin al'afdal aliastimae* 'iilayh," Cat said in Arabic. "I told him it's best to listen to you."

"OK, what's on your mind?" Agent Haddad asked.

"How many of the white supremacists have tickets for the festival?" I said. I saw a look of surprise cross his face.

"Is that in your planning?" I asked.

"Of course," Haddad replied. "There's no way to know how many."

"So, it could be hundreds," Buck stated.

"Could be." Haddad looked around the grounds. "Nothing we can do to stop anyone from buying tickets. There will be hundreds of plain-clothes officers patrolling in here, though."

I held my arms out left and right and pointed.

"Are you aware that two supremacist teams came to do recon outside the fence yesterday?"

"Yes." Haddad faced north where I was pointing. "I saw the video of Dr. Murphy confronting them."

"You mean beating the crap out of that guy?" Cat said proudly. "So why did they come this far up? We think they will create an incident that causes a stampede. It will happen at this end, producing a panic. There would be a flood of people to the main entrance."

"We've accounted for that." Haddad took a few steps forward and pointed toward Kelly Drive. "That fence right there, it's on wheels; same on the other side," he said, pointing to Spring Garden Bridge and MLK Drive. "There will be fifteen security personnel on each side. They drilled about an hour ago and they know what to do. They will get those gates open so that people can escape."

"Escape into what?" I let the question drift in the air as everyone eyed the scene. To our right, across the wide boulevard, was a large condo building, tall trees, and at least a hundred parking spaces. To our left was a series of high-rise apartment buildings—lots of places to conceal oneself and lie in wait.

"What are you thinking, Key?" Arin asked.

"Waiting on the other side are small units of disciplined militia." I pointed north toward the large condo building. "They'll be wearing jeans and T-shirts, looking all normal. None of them would have gone through security and metal detectors."

Agent Haddad looked at me like I had sucker-punched him. He was undoubtedly an elite warrior. He had likely run missions in places where I would have folded up and hidden in a corner, unprepared for the sheer violence. Where I might have died. He had served in the darkest, bloodiest corners of the unimaginable, like Cat, like Buck. I didn't know the crumbled alleys of Mosul, the caves of the Taliban and Al Qaida like he did. And therein lay his limitation. He couldn't imagine it happening here. He could *say* that he could visualize it. But it was a step too far to think that fellow citizens might lie in wait. I was probably wrong. But the riots at the Capital on January Sixth told me I could be right. That was the unimaginable.

"Does the show begin tomorrow?"

"What?" Agent Haddad had been writing on his electronic notepad. He tilted his head and then looked back at the screen. "Yeah, I assume you mean the Festival."

"The guy Arin confronted, Dit, he told Cat that January sixth was a dress rehearsal." I looked at the mainstage, where the VP will stand.

"If that was the dress rehearsal, does the real show begin tomorrow?"

Haddad removed his FBI cap and rubbed the back of his head before returning the cap.

"Assume the answer is yes. We're here to stop it. So, let's go." Haddad lowered the smart tablet. "Captain Fahey, I want you to think like you would if you were stepping onto the streets of Fallujah."

Buck and Arin started walking behind Haddad. Cat stood frozen in place at the mention of Fallujah. I assume she fell into a dark hole of unkind memories, smoke and the odor of cordite, the stench of flesh. I watched her shiver and then snap out of it. She tentatively stepped forward, then hurried to catch up with Agent Haddad.

Another figure moved quickly toward us. I reached out to tap Cat's shoulder, then nodded toward her boss, Scott Morrison. Morrison caught up with us.

"Agent Di Stefano told me that you are doing recon. I thought you could use another set of eyes." He reached his hand out to Agent Haddad. All smiles. "Hey, brother, how you been?"

Morrison faced Cat and Arin.

"That was one hell of a press conference, ladies. You certainly stirred the hornets' nest. Let's try to think like them. How will they react?" He raised his arm like he was going to offer a high five but straightened the sleeve on his jacket instead.

"They won't," I said.

"What makes you say that?" Morrison asked, regarding me as if my input suddenly mattered.

"They maintained discipline in the hotel. They watched Cat and Arin ridicule them. They had to be tempted to retaliate right then. But they did nothing, didn't break their silence."

"So, whatever they had planned hasn't changed," Buck added.

Haddad briefed Morrison on our earlier conversation, the possibility that there could be small bands of extremists mixing with the crowds, waiting for something to trigger a stampede out of the Festival area. All conjecture. All possible.

The busy Festival area was a quiet oasis compared to what it would look like when the gates opened tomorrow.

"We all know that the city is laid out in a grid. The numbered streets run north–south; the name streets run east–west. Are there gates that can open quickly at all the intersections?" Cat asked Agent Haddad.

"Yes, for emergency vehicles."

"How many police will staff them?" She didn't wait for an answer. She hustled us to the north side of Twenty-Third Street, where one security person stood guard at the gate. No traffic. The north–south roads had been closed. Trash trucks blocked the entry.

"My notes show five officers stationed at each location, on the north and south gates," Haddad reported. He punched in some info on his smart pad. Twenty seconds later there was buzzing overhead. We followed his eyes to see a drone about one hundred feet above us. "I'll get photos and videos so we can analyze the terrain."

Cat straddled her arms over the gate and scanned the area. Many young people hung out, watching the Festival area get its finishing touches. The Von Colln playground sat one hundred feet from us. Kids were on the swings. Teens played touch football; others chased a soccer ball. The normal things that kids were supposed to do. But I imagined that Cat saw something very different.

"I would make sure these gates couldn't open, if I were the bad guys. Control the gates, keep the people trapped inside, forced to exit through the main entrance. It becomes complete panic." Cat glanced up to the buzzing drone. "Tony, you need twenty of the best cops at each gate, ten outside, ten in."

Agent Haddad looked up from his smart pad.

"That's a City decision, but I can recommend it."

"Buck, call Deputy Commissioner Cruz; we don't have

time for recommendations." Cat turned to her boss. "Scott, your thoughts?"

Scott Morrison looked all modeled up, could easily be on a Times Square billboard or a Paris runway. He pointed down the Parkway to his domain, the Philadelphia Museum of Art.

"It's a fortress, from the main stage to the rear entrance. Homeland and the Secret Service now control every inch of it. I don't get it back until the Vice President leaves." He did a 360 sweep with his eyes. "I agree with the Captain. "I'd suggest that you run a drill with whoever is in charge of each gate. If something does happen, the gates are your relief valve."

Haddad made notes then continued down the Parkway, Cat and Buck following. Morrison stood in front of Arin and me, looking as if he had something to say.

"What's up," I asked.

"These aren't nice people; your concern is valid, Key. They probably will have thugs out on the streets," Morrison said. "Take them seriously. You need to be very careful after that altercation yesterday and the press conference today. It seems to me, if they want you dead, you'll be dead."

Arin gripped my right hand, hard, her nails digging into my flesh. I felt her go off balance. I steadied her. Those words. The echo. Two years ago, but like it was yesterday.

CHAPTER 26

FRIDAY, SEPTEMBER 3, 2021.
FESTIVAL SITE, PHILADELPHIA

We followed Cat down the Parkway as she continued her inspection. Arin tugged at me, hurrying me, creating distance as she looked back at Morrison and pulled me off to the side.

"What the hell, Key? You heard what he said."

"It was no secret. We told the entire world about those words."

She gave me *the look*, squeezing her eyes tight, scrunching her nose.

"What, you think he was part of it?"

Someone hollered into a microphone, "Testing, one, two, three,"

"I don't know. Morrison gives me the creeps. There's something off with him," Arin said when the sound check stopped.

"I can't argue with that, but I'm sure it's nothing." I took Arin's hand and started to where Cat was walking, several yards ahead of us. We made our way around the Ferris wheel, a light show flashing over its many spokes, a kaleidoscope. It would have been fun to hop on and forget that we were in the middle of craziness. As we got close to our entourage, Arin's phone buzzed. She paused, read, then handed me the phone.

"From my mom."

I scrolled through photos from the front pages of the major newspapers in Jamaica. They each featured stills of Arin hitting Dit's guy with her elbow. One headline read, "Anthropologist Deposits DNA on White Supremacist's Jaw."

I read her mother's text: *Everyone is talking about you. Nonstop. The Gleaner conducted a poll. If you ran for Prime Minister today, you would win in a landslide.*

My stomach churned. I realized, with cold dread, that I didn't want her to be Prime Minister. I didn't have a clue as to how I would fit in.

Cat, Buck, and Scott Morrison were talking, and Haddad took notes as we arrived at the site's main entrance. There had to be thirty metal detector stations to process the sixty thousand people that would arrive tomorrow. If there were a stampede for the exit, this would be a nightmare of bottlenecks. Luckily Cat was thinking the same thing.

"Tony, you will need at least thirty to fifty cops here, from seven until the VP leaves. If there is a rush for the exit, these things need to get moved. Most people will be down by the main stage, so they will have about three minutes to create a large opening."

"I'll send that info to Cruz," Buck said while texting.

Vendors were heading in and out through the detectors. Suddenly one of the machines was beeping like crazy. A young Black man backed up as the security guard signaled him to step away from the machine. He looked like a jewelry store display, with gold necklaces, plural, and rings on each finger.

"I'm one of the artists. Late for a sound check, man, hurry me through."

We watched in amazement as he dropped twenty pounds of metal into the security bin.

"At least we know they work," Haddad said.

We shook hands with Haddad and watched as he hurried into the Festival grounds. Cat turned east and walked toward a marble pillar, the Civil War memorial, forty feet tall. Arin and I followed her.

"I've always wanted to stop and look at these. Just haven't done it," Cat told us. Buck and Scott Morrison stood next to her and were looking at the monument.

"They are impressive. This one was for the Navy. That one," Arin pointed to the north side of the Parkway, "was for the Army."

These two sentinels anchored the entrance to the Parkway. Arin and I had visited here frequently.

"My great-great-grandfather, Mack Murphy, came from Jamaica to fight for the Union. I like to stop here and read the inscription," Arin said, looking upward. Cat followed. The bodies and faces of sailors were sculpted into the towering monument, the angel that stood above them held a sword. An eagle topped the memorial.

Cat read the words aloud: "In giving freedom to the slave we assure freedom to the free."

"Abraham Lincoln wrote those words," Arin informed her. But Cat had closed her eyes, her lips moving, though I could detect no sound. She remained in that trance-like state as cars rushed by just beyond us, and voices of passers-by reached our ears. And then tears ran down her face. Her eyes slowly opened.

"Tell us," Arin said softly.

"That's weird," Cat said. "I just recalled a memory that I had early this morning. I forgot to tell you." Cat rubbed her temples.

"Martin introduced Frederick to a crowd. It was in Cork. I know, because he thanked the people of Cork for such a warm welcome. I think they were in a Quaker Meeting House, but I'm not certain. 'I witnessed the unbound anticipation in their faces as Frederick stood tall, fierce even, and read a passage from his book.'"

Cat took Arin's hand and closed her eyes while recounting Frederick's speech.

"'I have often been awakened at the dawn of day by the most heart-rending shrieks of an own aunt of mine, whom he used to tie up to a joist and whip upon her naked back till she was literally covered with blood. No words, no tears, no prayers from his gory victim seemed to move his iron heart from its bloody purpose. The louder she screamed, the harder he whipped; and where the blood ran fastest, there he whipped the longest. He would whip her to make her scream and whip her to make her hush; and not until overcome by fatigue would he cease to swing the blood-clotted cowskin.'"

Cat released Arin's hand and brushed her forearm over her eyes. "I could feel the tears running down Martin's face, and I could see in his memory that this revelation had shaken every man and woman."

Cat shook her head.

"I'm strange, right? I can't remember to eat some days, but I can remember things like this, word for word. It's the part of my brain that makes me think like Nine."

Buck and Scott Morrison's phones buzzed at the same time. Buck was the first to react. I didn't love the tension in his face.

"What?"

"From the task force." Buck nodded his head to Morrison.

Morrison held his phone out in front of him.

"A police station in Portland, Oregon was firebombed. Two cops are dead. Antifa claimed responsibility. They said in a statement, 'We stand in solidarity with our sisters, Arin

Murphy and Cat Fahey, as they face down the fascist white supremacists in Philadelphia.'"

Buck looked up at the Angel with the sword.

"Gonna need her. You two are shit magnets."

————

We arrived in front of the main stage as FBI Agent Di Stefano and Homeland Security Agent Noreen Casey made their way to us.

"There's been another one," Joe said. "An African American church in Wilmington, Delaware, not far from the President's home. A crucifix was lit on fire and they spray-painted the church wall. It said, 'Jews and Blacks will not replace us. We will Stop the Steal.'"

"The President was scheduled to speak at a prayer service there on Sunday." Noreen looked straight at me as if I had answers. I didn't.

"It's all too wrapped up in a bow." I rocked back and forth on my toes. "I keep feeling like we're being played. What about you, Scott?"

Morrison seemed to study his hands before lacing his fingers and snapping them, a loud crack of his joints.

"I think the Feds need to get back to work. We have a VP to protect tomorrow."

With that, he turned from us and headed to the museum steps. I couldn't shake it. Something bad was going to happen in this area to cause a stampede.

"Look, I'm going to feel better if I know you are safe." Agent Di Stefano interrupted my thoughts. "The death threats against Arin and Cat are increasing. Do me a favor. Go home, all of you." Di Stefano directed his plea to me as if I was the ringleader. "Have a few beers, burgers, relax. It's Labor Day weekend. I need you off the streets where the crazies might find you."

"And we need you back tomorrow, fresh," Agent Casey pleaded, then placed her hand on Cat's shoulder. "We have hundreds of the best on this, Captain Fahey. What we need from you are the things we cannot see. Let all that happened today get sorted. Call Agent Di Stefano the moment you have something."

The entire perimeter of the Festival grounds was fenced off. I tried to picture sixty thousand people inside, nowhere to hide.

"Let's go. It's going to be a long day tomorrow." Buck started walking to his car.

I walked in the other direction, east, toward the Civil War memorial, toward William Penn, towering over the city. Toward Independence Hall, where our founder's words were written: "We hold these truths to be self-evident, that all men are created equal, that they are endowed by their Creator with certain unalienable Rights, that among these are Life, Liberty and the pursuit of Happiness."

As I walked in the direction where the *Declaration* was written, I wondered if we had lost the right to those words. I felt a hand reach me, stopping my forward progress. I met Arin's gaze.

"I need some time. I'll walk home by myself."

"But the threats, as Joe just said."

"The threats are to you and Cat. I'll see you in twenty minutes."

I let her hand drop and waited a moment as she walked to Buck's car, Cat and Buck standing beside it. For the first time in two years, I couldn't find where she belonged, where I belonged.

As I walked toward the exit, I noticed a smell. Caustic. The floodwaters, the pollution, mixing with the grass, and the emerging Festival city. All bundled up with the distinct, noxious taste of having no idea of where the world was going.

The Vice President might die. Arin could easily be the Prime Minister. We might need a new Civil War memorial to commemorate a second civil war.

I increased my pace and exited through the metal detectors. Fifteen feet in front of me stood the pillar celebrating the soldiers of the Civil War. It depicted a wounded soldier, his comrades embracing him as they pushed forward toward victory. My eyes climbed the pillar, resting on the sculpture of a woman, a battle axe in her right hand and a small female angel standing in the palm of her left hand. Capping the monument was the American eagle. Just under the eagle was the inscription that I had read so many times:

One Country – One Constitution – One Destiny

I'd often thought about that word. *Destiny.* Were Arin and I destined to be together? Or did I win a random lottery? It would have been easy to say that destiny had joined us; it was very romantic. And perhaps it had. We shared a family tree. Centuries separated our DNA, but her family had searched for the missing pages of the *Book of Kells* as had my family. But then what? Did fate keep you together, or did a random universe slap you around and test the Destiny theory? And if the daily vagaries of life were complicated for two people, what about a nation? America loved to think of itself as destined, as if a divine force bound it and protected it. It had become sacrilegious to think otherwise. But Lincoln said we would never be destroyed from the *outside*. If we lost our freedom, it would be because we had destroyed ourselves. That rang true. Today. The day before the shit might hit the proverbial fan.

"Hey, aren't you that memory guy?"

I was startled out of my daydream. The girl was somewhere around fourteen. A group of kids looked up at the monument, as I had been doing.

She seemed confident. Like craning her neck to look at a six-three thirty-two-year-old with red hair was just a normal thing.

"Yeah, I'm Key Murphy. What's your name?"

"Tawanda."

She was wearing jeans with holes in them that were designed to be there. She held her skateboard in her left hand. Her friends gathered around her and stared up at me.

"Your wife is a badass. I can't believe she's a professor and all that. Put a beating on that guy. I read that she's like Indiana Jones."

"She kind of is, you're right. But she's not my wife."

Tawanda tilted her head and looked at me sharper, the right corner of her mouth pulled up.

"You have the same last name."

"True."

"And it's obvious you're in love."

Tawanda's friends laughed. One of them pushed her lightly on the shoulder.

"Obviously, Tawanda in love."

Her friend blushed. They all laughed, except for Tawanda.

"I'll tell Arin that you said she's a badass. She'll like that."

Her friend added, "Tell her if she don't marry you, Tawanda's waiting." The friends laughed hard.

"Nah," Tawanda pointed to the inscription almost forty feet above us. "It's Destiny for Mr. Key and Dr. Arin. You don't mess with destiny. Right, Mr. Key?"

CHAPTER 27

FRIDAY, SEPTEMBER 3, 2021.
PHILADELPHIA

Tawanda and friends skateboarded west on the Parkway, and I headed down Twentieth past the science museum. It was bustling with families heading in and out, ice cream trucks pulled up to the sidewalk, lines in front of them. It was in the low seventies, a bit overcast, pleasant. Most adults wore masks, but it didn't hide the energy in the air, laughter, animated voices. I stopped to take it all in, like that feeling in spring when the first flowers poked through the ground: hope, freshness, possibility.

It was quieter as I got a few blocks away, and thoughts of buying an engagement ring played in my head. Destiny? Two guys turned the corner from Cherry Street onto Twentieth and stopped cold, three feet away from me. I hadn't been paying attention. I was still contemplating Arin and was taken by surprise. They were big, rough-looking. A black van screeched to a stop. The driver got out, slid the side door open and grabbed a baseball bat. Fuck.

"Your bitch isn't here to protect you." The guy in the

middle stepped forward and slammed his fist into my gut. I was able to take some of the power out of it with a partial block, but it still rocked me.

I leaped in close, giving him no room to maneuver, knowing he would have no choice but to push or grab me.

He used his right shoulder as a battering ram to shove me backward. I took hold of his shirt while I stepped back and yanked him forward and off balance. My right palm caught his nose in a wicked uppercut, blood spouting immediately. Before he could drop to his knees, I thrust him into the guy on his left.

Baseball Bat man had closed the distance and lined up a swing to my head. Dumb. Go for the legs, the torso: hard to miss. I offered my head as the target and he took a deadly swing. I went under it as his momentum propelled him to the left, exposing his back to me. I delivered two powerful kidney blows, threw my arm around his neck, and slammed my heel behind his knee.

The third guy had gotten behind me. I felt his arms slip under mine, his hands reaching for my neck. A headlock. If he succeeded, I was in a world of hurt. Using my height to my advantage, I spread my feet apart, squatted low, and got my ass under his pelvis, my body now a fulcrum.

Baseball Bat guy was on his feet, the bat over his head this time, coming in like an axe chopping wood. I grabbed Headlock man's forearms; the front of his body was pinned to my back. I dropped to the ground as the baseball bat landed full force on Headlock man. His scream was horrific.

I got out from under him, but Baseball Bat guy was waiting for me. The bat had bounced away a few feet, but he rushed me, a right hook to my head. He caught a bit of my cheek as I dodged, his fist catching my shoulder. I wobbled back a few inches as he sent in a front kick. It knocked me on my ass. He caught my shoulder with another kick as I tried to get up. I was on my hands and knees and saw him line up a kick to my exposed face. I leaped upward and came crashing down on his shin with my elbow just as his kick gained momentum. It hurt like hell. But it hurt him more. He screamed at the pain. I clamped my hand around his throat and felt like squeezing.

"Tell your friends, don't ever call Dr. Murphy a bitch. Next time I'll kill you." I knuckle-punched him in the solar plexus and his face went crimson as he gasped for air. I saw zip ties in his back pocket as he dropped to his knees. I looked at the van's sliding door, open, their plan apparent.

Adrenaline was coursing through me hard. I was pissed. Clearly, they had followed me. There was nothing random about this. I considered giving them another round of hurt. And then I deflated, like the adrenaline was sucked back into wherever adrenaline comes from. My chin throbbed and my torso felt like it had been struck by a battering ram. I rested against the brick wall of the building next to me, my fingers brushing against the rough surface. All I wanted to do was get back home to Arin.

I wiped my hand over my face and came back with blood from my lip. I had an N95 mask in my pocket and slipped it on. A quick check of the street; no one was nearby. I hurried away. If the police had come, I would have been tied up with them for hours giving statements.

Arin must have heard the door opening and hurried to greet me. She stopped a few feet away as I pulled the mask off, alarm in her eyes.

"What happened?"

"Buck and Cat are in the kitchen?"

"Yes."

"Then I may as well tell everyone at the same time."

Arin wrapped her arms around me and I winced. One of my ribs must have taken some of the punch. She pulled away, but I coaxed her back. Her hand brushed my face. Her eyes melted me. Her lips mouthed, "I love you." I leaned in to kiss her. She stepped away.

"I love you, but you need to clean up that ugly mug before you get to kiss me. Have you seen yourself?"

I shook my head.

"OK, pretty boy, let's show you off before we clean that up."

Cat and Buck looked our way as we entered the kitchen. Cat gasped. Buck had a good stare, went to the freezer, pulled out a frosted Yuengling. "I put a few in the freezer thirty minutes ago."

He twisted the cap, handed it to me. "Please tell me the other guy looks worse."

"Other guys." I held up three fingers.

"Oh my God." Arin's hands had been on her hips; they were now covering her mouth.

I drank some of my beer and was surprised how much my lip and tongue hurt, but the cold felt great on my throat, so I swallowed some more. "Yeah, they look worse. I hope. But I haven't seen myself yet. I thought I would give you the pleasure."

I sat down and recounted what happened.

Arin had filled a bowl with hot water and began wiping my face, the blood from the cloth clouding the water.

"Did you call it in?" Buck asked.

"Hell no. I'd be sitting at a detective's desk for three hours answering questions. No time for that."

"You shoulda called me after."

"Come on, Buck, you'd have to play it by the book. Those guys likely got out of there as fast as they could." I took the final sip and held the empty. "Pretty please."

Arin went to the freezer for another beer and touched the ice-cold bottle to my jaw.

"You're going to need ice on that."

"Thanks, Dr. Murphy."

"Key's right," Cat said. "No way they want to talk to the cops. They were watching all of us at the Festival grounds. We got in the car, and Key walked. They followed you. But what's the point?"

"No point at all," Buck said. We waited for more explanation.

"Look how disciplined they were at the hotel. They were biding their time for whatever they have planned for tomorrow." Buck stood. His festival ID lanyard bounced on his chest. "Maybe your attackers were lone actors, some other militia group that wants to make a mark but is not part of Dit's group. That attack broke the discipline we saw today."

My jaw hurt. I felt my left eye closing, blinking, watering. My chest ached as I inhaled. Yet the ale washed nicely, softly. I thought of Aedan as he walked to the village and his surprise at seeing the Viking invaders.

"You know, Cat, it occurs to me that Aedan's job was to get the *Book of Kells* from Scotland to safety in Ireland. Martin's job was to get Douglass from America to safety in Ireland. Maybe we should kidnap the VP and get her to safety in Ireland."

My three amigos looked at me as if my brain had been rattled. They might have been right.

"Give it some thought. I need a hot shower and a short nap. I'll be back soon."

Arin followed me up the steps and into our room. She gently pulled my T-shirt up and slid it over my head.

"Not too bad." She brushed her fingers lightly over the emerging bruise just under my ribs. "Does it hurt?"

"A little."

She ran the shower hot.

"Get in here," she instructed while tossing her Beatles T-shirt to the floor. "Let the water run down your back."

I gladly obeyed and felt the pleasure of her soaping me

and running her hands over my aching back and legs. She made me turn, carefully washed and caressed my chest, then the rest of me. I thought I was too tired to respond, but that was evidently not the case.

I reached for the soap so I could wash her.

"No," she began washing herself. "Go lie down."

"OK, boss lady," I said. I toweled off then sat on the bed, waiting.

Arin came out a moment later, towel wrapped around her body, hair wet. She reached for my hand and guided me to where the towel tucked into itself. She had me pull on it so that it fell to the floor, then she moved my hand over her breasts, her nipples responding to my touch. Her fingers brushed my hair, my cheek, my chest. She leaned over and let her lips play softly over my ear, then down my neck, her breath alone an aphrodisiac. She pushed me back, my head on the pillow as she straddled me.

"Just call me Doctor Murphy," she said, guiding me into her.

She moved softly, slowly, being careful in her stride. Her pace increased, at first rhythmic, slight moans escaping her. Then her movement became wild, urgent, rough. I was lost in our unleashed pleasure until I looked into her eyes. There was no pleasure there, only frantic release. I laced my hands over her back, calming her until she slowed, then she lay peacefully on my chest, our breathing rising and falling. Arin rolled to my side. Her head nestled on my shoulder. She reached her lips to my cheek, my neck, then closed her eyes as sleep claimed her.

Sixty thousand fenced-in young people, three thousand white supremacists. And we would be right in the middle of the storm.

CHAPTER 28

Getting past the firewalls was relatively easy. Anwulika and her team had built a program that mirrored the TOR browser. TOR provided anonymity for searching the Dark Web. Anwulika's browser was faster and utilized double or triple the number of relay stations. If her entry was detected, the trail would end at a computer repair shop in Ponce, Puerto Rico. It would switch to a restaurant in Athens, Greece, after a few minutes.

What surprised her was the sheer volume of transactions under five thousand dollars. She wanted to know where it came from, how it was laundered, and who was receiving it. That would have to wait. The only question that mattered now: was there anything here that threatened the VP?

She cursed her weariness as she considered a brief nap. Age. She frowned.

The carriage house had no windows. Anwulika walked to the door, pressed her code, and opened it to see that the sun had risen. It was Saturday. VP-in-Philly day, and she was running out of time. She sent an SOS to her two most trusted geniuses, Lihua and The Edge. It would wake them.

"I need you now. Bring coffee."

CHAPTER 29

Li Chen arrived at the Trident Hotel, one minute down the road from the Trident Castle, both gleaming white against the turquoise waters of the Caribbean. The concierge reached his gloved hand to the car door and opened it. Chen emerged, followed by his bodyguard, who was ordered to be discreet and remain at a comfortable distance. The concierge directed Chen to the Veranda Restaurant and the table where Xi Liang awaited him.

None of the guests paid him any attention. There was no pomp or press. The plan was simple: be seen together, word of which would be leaked to the society pages, that the two colleagues enjoyed breakfast together before Mr. Liang departed for Miami.

The two tables closest to them would remain empty. Some twenty feet separated them from other guests. Their table overlooked the calm morning waters, the sun warming this Saturday morning; a luxurious cool breeze blew in from the sea. Xi Liang was a guest at the hotel. Chen had no doubt that at least two women were still sleeping in his bed.

Chen waved the waiter over.

"Coffee."

"Would you care for a mimosa, sir?"

"No. Tell the chef that I'm here. He knows what to prepare."

Chen waited for his coffee to be poured and Liang's tea to be refilled. Chen regarded Liang.

"News?"

Liang sipped his tea and returned the cup to the table.

"Not really. The clock is ticking; continue to monitor the situation."

"You understand, if the VP dies, the United States will not rest until they find who is behind this."

Liang leaned closer to his protégé.

"And that's why you will point them in the right direction."

Chen nodded. His mentor was a decade older and had grown soft and fat. Chen no longer needed him, other than as a conduit from Beijing.

Liang turned toward the ocean.

"It doesn't matter if she dies or not, just that there is chaos." Liang beckoned Chen to lean closer. "Russia will place one hundred thousand troops on the Ukraine border in November. U.S. intelligence agencies will move resources. They'll be preoccupied with Ukraine. The build-up will continue. Russia is counting on NATO being weak and divided. We are not so certain. Beijing will watch and analyze as we continue destabilizing Taiwan, waiting for our moment."

Chen nodded, an inward smile. Liang was telling him this for one reason. He would be involved—another very big payday.

"So, our campaign was designed to aid Russia?"

"Beijing doesn't care about Russia. They are a tool. The new U.S. President is far more dangerous than the last one. He's been around a long time. He sees China as his main adversary and competitor." A seagull walked the sand a few feet from Xiang. He broke off a piece of bread and tossed it to the bird. "While the U.S. is screaming about China and Covid, threatening tariffs, building alliances with our Asian neighbors, our job is to distract them with chaos on their doorstep. Then we simply turn their ire towards Russia. Beijing is pleased with your results so far."

Li Chen nodded to his superior and then sat back as the waiter delivered plates of shumai, dim sum, and steamed fish basted in a heavenly oyster sauce.

"The whole secret lies in confusing the enemy so that he cannot fathom our real intent," Chen quoted Sun Tzu while spearing a shrimp shumai with his chopsticks. "To secure ourselves against defeat lies in our own hands, but the opportunity to defeat the enemy is provided by the enemy himself."

"Just remember, if anything goes wrong, you and I become the enemy." Xiang took a dumpling in his fingers and placed it in his mouth. He let the juices flow over his tongue and allowed a contented *"hmm"* to escape his lips. "Our masters will not leave a trace. Of either of us."

CHAPTER 30

SATURDAY, SEPTEMBER 4, 2021.
PHILADELPHIA

I popped onto my elbows, uncertain where I was. My head hurt, my ribs ached. I reached over for Arin but she wasn't there. I assumed she had gone downstairs to get some dinner with Cat and Buck. I put shorts and a T-shirt on while recalling Doctor Murphy's treatment plan. A glance at the windows told me the sun had set. I'd slept an hour or two, I guessed. The house was dark, except for a glow in the kitchen —5:37 a.m. The digital clock on the stove told me so.

"Coffee's fresh. I just came down a few minutes ago." Arin startled me. She was on her stool, across from mine. Funny, our little habits.

I was in a daze. Tuesday, I was in Scotland. Wednesday, I was sitting across from where Arin was now. Thursday flood. Friday, punches and kicks. "It's Saturday?"

I poured, hoping the caffeine would create a fog-clearing miracle. I sipped.

"The VP goes on in sixteen hours, Key."

That woke me up.

I reached for the light switch and put the dimmer setting on low, just enough light to maneuver. I heard the steps creak and a moment later Buck and Cat walked in: T-shirts, gym shorts, and a telling glow. Cat looked surprised to see us and seemed a bit embarrassed. Arin waved her over and kissed her cheek.

"Good morning. I'm guessing you two spent some time discussing strategy," Arin winked.

"Best layyyed plans," I said. Everyone groaned. If that wasn't bad enough, I added, "Cat's out of the bag."

"Stop," Arin pleaded.

I took Buck by the arm and walked him toward Cat.

"Not until I pass the Buck."

"OK, you win." Cat put her arms around Buck. "The Buck stops here." She smiled. So did Buck.

"Coffee up, everyone; we need to put our heads together." I pulled bagels out of the fridge and Buck cut them and began the toasting operation. I grabbed cream cheese, peanut butter, some cheddar cheese, and raspberry jam. Arin had put plates and knives on the counter. Cat remained seated, staring into the void.

"I don't get it."

"Get what?" I asked Cat.

"This memory thing we have. It makes no sense."

"Of course it makes no sense. Scientists are still trying to understand how it works."

"How *does* it work? Give me your elevator pitch." Cat folded her arms, waited.

"You want me to give you six years of scientific research in twenty seconds?" My voice was strained. I still don't really get it. I tried to conjure Dr. Garcia.

"If anyone can, it's you." Buck loved putting me on the spot.

"OK ..." I drew the sound out slowly. I took some jam and dropped it into the center of my bagel. "Picture this in your mind." I pointed to my display. "It's now a potential memory embedded in the neurons in your brain. Agree?"

Cat nodded.

"They believe that the gene is randomly passed down your family tree. The gene carries those embedded memories. If the gene activates, then some of the memories become embedded in your own neurons."

Cat sat silently while her body started to move side to side, like a gospel singer in a choir. Her arms went up, not in praise but in frustration, beseeching someone or something.

"It stinks that they don't have something you can take to stimulate it."

I took half my bagel and spread cream cheese and jam over it. "They do have something."

"What?" Cat put her coffee down. Her eyes bored into me. "Why didn't you tell me?"

I chewed and then sipped some coffee.

"Because it takes two weeks for it to have any effect."

Cat held her harmonica in her right hand and slapped the countertop with her left, her lips pinched together.

"Seriously. You didn't think maybe it would work differently on me?" She stood and threw her arms in the air. "What harm would it have done? None."

"You don't know that."

"What's that mean?" Her hands bunched, tightened. I thought she might crush the harmonica.

"No way Dr. Garcia would administer it to you without being in a controlled situation." I needed to manage this. Keep Cat calm and focused.

"Why?"

"Your PTSD, possible brain damage. There are risks." I glanced at Arin; her complete focus was on Cat.

"Fuck you, Key. Fuck all of you. The VP is coming here and everything in me says she's in danger. And we don't have a clue."

"Look—"

"You look." She slapped her chest and appeared ready to tear my head off. "I'm Captain fucking Fahey. I'm Nine. You think some little pill from Dr. Garcia scares me? You think I'm worried about getting damaged? Look at me. I *am* damaged. You want me more damaged? Let the VP die on my watch."

She crossed the room to me, arms swinging by her side.

"You got that? You fucking got that?" She slapped my chest, and my rib screamed as she stormed out of the room.

Arin started to follow her but Buck blocked her way.

"I've seen this before. Give her a minute." Buck rested his hand on Arin's shoulder. "PTSD's no joke. But we got her. The same way we have each other, same way we give each other space."

Arin got up and walked down the hall. Buck didn't try to stop her. Their voices reached us: gentle, consoling, the way Arin does; the griot, the seanchaí, the ancient healer.

I watched Cat and Arin walk toward us, arm in arm, as they returned to the kitchen.

"I am so sorry, Key. Everyone." Cat looked down at her hands.

"No need, Cat," I said. "That's exactly how I felt the night my parents were kidnapped. It took everything I had not to go into a complete meltdown. Arin coaxed me out of it. But the stress stimulated the memories, helped us learn where the treasure was."

"OK, now what?"

"Now, you go play harmonica and come back when you're ready."

Cat sat at the counter and laid her harmonica in front of her, its silver casing reflecting the overhead light. She lifted it, tenderly, her index finger caressing the small but powerful extension of this woman warrior.

"I can only play in front of people I trust."

She moved the instrument tentatively to her lips. Her

hand trembled for a moment, her lips quivered, uncertain, and then a long, thrilling note rang out, and the melody of "Stormy Monday" took my breath away, steering her blues between sweet and sorrow. As she finished, there seemed a renewal of her being, a lifting of her chin and back. She looked at me.

"Thank you, Key. Time to get back to work."

Buck had quietly moved next to her while she was playing. She did a slow turn of her head, veering up to meet his eyes, then turned to Arin.

"Take me back. Take me to what it was like when Frederick and Martin stepped onto the shores of Dublin."

Professor Arin Murphy had been summoned, a woman whose fingerprints touched Africa, Ireland, and the Caribbean. She had breathed the intersections of the slave trade, the British prison trade, the path of freedom, and the new life people carved from it. Arin came from those people. She studied them. But most importantly, she loved them. She had told me that Frederick Douglass and Daniel O'Connell still reached across time to instruct us.

"Only through the lens of history do we know that a great wave of human misery was marching from the west of Ireland on the day they stepped off the ship. What we know as the 'Great Hunger' had begun. The potato crop was failing due to a blight, a fungus. Potatoes were not only food. They paid the rent. And the rent was owed to landlords in Britain." Arin slapped her hands on the table. "Poverty sucks the life out of people, out of a country. Jamaica knows all about that."

She took a sip of her now lukewarm coffee.

"If the Irish farmers didn't pay, they were evicted. One million died. Another million would flee, mostly to America. But that would not be apparent to Douglass. It was just beginning." Arin took her phone in hand and toggled the screen. "I want to read you something. There was a French sociologist named de Beaumont. He had visited Ireland; I think it was

1835. Give me a sec to find my notes." Arin toggled some more.

"Got it. Here's what he wrote. 'I have seen the Indian in his forests, and the Negro in his chains, and thought, as I contemplated their pitiable condition, that I saw the very extreme of human wretchedness; but I did not then know the condition of unfortunate Ireland. In all countries, more or less, paupers may be discovered; but an entire nation of paupers is what was never seen until it was shown in Ireland.' It was only ten years later that Douglass stepped onto Irish soil."

Arin broke off a bit of bagel and scooped some cream cheese onto it.

"Catholics could not own property in their own country. They couldn't vote. Their language and religion were outlawed. O'Connell was their Martin Luther King. O'Connell hated violence. He was schooled in France as a young man and witnessed the mob rule and bloodshed of the French Revolution."

She lifted her coffee mug to me. I filled it and topped off the other cups. "Douglass rejected violence on religious grounds but was the driving force in convincing Lincoln to bring Blacks into the army. His efforts created the USCT, United States Colored Troops."

"My people went back to that time," Buck added. "Word went out that Lincoln was forming divisions of Black soldiers. They couldn't join fast enough."

Arin sipped some water and looked off into nowhere for a moment. It was quiet, no intrusions of sound from the outside world—just us at our little kitchen oasis. "Douglass stepped into the land of great contradictions. Dublin was a city of landed gentry and Anglo-Irish affluence. It was also a city of poverty and desperation."

Cat rubbed her fingers gently over her harmonica.

"We know Douglass returned to America after a

successful tour of Ireland and Britain. We know that O'Connell's health was fragile and that he died in Italy two years later. We know that O'Connell warned Douglass that he was under threat. What we don't know is what happened next. Is there anything written about this in the history books?" Cat asked.

"Nothing," Arin said firmly.

"It's so frustrating." Cat put a finger on her temple. "It's in here somewhere. But sitting on my butt has never provided answers. Let's go where the action is."

CHAPTER 31

"Are you people nuts?" Deputy Police Commissioner Cruz was hollering into the phone. "Detective McCoy, I'm ordering you to stay in the house with them until I send for you."

Buck had called to tell him that we were going to Independence Hall to observe the supremacists' parade to Love Park.

"You can order me all you want, Sir, but I can't order them." Buck raised his eyebrows to us. "And they're getting ready to leave."

Cruz was quiet.

"OK, listen up, all four of you. I'll send a van for you. You can observe from inside."

"Commissioner," Cat began, "you want us to be mobile. Being confined won't work. We'll be as incognito as possible."

"*Que dolor en mi culo.*"

"I think you mean me, Sir. I'm the pain in the ass," Cat replied.

I heard a muffled sound, likely Cruz stifling a laugh.

"No, I mean all of you," the Commissioner answered. "Listen, this rally could be highly volatile. I cannot afford you inciting any confrontations. And stay away from reporters. Please." He disconnected.

Arin had on a Temple cap and T-shirt. Buck wore his Eagles cap and a button-down over a black T to hide his gun and badge. I grabbed one of my old Penn State caps for Cat. I had a Flyers hat. All four of us wore our masks and sunglasses—our attempt at incognito. We looked stupid. N-95 masks had a way of doing that.

We left through the rear door. The frame was steel reinforced, and a two-inch bolt lock made it almost impregnable. A camera was mounted three feet over the door, and a motion-detector spotlight sat above it.

As we started down the alley, we heard the screech of tires behind us and turned in alarm. Buck placed his hand on his gun. The van stopped fifteen feet away; the door slid open; Di Stefano got out.

"I just spoke to Cruz. He told me you were heading out. Get in. Let's make a plan."

We complied and pulled our masks off.

"Thanks, by the way. I had a wager with Cruz. I bet him there was no way you would stay put until this evening." Di Stefano rubbed his fingers together. "He owes me a case of Guinness and a bottle of Jameson. I'm bringing it to your place when this is over."

The fact that there were bets pissed me off a bit. I didn't want to be so predictable that someone felt secure in a wager about me.

"What do you have in mind, Joe?"

Joe Di Stefano massaged his forehead.

"Hundreds of counter-protesters are pouring into Independence Hall. There's not a single white militia demonstrator, not one." He checked his watch. "It's 3:27. The parade starts around four. No one, including Dit, has left the hotel in New Jersey."

Joe took a long slow look at all of us.

"We have a command center set up—cameras, sound, facial recognition. I want you to stay back with me. If you want to go into the crowds for recon, you need to do it individually. I'll have an agent tailing you just in case."

"No can do, Joe. I need to move instinctually," Cat challenged. "I can't be worried that I'm moving so someone can keep up with me."

"With all due respect, Captain, you can move about however you like. My agents will be invisible." He waved his hand over his body. "Under this calm exterior is a badass. Independence Hall is part of the National Park Service. Government property. I own it. This is my neighborhood for the next few hours. Am I clear?"

We rolled over a speed bump as Cat gave him a high five. A few minutes later we pulled up behind an FBI Mobile Command Center that looked like a luxury RV. We exited the van and followed Agent Di Stefano to the mobile unit. He entered a code on the keypad and opened the door.

"Mere mortals do not get to enter. Homeland Security has deemed you worthy."

Six men and women sat at consoles, monitors above them. Di Stefano walked us down to the far end of the vehicle. He gestured to the monitor.

"As you can see, this is from the hotel."

There was no one in the parking lot. The screen switched to the rear entrance for a few seconds, then to the front. We followed him to another console.

"This is a live map with GPS links to our assets on the ground. You can see the vehicle icons. The blue circles are agents. We have twelve on the plaza now."

"Sir," came a female voice. We turned to look. She nodded to the screen. We positioned behind her. "We have action."

Two vans had pulled up on Fifth and Chestnut, two at Sixth. Approximately fifteen men dressed in paramilitary uniforms were discharged at each corner. They unfurled Confederate and American flags, then converged in the plaza directly across from Independence Hall. I glanced at the GPS screen and watched as agents took positions closer to the new arrivals.

The crowd of thousands jeered at the white supremacists. The men took their positions and simply held the flags. No one approached the microphone that had been placed there. The men simply stared through the screaming crowd, unmoved by the taunts. Before long, the crowd began to quiet, unsure of what to do in the face of silence. Counter-demonstrators attempted to stoke the crowd with chants of "Down with Nazis" and "Racists not Welcome." But the chants died off quickly.

"Attention," we heard over the monitor. The supremacists turned in military formation and began their march west on Chestnut Street toward City Hall. Two police cars filled in behind them, one in front. The counter-protestors started to follow, maybe two thousand strong, to the thirty white supremacists.

Arin raised her hand. "I need to state the obvious. There's over fifty of them at the hotel in Cherry Hill, and thirty here. They bragged about having three thousand."

"The night is just beginning. They are setting us up for something else," I replied.

"I agree," Cat added. "Joe, I need to get out there and get in the crowd, listen, get the feel."

We all looked up at the monitor as the crowd continued to pour onto Chestnut Street.

"OK, I can't stop you. I will have a few agents watching

out for you. You are celebrities, after all." He folded his arms over his chest. "Thoughts, theories, anyone?"

Buck looked ready to contribute but was interrupted by the agent watching the scene in New Jersey. We moved to see his monitor. A bus had pulled up to the entrance of the hotel. The passenger door faced the lobby at an angle the camera did not cover. Shades had been pulled down on the bus windows. Some ten minutes passed and then a man walked in front of the bus and came into camera view. He pulled his mask down and raised both hands, middle fingers extended.

It was Dit.

CHAPTER 32

SATURDAY, SEPTEMBER 4, 2021.

CLONTARF, IRELAND

Lihua came through the door first, coffees in a cardboard carrier. The Edge carried a bag to the table and removed the contents; the intoxicating odors of spiced lamb reached Anwulika. The only thing greater than her weariness was her hunger.

"The twenty-four-hour kebab shops come to the rescue yet again," The Edge said as he placed a sandwich in front of Anwulika. "For our Queen."

Anwulika kissed him on his cheek. She thought of the three of them as a merry band of misfits. They had spent so much time together, knew each other's—what she called—" idiot syncrasies." All three were rescue pups, hackers that had crossed the line, made dangerous enemies and had been given purpose and protection by Padraig Collins.

Lihua was often mistaken for a boy. Her baggy clothes made her amorphous, androgynous. Around a year ago, she started experimenting with skirts, form-fitting tops, and occasional flourishes of make-up. In response to Lihua's change,

The Edge began wearing designer jeans and shirts, like the rock star whose name he borrowed.

Eight months ago, Anwulika said to them, "Why you try to hide it from Anwulika?"

They both just stared at her from their desks, a blank look.

"You two been fucking each other's brains out. You are happy. Don't hide it." Anwulika had put her hand on her chest. "Not from me, the goddess who knows all and sees all."

The three of them had laughed and hugged.

A new lightness and happiness permeated the office during those traumatic pandemic months. But the contrast of their happiness to hers began to eat at Anwulika.

Anwulika finished her sandwich and delighted in the coffee. She stood behind her friends, their screens filled with transaction information. Lihua was the resident genius at following the money.

"I see that the transfers stay under five thousand," Lihua said. "What's our goal?"

"The goal is to ignore everything that is not a direct threat to the Vice President of the United States. Look for bomb-makers, bomb ingredients, bribes to anyone in the security apparatus with access to the VP. Look for anything in Philadelphia and the surrounding areas. Look for payments to mercenaries in the U.S., to snipers. If you come across the name Andre Milo, let me know immediately. He was with the State Department, hasn't been seen in weeks."

"We only have a few hours," Anwulika started back to her desk. "I'm about to shove a flashlight down Milo's throat, and one up his ass."

CHAPTER 33

SATURDAY, SEPTEMBER 4, 2021.
STATE HOUSE, PHILADELPHIA

We walked along the familiar lawn of Independence National Park, the Liberty Bell Pavilion to our right and Independence Hall directly in front of us, as it would have looked had we been crossing it with Thomas Jefferson and Benjamin Franklin. Of course, minus the sprawling modern city that Philadelphia had become. The place had emptied and the reporters had followed the protest to Love Park.

It was not lost on me that men had just carried the flag of the Confederacy in front of the very building where the Union had begun. It was also not lost on any of us that our brilliant founders were deeply flawed regarding race. Most were slaveholders, including our first president. But strive we do toward a more perfect union. At least that's what I told myself.

Chestnut Street had been closed to traffic and the trail of protestors and counter-protestors was now a few blocks west.

As our feet touched the cobblestones of Chestnut Street, Cat froze in place, staring at the stately building. I sensed Cat was on the verge of experiencing a memory. She reached to touch Arin.

"This is so familiar. They were here."

"You've probably walked by here a thousand times," Buck said.

"True, but the images I'm seeing are not from this time. None of the modern buildings are there. And the smell of horse is potent. Arin, do you know if Douglass was here?"

"He must have been; he'd been to Philly many times."

Cat pointed to the historic structure twenty yards in front of us. "Did he give a speech here?"

"I don't know," Arin admitted. "Seems likely."

Cat shut her eyes, her head bowed slightly forward. Her eyes snapped open and she walked toward a park ranger, male. Not all of them wore sidearms, but this one did.

"Excuse me, sir, do you know where the State House Gardens are?"

I watched the Ranger's expression go from curious to confused. Cat stepped up on the curb.

"Please step back. The building is closed."

Cat's feet moved to the cobblestones.

"Why did you ask about State House Gardens?" Buck inquired.

Cat was staring into the horizon.

"Martin was looking at a flyer. It read, 'Abolitionist gathering, State House Gardens.'"

"Captain Fahey, Dr. Murphy." A female Park Ranger stood on the sidewalk about five feet from her colleague. She was somewhere in her late forties; her dark wavy hair was streaked with grey. "I'm Ranger Rashida Owens. I heard you ask about the State House Gardens. This is the State House." She swept her arms over Independence Hall. "That's what it was called for a long time."

"Thank you," Cat responded.

"Thank *you*, and Dr. Murphy. You gave those boys a hard time. Supposed to be thousands of them. I think you scared them off." Ranger Owens chuckled.

"Where were the gardens?" Cat asked.

"They're still there, just through the archways. Would you like to visit?" She pointed to three arches.

We stepped onto the sidewalk, then over the chain links dangling between metal posts, designed to keep vehicles from breaching the birthplace of the Union. I kept my eyes on Cat to see if she would react to the scene. She surveyed the surroundings, the rear of the State House, Independence Hall. Her gaze swept over the tall trees and flora, the statuary, and I wondered if she was comparing it to what she might have seen in a memory. She looked at me looking at her.

"Just some flashes; trees, bricks. Not much to go on."

"I can probably help you." Ranger Owens removed her Ranger hat and wiped her brow with a handkerchief. "Been here a long time."

"Did Frederick Douglass ever give a speech here?" Arin asked.

Owens put her hands on her hips as a smile crossed her face.

"That's not a question I ever get. People only ask about the usual cast of characters. As a matter of fact, he did. August 1844."

"Do you know where he gave it?" Cat inquired.

"Sure do, Captain. Same place most speeches were made back in the day." She began down a brick walkway and stopped in front of a statue. "This wasn't here then. The audience would stand under the trees there, and the speaker would stand where the statue is now."

I read the dedication plaque.

"This is Commodore Barry, Father of the U.S. Navy. From Wexford, Ireland."

"Here's one of those little historical facts. Douglass went to Ireland one year after his speech here, where we are standing, almost to the day." Arin ran her hand over the plaque. "He also gave a speech in Wexford during his tour."

I touched Arin's arm and nodded to where Cat was standing, eyes closed but facing the statue from where the audience would have stood. Arin moved quietly to her side. Cat gasped audibly. She opened her eyes to discover Arin next to her.

"What did you see," Arin asked.

"A few hundred people were listening to Frederick, just there." She pointed to the grassy area a few feet away. "He admitted to them that he was still a slave, not yet a freeman. The entire audience gasped as one." Cat shook her head. "Martin told him that the audience gasped because bounty hunters were constantly in the area. If informants were in the audience, trouble would be on its way. Martin tried to get him to leave immediately, but Frederick refused so that he could mingle with supporters."

"You having one of those memory things?" I noticed that Ranger Owens was watching this scene unfold. The look on her face was priceless, somewhere between star-struck and seeing a ghost.

"Sure am." Cat gave her a conspiratorial look. "And it's pretty weird."

Cat stared into the distance once again, then was startled by three pigeons as they landed in front of us; their search for crumbs was on. She watched them bob their heads.

"Martin was distraught with Douglass. He approached a group of Black men he apparently knew and addressed one as Reverend. 'I fear for our young friend,' he said, 'There is good money on his head. Bounty hunters might be on their way. I need you to get him to safety. He won't listen to me.'"

Cat scanned the area. "Frederick was talking to a group of

women. The Reverend took him by the arm, said something in his ear, and turned, Frederick hastily following." Cat looked toward Sixth Street. "One of the men whispered to Martin, 'We will secure him at Mother Bethel. Stay here. Send word if you see signs of the bounty hunters.'"

Buck pointed south. "Mother Bethel's just a few blocks that way."

"What the heck does any of this mean?" Cat said, throwing her hands up, her jaw tight, cheeks reddened.

Ranger Rashida Owens let out an audible sigh.

"Is it possible, my dear, that it's more than a memory? Perhaps it's a premonition."

Three people had been standing about one hundred feet away, mid-twenties, fit. Cat had spotted them following us on the plaza. FBI. Buck's phone rang.

"Di Stefano," Buck informed us and put it on speaker.

"We have a situation."

"We're all listening, Joe."

"The thirty or so that marched up Chestnut are in Love Park. There were at least five hundred men already there, they've been trickling in from every direction. We followed the bus from New Jersey. It's dropping men off in various locations, one at a time, where approximately twenty other men are waiting for them. Fifty-three on the bus, times twenty. They're walking through neighborhoods. Bandanas up, sunglasses on, hats, combat fatigues. Intimidating as hell. That accounts for over one thousand men. Now we know why only thirty showed up for the parade."

"What do you want us to do?" Buck asked.

"Get in the SUV that I sent for you. It's waiting on Chestnut Street."

· · ·

We drove past hundreds of counter-demonstrators arriving to protest the militias, signs in hand. Love Park sat at the confluence of the major roadways in Center City. The SUV stopped at the corner of Sixteenth and JFK Boulevard. An agent opened the door and escorted us into the old Visitors' Center, nicknamed the "Flying Saucer." The building was circular. It had a semi-submerged lower level, and a deck wrapped around the building one story off the ground. We climbed the steps and entered the glass building with a 360 view. We could see bands of the militia arriving from every angle, counter-demonstrators shouting at them.

Police had cordoned off access to Love Park, keeping the counter-demonstrators to the surrounding streets. I spotted National Guard on the Municipal Services Building Plaza. Di Stefano must have followed my gaze.

"Only thirty soldiers. The rest are in barracks a few blocks away," Joe informed us.

"Something's not right about this," Cat said, staring out at the growing crowd.

"I agree." Buck was reviewing the crowd. "I've studied the Alt-Right rallies, Charlottesville, January Six, others. There was barely a modicum of discipline: competing groups, pretty ragtag, chanting, screaming, egging on the police and counter-demonstrators …"

"This crew is completely disciplined," Cat responded. "Just like at the hotel."

The men had lined up side by side, row upon row. Silent. A man stepped in front of the LOVE sculpture. He blew three notes into a trumpet. The men who formed the perimeter of the crowd turned to face the counter-demonstrators. Another blast of the horn and the men raised their flags; the Stars and Stripes, a swastika flag, the Confederate flag, one after the other, the entire perimeter covered.

The counter-demonstrators raged. The police braced for a push forward, the militia meeting the jeers with utter silence.

Cat stepped onto the outdoor deck of the Visitors' Center, some fifteen feet above the crowd. We followed. I looked down the Parkway; the majestic Grecian columns of the Philadelphia Museum of Art stood in the distance, the sun reflecting a golden sheen off them. I rotated my head in the other direction: City Hall, a tower rising above the urban scape, its founder, William Penn, keeping watch from high above. He named it *Philadelphia*, Greek for "brotherly love."

"They will stand like this for two more hours," Cat said. "Until the VP comes on. Then the show begins."

Agent Di Stefano took one more look at them: male, white, in military formation. The only sound was from the counter-demonstrators yelling taunts.

"I'm afraid you might be right." He re-entered the building, leaving the four of us on the outdoor observation deck.

I put my arm around Arin. She slid an arm around Cat. Buck completed the line, his arm over Cat's shoulder.

A man below us held a Nazi flag. He noticed us, recognition and surprise obvious as he jerked his head back for a better look at Cat and Arin. I could feel Arin's body stiffen. I imagined a string of Jamaican curses would follow. Before the volley let loose, Cat leaned over the rail toward the man who held the swastika.

"I'll say a prayer for you," she hollered to him. Cat gave us a smile. "That'll fuck with his brain."

———

Li Chen sat glued to the CNN coverage of the rally at Love Park. E smiled.

"Everyting cris. Rabbit done good, boss, like you ordered."

"It's early. We'll see. The fun has yet to begin."

Diamond observed the drama playing out on the screen and quoted softly the most appropriate line he could conjure from the Bard: "Hell is empty, and all the devils are here."

CHAPTER 34

"Joe, I don't want a ride."

Agent Di Stefano stood in front of Cat, pleading with her to get in the SUV.

"I need to walk, see, get a feel for the vibe. The VP is on in less than two hours. I know how to do this."

Di Stefano betrayed a slight nod.

"Then I want you to do something before you enter the Festival grounds. Go to the L Hotel. We have a command-and-control center on the rooftop bar, overlooking the Parkway. They will give you a lay of the land and outfit you with an earpiece. You'll be in direct communication with us."

Masks went back on, hats in place, trying to keep Cat and Arin from being spotted. It was a short walk to the hotel. An FBI Agent greeted us in the lobby. We skirted the lobby bar and turned down a short hallway to the elevator. The elevator door opened; two security guards stood in the car, hands folded. The FBI agent escorted us to the rooftop bar. No cocktails or bartenders today. This was an operations center with a commanding view over the Parkway and the Festival grounds. Three agents were busy at computers. Four were viewing the scene below with high-powered binoculars, while two men and one woman operated sniper positions. They were relaxed, drinking water and chatting. They would be on full alert soon enough. Buck told me the rifles were long-distance M82s. *Please, may they go unused.*

Homeland Security Agent Casey came out of nowhere.

"Great view, right?"

"Hey, Noreen," Cat said.

She wore a DHS-emblazoned cap, her blonde ponytail hanging out the back.

"Agent Cohen is going to get you hooked up, Captain. In the meantime, there's a spread at the bar. Get some food; it's going to be a long night."

I didn't realize I was hungry until she said it. We made our way to the sandwiches and sat on the barstools, savoring Italian hoagies and tuna wraps. Cat was sitting on a barstool, looking north. As if in slow-motion her chest rose, her mouth opened. She suddenly walked to the guardrail, all glass but for the silver handrail atop, where she rested her arms. I slid off the barstool and joined her. She stared. I followed her direction, the golden crucifix crowning the aqua-colored copper dome of the Cathedral Basilica.

"Martin and Frederick visited there. After the Civil War. A commemoration, I think." Cat pointed to the church. Arin had quietly slid beside me. We waited. Cat finally noticed we were there, her face serene. She began narrating her experience:

"How does it end, Sir?" Frederick asks.

We are enjoying a warm afternoon walk in Merrion Park. The Liberator moves slowly, shuffling a few feet forward, stopping to claim his breath.

"How does what end?"

"Any of it. Slavery, injustice, the treatment of Irish Catholics. How do you get your country back? How do we Africans make a place for ourselves in America?"

"Agitate, agitate, then agitate some more." The great man clears his throat and spits his phlegm on the grass. He spots a bench, and Frederick takes his arm and leads him to it.

"I will not live to see a free Ireland. I just pray that my actions have pushed the boulder over the hill. You, young Frederick, will see the end of slavery. But you will not live to see the end of oppression and intolerance. We end the evil that we can and start the next fight while we have breath. God made the likes of us to be a pain in the arse to the powerful, who are a pain in the arse to the powerless."

Cat ended her narration.

"I guess I should be proud to have been a pain in the ass." She laughed.

We made our way back to the food. Cat lifted an Italian hoagie from the tray; the capicola, prosciutto, and other meats and cheeses bulged from the crusty roll. She took a bite.

"Damn, that's good."

There's something special about the smells that bring back fond childhood moments. The scent of an Italian hoagie is one of them. I think it's the oregano blending with onions and olive oil. At the end of football or baseball games, some kids would head off to Mickey D, but my friends and I always went to the hoagie and cheesesteak emporiums. I wondered what it was for Cat. And Frederick Douglass. Or Martin Fahey. I wondered what it was for Dit. And why he wanted a Civil War. I wondered if one of the FBI snipers would have him in their crosshairs before the day was over.

· · ·

Cat tested her earpiece and then Agent Cohen led us to the elevator. Ten minutes later, he guided us through a secured entry at the Festival, guarded by heavily armed DHS Agents.

"Oh my God, this makes me feel old," I said. It looked like the average age of the crowd was eighteen.

"You are old," Buck replied.

"You got six years on me, old man. You could be one of these kids' daddy."

"Or granddaddy," Arin added, laughing.

The place was packed. There were three stages, a mini amusement park, beer gardens, the greasy but inviting odor of fried something, and the almost overwhelming thump of bass lines.

We made our way to the amusement area, weaving between boardwalk-style arcades: basketball tosses, Skee-Ball, water guns shooting into clowns' mouths, stuffed animals as prizes. Cat stopped about twenty feet from the Ferris wheel.

"I've already spotted three two-man teams." She looked at Buck.

"I didn't notice. What are you looking for?" Buck asked.

"Those two, over at the pulled pork food truck."

There were two young men in line. Both wore jeans, Ts, around twenty-seven years old or thereabouts. Nothing out of place to me.

Buck was nodding his head.

"What? What am I missing?" Arin asked.

Cat waited for Buck.

"Observe the behavior of everyone around them," Buck instructed, "then focus on them."

The pattern emerged. I was about to comment, but Arin beat me to it. "Everyone around them is talking, taking selfies, texting. Those two are observing."

"Their build," I added.

"Yeah and no," Cat responded. "You'll see a lot of guys around here that are gym rats, tatted up, biceps like melons.

What separates them is their bearing—years of military discipline. Buck still has it. He knows how to stand quiet, no cell phone every five seconds, focus."

"Seventy percent of the ones back at Love Park were completely out of shape," Arin said.

"That's why the young, former military guys are here and not at Love Park." Cat kept her eyes on those two. "I should call this in."

She pressed the call button attached to her shirt and gave the person that answered her an update. "And don't let anyone approach me with FBI written all over them. Clear?"

Two minutes later, Agent Cohen stood next to us. Cat pointed out the men.

"We'll keep an eye on them. Let me know if you spot others; we'll get someone on them." Cohen disappeared into the crowd.

"You're amazing, Cat." Arin stood almost shoulder to shoulder with her. "We're here fifteen minutes and you spot three teams."

The sound of the explosion jolted us. Cat had lowered her body and pulled Arin down with her.

"It's OK, guys. It's just a flash pot on the stage." Buck pointed to the area just a bit north-west of us. "The smoke is red."

The grungy sound of an electric guitar filled the air while a few thousand kids swayed their hands and began shouting, "yay oh" to the beat.

Cat remained crouched, trembling. Arin knelt silently beside her. Cat reached her right hand a few inches forward, her fingers closing as if taking an invisible hand into hers. Her features were now soft, her eyes moist and longing. She spoke the words aloud.

"History will have no use for me, Mary." I squeeze her hand, wrinkled like mine, her beautiful skin now transformed by time and hardship, softened by a life of love and kindness. "Teach our grand-

children that not everyone gets to push the great boulder of history over the hill and transform the future. It is enough to stand behind the ones destined to change history, steady them, and push them when the boulder threatens to slide back."

Cat's hand dropped to her side and she began to weep. Arin rested her fingers gently on her shoulder, and Buck and I stood in front of her to give her privacy. She wiped her tears, her eyes to the ground.

"I'm not crying for Martin. He was at peace." Cat put her fingertips together, palms parted, as if in prayer. "I was able to see my great-great-grandmother."

I had to turn away. The familiar anxiety crept into my skin. Cat was weeping, and I had a deep sense that she was fearful that there would be no one to hold her hand at the end. I breathed deep, hoping my exhalation would force my demons to flee.

Cat and I shared the same fear.

CHAPTER 35

Saturday, September 4, 2021.
Clontarf, Dublin

The Dark Web. Most think of it as the cyber den of iniquity. And it is, in part. Ninety-two percent of all internet traffic happens here; only a fraction of it is nefarious. This is where your bank transactions hide from prying eyes. Your social security and medical records and all the data you want to keep secret lurk here, behind firewalls and encryption. So do illicit drug sales, illegal gun transactions, human trafficking, child pornography, and insurrectionists. It is also where Anwulika concealed her chat room.

Four. That was the number of people who had access to her room. It had never been breached. Never. The four were in the elite of the hacker world. When they had something of use to Padraig Collins or one of his many companies, this was where the transaction began and ended. Anwulika's computer chirped a notice and she entered the chat room. Adrenaline pumped into her bloodstream; her body stiffened.

"What the hell is going on here?"

She heard The Edge and Lihua turn in their chairs toward

her. She ignored them. The message from the intruder read, Milo = http://890nkjnbji#9796%zq; a Dark Web address. She scanned it for malware and spyware. Negative.

Anwulika took a photo of the address and moved to a different terminal. This terminal contained no data and ran on a separate router. If someone could trace it and break through the encryption, they would find nothing, nada, zip. Someone knew she was looking for Andre Milo and had provided her with an address. "Only one way to find out if it's real," she whispered, followed by "oo chimoo," as the door opened into the private world of Andre Milo.

Milo had gone off the grid. Government employees going off the grid was a cause for panic, especially if they had security clearances. Like her own chat room, there appeared to be a small number of people that interacted here in Milo's. It had clearly been in use for quite a while. But there was no time now for Andre Milo history lessons. She scanned and scrolled, looking for anything that might lead to a plot against the Vice President, wondering who sent her the information and why.

Like all internet chats, the entries went from last in to first in, and it was a long scroll to the first. The most recent entry:

R: *Interpol warrant issued for your arrest on 8/23.*

A: *Don't worry. I'm burrowed—all on track. Boland and Walsh have dispersed funds as planned.*

Anwulika had found these two and the plot to terrorize the voting commissioners. She wrote down the names and took them to Lihua.

"These two are nasty. I just sent you the short file. See if you can dig deeper."

Anwulika returned to the terminal, searching for any scrap of familiar wording. Most escaped her. Until it didn't.

R: *Training and coordination of the various militias all good. Maps and schematics of the Capital Building in hand. Leaders will be in D.C. on 1/4 to do recon. Final prep for 6th.*

A: *Funds Dispersed. I hope they can do something about that Jew bastard running the Senate.*

Anwulika texted Collins: *Need you here. You must see this.*

She continued to scroll for any scrap and stopped at an entry from 2019. She read it twice.

A: *I pushed Ukrainian foreign minister to soften the ground. Zelensky is desperate for stinger missiles.*

A: *POTUS won't give him shit if he doesn't play nice.*

CHAPTER 36

Beer had flowed—lots of it. So had money, at twelve bucks a pop. And pot. The energy was high and so was half the crowd. Worrisome, if some crisis occurred. Nothing we could do about it except stay on alert and hope that the Department of Homeland Security had an impenetrable force field over the VP.

The signs everywhere read MASK REQUIRED. That failed. At this point in the evening, barely twenty percent of the crowd wore one. The four of us were compliant. We needed to be, for anonymity. So were the teams of men that Cat had spotted. It was up to eleven. Three of the teams were male and female.

It was the first time we had encountered women associated with the Alt-Right protestors. Cat assured us they were former military as well. The FBI had someone tailing each team.

I had to pull my mask down for a moment and suck in some fresh air, wipe the sweat from my face. I spotted a lemonade stand and made for it. I ordered four, handed over a fifty-dollar bill, got two dollars back, and dropped them in the tip jar. The temperature was in the high seventies, not too bad, but the humidity was rough and the air motionless. The outside of the plastic cups sweated. So did we.

We moved to the side and stood next to a booth with a sign that read "Creative Arts in the Black Community."

We lowered our masks and gladly inhaled the ice-cold drinks through straws.

"Hi, can I tell you about our program?"

We turned to the voice. A young woman with long braids smiled and started her spiel when that look of recognition crossed her face.

"Oh, you're. Oh my God. I've watched the videos like a hundred times." She came out of the booth, phone in hand. "James!" She waved her hand vigorously at the booth next to us. "Look who I got. Come, take our picture."

Neither Buck nor I existed, thankfully. She slid between Arin and Cat. James was next. Others gathered, in hopes, I think, that one of the music stars was here. Some got excited, while some remained clueless about who Cat and Arin were and walked away. Before long, the line for photos was fifty-plus. I told Buck we needed to get Cat and Arin out of there and back to work.

But before he intervened, Cat said to the crowd, "Sorry, folks, gotta go."

"I received a message." She touched the headset in her ear. "One of the male–female teams was over there watching us. Di Stefano wants us to get behind the security barricade in front of the main stage."

I watched as Cat's shoulders tightened, lifted, bunched up.

We were two hundred yards from the main stage when the band started. I thought my eardrums would burst. Cat took hold of Buck's arm.

"I need to sit for a moment."

We looked around. A first-aid tent was just to our right. Fire Department EMTs stood in front. Buck held up his badge.

"I need to use the tent for a few minutes."

One of the EMTs checked the badge.

"Anything we can do?"

"Thanks, just give us privacy for a few," Buck answered.

The EMT held the tent flap open then let it fall as we entered. Buck guided Cat to a chair.

"You OK?"

She stared ahead.

"Cat?"

"Hell no, I'm not OK. We got these white supremacists inside the Festival grounds. Fucking inside. They're not here for the music. Over two thousand of them are less than a mile away. And how many are just outside the grounds waiting for something to happen?"

Buck didn't respond.

Cat's hands balled into a fist. She stood and looked into Buck's eyes as the words poured out.

"Jaysus, Mary, and Joseph, Frederick, how can you be so calm? They are here to bloody kill you."

"It's not my time, Martin. They've been killing me since I was born, yet here I am."

"You are a Christian man. You know full well that we don't determine our time. It could be today."

Frederick reaches to me and taps his hand on my shoulder, like a fatherly figure, though ten years my junior.

"I would never assume to know God's will, but I believe, with everything in me, that he will not abandon his children."

I witness the power in his knowing eyes, the calmness, and the boundless sense of destiny he had acquired since stepping on these shores. I feel a sliver of hope that his life will be long, that he is a vessel of the Almighty, but I also know that if we don't leave in the next ten minutes, one or both of us will die.

I take my young charge by the lapels of his greatcoat. He seems surprised, attentive.

"Three of O'Connell's men just left my room. The two assassins from America are here in Belfast. Except they are not assassins. They are journalists coming to document your story. It was a lie, planned and planted to distract us."

Frederick's face brightens.

"Then why are you afraid?"

"The real assassins are in the building across from here. They were hired by British lords. Lords who profit from American slavery. They will frame the two Americans and deflect their guilt to them. They want you to die here and blame it on the Americans. They do not want you to reach their shores."

I stare into the freest man I have ever known, though birthed in shackles—a man who refuses to bow, to be broken.

"The plan is to rain bullets down on us as we leave the building. The room they will shoot from is let in the name of the two journalists. Stories will run in the papers that the slaveholders in America contracted the assassins to kill you."

"And so?"

"O'Connell's men will meet us in the hall and lead us secretly to the ship that will carry us to Glasgow."

Frederick looks to the window of his modest room, the stone façade of the assassins' hotel just across from us.

"If they do not see us on the street, then they will come to this room, Frederick, soon. You must die, and someone must be blamed."

CHAPTER 37

Lihua had little use for words. They had never served her well. Her connection to data, to numbers was much stronger; they spoke far more clearly, resonated deeply, a language that her brain comprehended with such speed and force as to sometimes cause ecstasy. She felt that moment approaching as the lines of code gave way to her commands.

She sensed The Edge, just two feet away, stealing glances. She felt his smile. His desire. She had never known, until recently, that her body could have these sensations. Sensations that could overpower the outrageous high of cracking code. But it did. And today, at this moment, the two melded. Every nerve ending wanted him, imagined him roaming his lips over her body. The electricity of her brain, unrelenting, sent her fingers chasing digits that held secrets. The two sensations threatened to overpower her, but she commanded them to merge, and at the crossroads of lust and numbers the unknown became revealed, the patterns emerged.

She snapped her fingers rapidly, arm held high in the air.

Anwulika knew the signal and moved to her side. The Edge pulled his chair closer. Collins had entered the building and stood next to Anwulika.

"Thirty million, that's my rough count. All between four and five thousand dollars. That's not the big reveal, aye." Lihua spoke with a Chinese-laced Canadian accent. She struck some keys. "I've found fifty-eight thousand dollars, so far, deposited to Jennifer Androv, at a bank in Stroudsburg, Pennsylvania. Jennifer is eight years old."

Lihua turned her chair to face Anwulika towering over her. "Jennifer's father is the head technician for a drone light show company. That company has the contract for the Made in the USA Festival."

CHAPTER 38

"That's it. That's the message." Cat paced excitedly inside the EMT tent. *"You must die, and someone must be blamed."*

"Details? What's your thought?" Buck asked.

"They'll kill her and lay a trail back to someone else." Cat was still pacing. "Just like I told you yesterday with Ukraine."

"Who will kill her?" Arin asked.

Cat stopped abruptly, hands on the back of her neck, massaging.

"I don't know."

"Bloody hell," I shouted.

The tent flap opened and an EMT peered in. Buck signaled him to close the tent.

Arin, Buck, and Cat stood waiting for more. It was me pacing now.

"Yesterday, when we were with Agent Haddad doing the recon, Scott Morrison came over to Arin and me."

Alarm spread across Arin's face. She knew where I was going.

"Morrison warned us to be careful. Said we'd pissed off the militia guys. Then he said, 'Seems to me, if they want you dead, you'll be dead.'"

"Holy shit," Buck's eyes widened. "You didn't think to mention this?"

I sat on a bench and ran my hand over my face, my jaw still aching. "I brushed it off. I thought it had to be a coincidence. Thirty minutes later, I was fighting off three guys."

"Cat, you work for Morrison. You served with him. Your take?" Buck waited while Cat processed the question.

Cat took her harmonica out of her pocket and gripped it tight, like a nicotine addict who needed a smoke.

"He's a bit of a nut-job, but people say that about me. And remember, he has security clearance from the Secret Service and Homeland. They would have investigated him thoroughly."

"Buck, call Di Stefano," Arin said, then sat down next to me.

Di Stefano picked up on the third ring; Buck had it on speaker. "Talk fast. We are right in the thick of it."

Buck held the phone close to me. I gave him the story. "Joe, you already know that Arin and I were threatened with the words, 'If we wanted you dead, you'd be dead.' Is Morrison on your watch list?"

Silence. Then words.

"No, but maybe he should be. No time for that now. The VP's in the house. Cat, I want you in front of the main stage, eyes on the crowd. Go there now."

We walked to the main stage and badged our way behind the security barricades that kept a twenty-foot perimeter between the audience and the stage.

"Come with me for a minute." Cat walked in front of the stage to the north side. She pointed to a raised platform, two police officers stood there, scanning the crowd.

"Buck, I need to get up there. Can you ask them to step down for a few minutes."

A moment later Cat was peering through binoculars. Her position froze, focused on the area where the gate could be wheeled open for emergency vehicles. She abruptly switched to the corresponding south side gate. After a moment she lowered the binoculars, descended from the platform, and spoke to the two officers.

"I told them that I saw militia teams forming outside of the gates." Cat pointed to the cops on the platform. "They are getting ready for something out there. I called it into Agent Cohen."

"Cat and I need to stay in front. I want you two backstage. One problem," Buck said.

"What?"

Buck tapped on the ID around my neck.

"You don't have the clearance to be on stage when the VP is here." Buck lifted his phone. "Let me call Di Stefano." He walked a few feet to a slightly quieter patch.

George Washington rode his horse high above the crowd, the sun was bidding farewell, and night-time electricity was rippling through the crowd.

The VP was due to come on in about thirty minutes. She wasn't giving a speech, just a few words about hip-hop, rap, rock, and the vibrancy of our multicultural society. She would be joined on stage by some of the biggest names in music, most of them not even performing this weekend, just wanting to be part of a public celebration after nineteen long months of isolation. I suspected this twenty-something crowd was more excited about seeing The Bieber than the VP.

Buck signaled for Arin and me to follow him. I looked over to Cat; her expert eyes were scanning for trouble. She turned to us suddenly, waving her arms. We stopped as she hurried to our side.

"I just recalled something from the earlier memory."

The music was so loud that I had to put my hand to my ear to signal that I couldn't hear her.

"When O'Connell's men were trying to rescue Martin and Douglass, one of them said, 'They plan to rain fire down upon you.'" Cat had raised her voice. "Buck, they need to do another check of the fireworks. They could put an incendiary guided projectile right on top of the VP."

"I'll talk to Cruz, get some dogs to sniff around," Buck added at the top of his voice.

Cat made her way to where she had been standing and continued her observations of the crowd.

I didn't know how she could spot anything. All I could see were tens of thousands of young people bobbing up and down, one arm raised, index fingers pointing and waving to the incantations of the musicians on stage. Then I had a recollection, the crucifix holding the photo of the VP, a bullet through her forehead. Agent Di Stefano's words came rushing into my brain; "How many cops and vets were involved in the Capitol Riots? Their ranks are growing." Followed by my words to him; "OK, got it, there is a traitor in your midst. Am I right?" And his answer; "I cannot confirm or deny."

There were at least a thousand law enforcement officers with guns roaming the grounds. All it would take is one good shot to her forehead.

Buck walked us to the south side of the stage and stopped in front of a security gate; three cops on our side, three on the other side, and one woman wearing an FBI vest and cap.

Buck lifted his ID pack to her and then nodded to the police to open the gate. The agent held her hand up, studied our ID, and asked us to remove our face masks. She snapped our photos, forwarded them, and stood silently waiting for a response. The band started another song, the roar of the crowd deafening. The agent signaled us to walk with her.

"Secret Service isn't happy. I suggest that you stay out of the way. I'll give you a place to stand. When the VP arrives, just stay put. Other than that, you can do whatever you are here to do."

We followed her to the rear of the structure, emptied our pockets, walked through the metal detection scanner, then climbed the stage. We were told to remove our masks and keep them off. Secret Service needed to be able to see our faces.

I had never been backstage at a large festival. I was expecting a frenzy, but it was calm, with professionals moving instruments into place, getting ready for the next band.

Philly police were on the art museum steps, some forty to fifty strong. FBI K9 teams roamed the perimeter, and sharp-shooters were barely visible on the top of the steps and the roof.

Secret Service agents stood at the bottom of the steps where we had passed moments ago, two more at the top. We were told the VP was in the museum, getting touched up for the cameras. She would descend the steps and join the music royalty that was just gathering on the stage.

We were ensconced in a fortress. Law enforcement of every variety had every inch of the rear covered. There were more ways for things to go wrong once you reached the front of the stage. Tens of thousands of screaming fans, acres and acres of trees and buildings all faced the stage. Three thousand white supremacists were roaming freely at this point—an invitation for chaos.

The agents and the police all stirred and turned their attention as a group of black-suited men and women descended the museum steps; a bright blue suit stood out in the lights that flooded the area. The group reached the main stage. Two agents climbed the stairs then conferred with the Secret Service agents that were in place. One of the agents nodded approval to the waiting entourage.

The VP took the steps energetically and dove right into greeting the VIPs who would accompany her on the stage. The band was still playing while the VP assembled with the famous musicians for an official photo shoot. One of the stage managers approached the group and bellowed instructions. They began to form up in what I assume was a pre-arranged order.

The VP stepped away from the group to take a call, and four agents formed a protective box. Arin and I stood about ten yards away, watching her. As she ended the call, she happened to glance our way, then turned back to join the group, stopped, looked back at us, and stared. The Vice President rushed forward.

"Oh my God, Dr. Murphy?"

Arin looked gob-smacked.

"Madame Vice President."

The VP took Arin by the hands.

"My assistant just showed me the video ten minutes ago. I couldn't stop laughing. Dem stupid, gwon mess wit a Jamaican woman dat way."

I recalled that her father was born in Jamaica and that she had spent time there as a child. Her accent matched Arin's; her Patois seemed perfect to my amateur ears.

The Vice President turned to me, extending her hands.

"You must be Key. I have followed your story for, what, two years now? I have so many questions for both of you." A young woman had moved to her side. The VP glanced her way. "Look who I found."

The young woman looked star-struck. So did the VP. Both stared at us like we were Hollywood stars. Weird.

"I'd like a photo with you if that's OK." The Vice President turned to her assistant. "Charlotte." Charlotte was already fishing her phone from her purse. The VP nudged between Arin and me, and Charlotte snapped away. The VP reached for the phone. "Your turn." Charlotte stepped in, arms around us. The VP clicked several shots.

"Promise me that you'll join me for dinner in D.C. Give Charlotte your contact info. She'll arrange it." She began walking back to her entourage, then reversed course. "Have they made you stay put back here?"

"Yes," I answered.

A new sparkle showed in her eyes, and a mischievous smile hit the corner of her mouth. "Let's piss off the supremacists. I want you out on the stage near me." The VP beckoned one of her protective detail. She told him to bring us on stage shortly after she entered.

"Wait here until I get you," he said to Arin and me.

Cat's boss, Scott Morrison, stood fifteen feet away, watching our interaction with the VP. He smiled and nodded to us. I wanted to kidnap the VP and get her to safety.

Arin and I were taking it all in. Everyone backstage looked lit-up with excitement. The only people standing still were the VP's protective detail. Plus Arin and I. Everyone else was bopping to the music; deep, rhythmic drumbeats embraced the earth, while blazing piano keys soared to the heavens. I felt it deep in my marrow; sometime in the next few minutes the world was going to turn to shit.

An announcer said, "Philadelphia, put your hands together for Made in the USA musical royalty." The curtain had parted and the musicians began their procession. The VP was queueing up. I noted that someone familiar was hurrying to get outside of the security fence. I pointed him out to Arin. Scott Morrison was rushing toward the Spring Garden Street Bridge. He had reached inside his jacket, and out came a face mask, a cap, and sunglasses. It was getting dark. I heard Arin say, "What the actual …" I called Buck and told him. Something was not right.

"Let's go." I took Arin's hand and hurried to the steps.

The Secret Service agent stepped in front of us.

"You're supposed to wait over there for me."

I said the magic Covid words while I nodded to Arin. "She's not feeling good."

He couldn't back up fast enough.

We rushed out of the gate and made our way onto Spring Garden. Though it was called the Spring Garden Bridge, it was more of an overpass that connected West Philadelphia to Center City. It went over the river and expressway but also had pedestrian sidewalks. The bridge was closed to traffic and was packed with lawn chairs, coolers, and the occasional barbecue grille. Unlike the Festival, the bridge was crowded with people aged forty and above. I guessed they wanted to be near the youthful energy and the fireworks that would soon begin.

I struggled to find Morrison through the sea of people. He was distinctive in form and gait. I looked for a pattern. Ninety-nine percent of the people here would be relaxed, having had a few beers and several tokes; a party weekend vibe. Morrison would be the opposite. He abandoned his battle station, the Museum of Art. He broke ranks in a hurry and his kinetic energy would be evident. I saw someone separate from the crowd. A cap. An athletic body. Sharp in angles. Like a torpedo shooting into a calm sea. He reached for a door and disappeared.

Arin and I pushed forward until we were out of the crowd. Thirty yards in front of us sat a three-story building. A coffee shop occupied the front half of the first floor. Then I saw the door where Morrison had gone out of sight. I dialed Buck and told him we were heading in.

"Wait for me; you don't have a gun."

My phone rang as I disconnected from Buck. It was Collins.

"Padraig," I answered.

"No time to explain. Is there a drone display at the Festival?"

"Might be, I don't know," I answered, looking back toward the grounds.

"Who would know?"

"Let me add Buck." I did. I told him what Collins had asked me.

"They are going up now. It's a huge American flag in the sky," Buck reported.

"Get the VP out of there. Now."

"What? Why?" Buck's voice was filled with alarm.

I could hear Collins heavy breathing, about to explode.

"Just fecking—"

"One second." Buck was talking but I couldn't tell with whom.

"Cat just told me the same thing Padraig. I'm on it. Key, I just gave my gun to Cat. She'll be there in a minute. Wait for her. I'll call Di Stefano."

———

Secret Service and the FBI occupied a mobile control van adjacent to the Rocky statue; its glass wall faced the stage and the city. Agent Di Stefano took Buck's call. His eyes shot upward at the mention of the drone display. Secret Service Agent Williams saw the alarm on Di Stefano's face.

"We need to get those drones down. Tell your people to extract her."

Di Stefano raced out of the van, two agents in his wake.

They crossed to the opposite side of the Rocky Steps. A man and a woman looked up from their computers, startled by the arrival of three breathless FBI Agents.

"I need you to get those drones down," Di Stefano commanded.

"Excuse me?" said the blonde woman.

"Get the drones out of the sky now."

"Sir, it's computer programmed." She waved her hands over the screen and keyboard.

"Override it," Di Stefano screamed at her.

The woman scanned her colleague. They did nothing.

"If you are a part of this, you will rot in Guantanamo."

"Part of what?" asked the twenty-something sitting next to the blonde.

"You have ten seconds to override the program. I want them landed behind the museum," Di Stefano said in barely controlled rage.

Agent Williams and three members of the Secret Service had arrived behind Di Stefano.

"Do you have a warrant, Sir?" the woman asked.

Di Stefano and Williams shared a nuanced look. Williams gave an approving nod to his crew. They lifted the woman out of her chair and dragged her across the plaza while Di Stefano took her seat. He quietly held his gun and slipped it between the legs of the young man, pressing lightly into his balls.

"You have five seconds to override the program and land those damned things."

The Vice President had stepped to the microphone, the megastars of rap, hip-hop and rock applauding behind her, the crowd cheering.

"Hello Philadelphia, hello America."

Hundreds of points of light began amassing in the sky; red, whites and blues, forming the American flag.

"Like the Constitution, our music also formed and informed America."

The multicolored drones began to move. The VP paused as a man approached and whispered into her ear. Her eyes looked upward as the drones wrote in the sky: *Made in the USA*.

"Please give huge applause to the men and women who bring that music to us." She stepped back as the musicians moved forward for a thunderous welcome. The VP looked over her shoulder as four blue-colored drones descended slowly, like teardrops from the heavens and then reversed course.

After the drones had landed on the back lawn of the museum, FBI and Philadelphia Police K-9 units were sent to inspect them. Eight minutes later, the captain of the K-9 unit reported to Di Stefano and Williams.

"Four of the units had been outfitted with aerosols. We haven't identified the contents, but it's safe to say you won't like what you hear."

———

Cat came bursting through the crowd, almost knocking people over. The gun in her hand and her police lanyard must have cleared the path.

Arin and I had been staring up at the drones that lit the night sky. Old Glory, in a modern light show. And somehow it was a threat.

Cat stopped and followed our gaze. Her eyes bulged; her mouth dropped open.

"Oh shit. Oh my God."

"What?" Arin asked.

"The memory, Martin telling Frederick, 'I am told that the plan is to rain fire down upon us.'"

"You were right Cat, your great grandfather was trying to warn you," I said. I left out my concern that a law enforcement officer could be an assassin.

"I hope they got her out of there." She examined Buck's gun. "Where did Morrison go?"

I told her.

"Might mean nothing. Maybe Morrison has a lover in there," I said.

"Do you believe that?"

"No. But we need to account for it," I answered.

"We don't need to account for it. Scott left his post." Cat took a glance at the surrounding area, empty but for us. "Wait here."

"Not a chance." Arin stood her ground.

Cat ran for the door that Morrison went through. It was locked, an electronic keypad. She surveyed the first-floor layout in a glance and then took giant steps to the coffee shop entrance. Arin and I stayed with her. She walked to the counter. The woman behind the cash register flinched at the abrupt stranger.

"Is there an entrance to the other floors from here?" Cat held her police lanyard out for her to see.

The woman stared at Cat with disdain.

"I don't talk to pigs."

Cat walked around the counter.

"Nice legs." She raised the gun. "Which one do you want to keep?"

"What?"

"I'm going to shoot one of your legs," Cat said, as if this was a normal thing to discuss. "I'm offering you a choice as to which one."

The panic, the trembling, the expected response to the unexpected.

Arin stepped between Cat and the barista.

"The Vice President is under threat. There is someone in the building who might be involved. We need to find him."

"Why didn't you just say so? I love the VP." Seconds later, she pressed the code that let us into the hallway. "I know the people on the second floor. Don't waste your time. Go to the third."

I texted Buck our location and told him we were inside, hunting for Scott Morrison. I recalled Cat saying he was one of the best operators she had ever known. And I didn't have my gun.

We raced to the second-floor landing and looked up the stairs to the third floor.

"You're right, we can't go in guns blazing. We need to account for him having an explanation," Cat said.

We hurried to the third floor. One door. One unit. Cat knocked. Nothing. She knocked again and then tried the doorknob. Locked. A moment later it swung open. DHS Agent, Noreen Casey, stared at us in alarm. "Captain, what are you doing here?"

The three of us froze in place. I tried to shake off my confusion. "What are you doing here?" I asked.

"I asked first," Agent Casey answered.

"We saw Scott heading over the bridge, figured something was wrong. Where is he?" Cat waited for an answer.

I watched Casey's normally bright and cheerful eyes narrow, darken, and her jaw tighten. She held the door tightly and protectively. "We're on assignment here. You need to leave."

Her voice was deep and commanding. She began to close the door, but Cat pushed through, crossing the threshold, Arin and me behind her.

"You are compromising an operation," Agent Casey seethed.

The bedroom door to our left swung open. Scott Morrison pointed at us with his left hand, his right hand obscured by the wall.

"Are you out of your mind?" His face reddened.

"I have questions, Scott," Cat responded.

Morrison's bearded jaw jutted forward, quivering.

"What you have is five seconds to get your ass out of here."

Cat reached behind her and came out with the gun pointing at Morrison. "Show me your hand Scott, slowly."

"What the hell is wrong with you? You barge into my home and aim a gun at me?"

I had a quick survey of the room. An ugly couch. Two stools at the kitchen counter. Nothing on the walls. All wrong. Morrison was Mr. *GQ*, rarely a hair out of place. He would never live like this.

"Your hand, Scott" Cat gripped the pistol with both hands. "Now."

Morrison revealed his empty hand and stepped into the room.

I kept my eyes on Casey, a stern look on her face, her DHS-emblazoned windbreaker unzipped.

"I don't know what you think is happening here, Captain. Holster that gun, or I'll have you thrown into a deep dark hole." The agent shook her head. "You are interfering with a DHS operation."

"Bullshit." Cat aimed at Casey.

"I saw the micro-expression she gave you," Cat said to Morrison, "the tic of your right cheek in response."

"You're out of your mind, you stupid bitch. Noreen, me, we are on assignment here."

"Lace your fingers on your head and spread your feet, a foot apart from your shoulders," I commanded Morrison.

He did a slow-burn twist of his head. Cat steadied her pistol in both hands as Morrison followed my orders.

"Shoot him if he blinks," I said to Cat, then nodding toward Casey. "Her too."

I touched Arin on the shoulder. She acknowledged. She would stand guard with Cat. I walked toward the bedroom and steeled myself as I passed Morrison. I glanced into the nondescript room, bare naked but for a queen bed. I turned back to the main room and saw two silver aluminum cases on the kitchen floor. One contained some sort of weapon, the other a computer, and what I assumed was a satellite phone. A sheet of paper lay on the keyboard. I took it in hand.

"Explain." I held it for Morrison to see. It was obviously bank routing numbers.

He slowly unlaced his fingers, watching me closely, and took the paper. Morrison looked to Agent Casey. As if in slow motion, he returned his attention to Cat, addressing her even though I asked the question.

"Nothing that you would understand, Cat. You're a good person. I'm not. But I'm a rich little motherfucker, and you're poor as dung in the cow fields of Iraq. Homeless, brain all messed up. For what? Your patriotic duty? Do you think the men that sent you to war give two shits about you or the rest of us?" Morrison laughed at this. He lifted his wrist and glanced at his watch—a Rolex. "You're too late anyway. By now, the VP is dead."

I moved forward, ready to swing at him.

"Don't, Key. He's baiting you. He wants you to do it. Ignore anything he says. He's trying to rile us up, get us to make a mistake."

Casey took a step. Cat pointed the gun, rock steady.

"I didn't say you can move. Step back."

Casey obeyed. I walked to Arin's side.

"Is she really dead?" Cat's body seemed to drain of energy at the asking.

"I hope so," Morrison said casually. "But I don't get to take all of the credit." He pointed his thumb toward Noreen Casey. "I'm just a greedy little bastard, but Noreen, she's good people, Cat. A patriot who wants to save America from the socialists and global elites."

"You're part of the white militias?"

"Cat, Cat, Cat, come on." Morrison held his hands out like he was pleading his case to a five-year-old. "They are idiots … useful idiots, so convinced of their righteousness that they don't know they are being used. They made our job easier," Morrison said, glancing at Agent Casey.

I didn't like this at all. He was too confident and relaxed with a gun in his face.

"I have a dilemma. I could offer you money, but Arin is too rich. Doesn't need it. Key, you think you are a medieval monk; therefore, you're unstable. It's Cat who perhaps I could bribe, but that will never happen. She's a goddamned saint."

Morrison rubbed his chin.

"Arin," Casey said, now looking relaxed like Morrison. "I had your mother shot in the leg a few years back. You see, if Rabbit wants someone shot, they get shot. If I want someone dead, they get dead."

I couldn't make sense of it, wasn't sure if I heard her right. My shoulder jerked back at the memory of the bullet grazing my arm two years ago in Jamaica.

"You got in our way back then. Your mother was a little insurance policy in case we ever faced a moment like this. If we don't walk out of here soon, your mother won't live through the night."

Arin leaped at her; Cat reached out to stop her. Casey stripped Cat of the gun at blinding speed. Cat went for it before Casey could pull back out of reach. Casey fired two bullets into Cat's chest.

"No, no," Arin screamed and went for her again.

Casey raised the gun. I leaped past Arin and delivered a

head punch that sent Casey to the ground, but not before a bullet was fired. Arin dropped. Only instinct carried me toward the gun now lying on the floor. Morrison went for it. I landed a kick to his chest, but his momentum was taking him to the weapon. My foot caught his wrist as he raised it. The gun dropped and Morrison got to his feet. The slick *GQ* guy was replaced by a hardened soldier, his face tense, his body ready to strike.

Arin was lying in her blood. This had to end. I stood calmly, arms loose, as if I had given up. He did a side-kick. I caught his leg mid-air and thrust it higher, taking him off balance while I swept his other leg from under him. My right hand took hold of the gun as I made the sweep, low to the ground. Morrison landed hard but tried to get up. I fired a bullet into his knee. He screamed. I raised the gun, then lowered it. I wanted this traitor alive.

I moved to Arin while Morrison let out a torrent of curses.

"Arin ended up like Tanya after all," Morrison said.

The door flew open. Buck rushed in, gun up, beginning to shake as he took in Cat and Arin. Buck went to Cat, placed two fingers on her neck, shook his head.

"Get an ambulance Buck, get me a fucking ambulance." My hands shook uncontrollably.

Buck made the call.

"He's Rabbit," I said while trying to staunch Arin's bleeding.

"What?" Buck stood next to Morrison. "You're sure?"

"I'm sure."

Buck looked at Agent Casey, lying unconscious.

"They both are. They were partners."

Morrison was on his elbows, head raised, his eyes blinking wildly.

"My sister?" Buck said, his gun pointed to the floor, the tendons in his neck taut, straining to hold him upright.

"That had nothing to do with me. Shit happens when you're a junkie. She's your sister; that was on you." Morrison spat out the words and stared defiantly at Buck.

Buck had a glance at Cat. His arm rose.

Morrison snapped back, his head slammed to the floor, a bullet hole dead center forehead.

I was out of body, out of mind. Fear owned me. I reached my shaking hand to re-check Arin's pulse. She was bleeding from the chest, unconscious.

"I need that ambulance. Now!" My voice was shaky and cracked.

Buck was kneeling next to Cat. He lifted her hand and kissed it. The pain on his face will be etched in my mind forever. He joined me, compressing Arin's wound.

I could swear that I heard music from a Mr. Softy ice cream truck, and I wondered if there were ice cream trucks in Jamaica when Arin was a kid. I wanted to get her one. To get her anything.

I placed my hands on her cheeks. She was losing color, likely in shock. I wanted to say something. I wanted words to come out of my mouth, to stir the heavens and cause angels to come to our rescue, but the only thing I could whisper was, "*Please.*"

I heard action on the steps, and the EMTs entered. One came to Arin. One to Cat. After checking Cat's pulse, he shook his head and then checked Morrison. Then Casey.

"She's alive."

"Leave her," Buck said as the other EMT's lifted Arin onto the stretcher.

· · ·

I held Arin's hand as the ambulance raced to the hospital. I called on my ancestor Aedan to intercede with the heavens. I spoke to him for a moment, the shrill siren of the ambulance fading.

I floated above her—my Arin. Trauma coursed through her, her life force fighting back, but weary. I would not allow her soul and spirit to escape. I would keep watch, keep vigil. The first sign of her soul slipping into the ether and I would call upon the Almighty to leave her in my charge. "You, God, have a million souls to tend; please leave this one here with me."

The ambulance's rear door flew open and Arin was raced down the hall of the emergency room. I stood in a hollowness that I didn't know existed. I could sense Aedan's presence but not his comfort. I was abandoned in space and time and knew only one thing mattered in that loneliness. Love. Arin.

"*Please*," I whispered yet again.

———

Buck stood in the hallway and watched as the EMT's raced the stretcher carrying Arin down the stairs, Key in their wake. He turned to the wall, both hands forming fists, wanting his knuckles to meet the plaster. He gulped deep breaths, forcing the air into his abdomen until his fingers loosened. Buck turned to the arriving officers and asked them to wait in the hallway for a moment.

Entering the apartment, he called Di Stefano.

"Get over here right away. We found your traitors."

He disconnected and then knelt next to Cat. This was now a homicide scene, with protocols to be followed. He gently placed his fingers on her cheek and pulled his face tight to keep from loosening his tongue at God, raging against the world, from spilling tears. He heard the officers talking on the landing and then breaking into laughter. He violently pulled the door open; the officers flinched in response.

"An American hero is lying dead here. Show some respect."

The female officer looked past Buck to see Cat lying on her left side, her left arm straddled outward, blood puddled on the floor. She removed her cap, held it in front of her in both hands, and snapped her body to attention. Her two male colleagues followed suit.

Buck re-entered the room, his back to the officers, Captain Cat Fahey, Marine Corps, at his feet. His arm rose to military salute as tears rolled over his cheeks to his rugged jaw, making company on her body, a ritual baptism between lovers and soldiers.

CHAPTER 39

I had been ushered to a private solarium where I called Arin's mom. She would fly to Philly immediately. I phoned my parents and Padraig Collins. Collins would clear his calendar and fly to Philly as soon as he could arrange his pilots. My parents would join him on the flight.

Then I sat alone, knowing that Buck had to follow police protocol and give a statement before he could leave the scene. But it wasn't long before the door swung open, Buck bursting through, his eyes searching me for news of Arin.

"The doctor hasn't come out yet."

He sat next to me and draped his arm over my shoulder. I shook myself out of my misery for a moment to check on his; then it hit me.

"The Vice President?"

Buck leaned back and cupped his hands behind his head as if his weariness was so great that he had to hold it up.

"The information is sketchy, but Padraig was right. A few of the drones had aerosols that contained a nerve agent. The

268

VP was secured and the drones grounded. The crowd never knew it happened."

Buck put his hands on his knees. I placed one of my hands on his; the contrast of our skin, the symbiosis of our lives. Buck knew death, as soldier, as detective. It had also paid a visit to him as a child, taking his mother. Then his sister. Then his father. I was not new to death's intimate claim of anguish either. Tanya's overdose had rocked me to my core. But she had been sliding away for months, with a noxious sense of inevitability. It was the sudden breach of life taken and almost taken, the tear in what made life worth living.

"Big brother, I've never been so scared."

Buck's breathing was shallow, mine jagged. Buck placed his other hand on top of mine.

"I gotcha, Key. I gotcha."

"Mr. Murphy?" A woman in scrubs entered the room. I couldn't read her face; her surgical mask covered it. Buck and I stood.

"I am Dr. Shankar. Dr. Murphy is stable. She's a lucky woman. The bullet punctured her lung but we were able to inflate it. She has a few broken ribs. She's going to be fine but very sore. We need to keep her under observation for several days to assess potential long-term damage, but she'll recover."

I felt the world spinning, this time in the right direction, but dizzying nonetheless.

"You can see her now, but only for a few minutes."

I walked toward her. She put her hand up.

"I must warn you. She's lost a lot of blood and has experienced trauma. We have her on oxygen and intravenous. She's sedated. She will not look like the Arin you saw a few hours ago."

. . .

Buck had his hand on my shoulder. He guided me into the hallway. Somehow my feet knew what to do. The nurse stopped at the door. I turned away, trying to force my tears back into my eyes and resisting the urge to punch the wall as if Morrison's now dead face was etched there. Buck opened the door and I began to tremble at the sight of Arin. She was pallid, corpse-like. Death had been cheated. Barely.

"I fucking hate myself." My mind raced over the million and ten ways I could have changed the outcome.

"I know you do. That's normal." Buck took me by the arm and we stepped to her bedside.

I brushed her curls and then kissed her softly on the forehead.

"I know you don't want to hear this, but the best thing we can do for her is let her get some sleep," Buck said while gently touching Arin's hand. "Be fresh in the morning when she'll likely be awake."

"Doc gave us ten minutes."

"OK. Police are in the waiting room. They need to get your statement before we go home. I insisted they keep it short."

"I wish I'd killed Morrison. That's my statement."

CHAPTER 40

Saturday, September 4, 2021.
Moore Town, Jamaica

"Wha 'appened?" Li Chen screamed as loud as he could ever remember screaming. "Why are the drones leaving?"

The video feed from the Festival showed the Vice President at the microphone, the crowd cheering, the colorful drone display overhead moving in flight over the main stage. He leaned close to the monitor as a dark-suited man whispered into the VP's ear. Ten seconds later, she said goodbye and walked backward calmly, waving to the crowd. Her detail betrayed no panic.

"What the fuck! Why is she alive?" He felt the rising bile, the clench of his throat that caused him not to breathe for a moment. He had failed. It didn't matter if she died; it mattered that there was chaos. And there was none.

E and Diamond stared at the keyboard, shrinking into their chairs. They heard objects whirring, crashing, breaking.

"Tell me one. Calm me down," he demanded of Diamond.

Diamond grabbed the chair's armrest and squeezed. His mind went blank.

"What are you waiting for, ya ras clat son of a dog?"

Terrence Diamond wrapped his arms around his chest and forced his breath out and in, praying words would arrive.

> "To be or not to be, the question we all ask
> As we navigate through life's endless task
> We stake our ground, we make our claim
> Take wrong turns, improve our aim
> Hurt by love, healed by grace
> Hurl curses 'pon the human race
> What's done is done, a past we cannot change
> But moving forward, a new life we can arrange."

Diamond tried to gauge Chen's state of mind. The poem seemed to have its effect. "It means everytings gonna be all right boss."

Li Chen stood quietly, peacefully. Then the face of rage returned.

"Did you just say it's all right?" His body shook. "Nothing is all right. Do you think it's all right?" Chen grasped Diamond by the jaw. "One of you is a traitor. Is it you?"

His hand swept across the air, catching E in the jaw. E's lip opened, blood running down his face. While Chen concentrated his rage on E, Terrence Diamond turned back to the keyboard and entered a short command. He had sensed that the wheels might come off and had prepared his revenge if it so happened. He hit the enter button.

Chen had reached to his back and pulled out a small-caliber gun. "Did you betray me?" He placed the gun at E's throat.

"Or was it you?" He spun to Diamond and shot him in the forehead.

Chen's eyes were drawn to Diamond's monitor. He froze, calculating what he was reading. He had contingencies for this, plans within plans. Those plans did not include E. He fired two shots. The only sound in the compound was the whimpering of six Dobermanns.

―――――

An alert popped up on Anwulika's computer. The sound indicated a message from her Dark Web message platform. She read:

All that you seek can be found here. 18.0723° N, 76.4254° W.

She entered the GPS coordinates. The screen read *Moore Town Jamaica*. Padraig Collins had remained at Clontarf while events were still playing out. Anwulika called him to her side. He read the message and made a call.

Another message arrived:

I am a fan of you, the Nigerian legend. It may be too late for me, but you must follow the trail.

Anwulika put her fingers on the screen.

"*Ọ bụrụ na ị gafeela, ka nna nna gị hà na-ekele gị n'ọnụ ụzọ ámá,*" she prayed.

The Edge looked up from his screen, curiosity in his eyes.

"It means, 'If you have passed, may your ancestors greet you at the gate.'"

―――――

Li Chen had two possible options; remaining in Jamaica wasn't one of them. He wasn't worried about the Jamaican authorities. He could easily spread a few hundred thousand U.S. dollars among the right people and live peacefully. If the

U.S. made a connection between him and the threat to the VP, he would be arrested or dead in hours.

But the Chinese would get there first and erase anything connected to China, including Chen. Chen knew that at least six of the Chinese Embassy employees in Kingston were agents. Lethal agents. He likely had an hour. He would depart in ten minutes. Max.

Chen's Dobermanns stood guard in front of the carriage house. They snapped to attention as he crossed the yard to the main house. He moved a bureau in his closet and opened the wall safe behind it. He removed a satchel and placed the contents on the bureau: six passports and accompanying drivers' licenses and credit cards. Two of the identities were provided by the Chinese and traceable to him. Chen had secured the other four; therefore, he could be off the Chinese grid. He stuffed the satchel into a backpack that contained E's and Diamond's laptops.

Chen removed three pistols from the safe. One went in the backpack along with additional magazines. He secured the others in his jumpsuit. He left the house, the Dobermanns at his rear, and jogged to a shed hidden three hundred yards into the woods. He emerged on an ATV. The dogs sat panting, awaiting a command. He slid off the ATV and stood in front of his loyal canines. He rubbed their heads, one by one. A primal moan rose from deep inside them. He knew that they knew.

He took his seat on the ATV and commanded the dogs to stay, then rode the vehicle down the mountainous jungle paths to the boat slip where his speedboat was docked.

He would cruise two hours across the waters to Santiago de Cuba, where his contact would drive him to an airfield. Chen would board a small aircraft for the secret flight to the Dominican Republic. A few hours later, a man who bore a remarkable resemblance to Chen would board a flight at the Las Americas International Airport in Santo Domingo. Final destination: Ivory Coast. The look alike had been paid handsomely.

Chen's actual flight would take him to Abu Dhabi, where four airlines were booked to four destinations by four different passengers. All four passports held photos that resembled Chen. He would board the flight that would take him close to China, where he would hide in their shadow as they searched for him in other parts of the world.

From there, he would advance China's agenda and rehabilitate himself in their eyes. Should he live long enough.

CHAPTER 41

I walked into the kitchen and stared at the empty counter, four stools, a harmonica sitting lonely in front of one of them. Buck carried a bottle of whiskey and four shot glasses. He poured and then moved two glasses to where Cat and Arin had been sitting earlier. He raised his glass, and I copied him.

"To Nine."

We drank and Buck immediately refilled our glasses.

"To Arin."

I took the bottle in hand and poured another shot. I thought of my mother, and Arin's mother, and clinked my glass against Arin's and Cat's.

"To women who take no shit."

Buck downed the whiskey then slumped, arms on the counter, his head buried in them. After a moment he stood, hand on my shoulder.

"I need some alone time and a few hours' sleep. You gonna be OK?"

"Yeah."

Buck went to his room. I stood over Arin's stool, our place of morning coffee and night-time wine, of lips meeting and quiet confessions shared. I brushed the top of the stool with my fingers; her energy, her life force seemed to enter and embrace me. I climbed the stairs and stopped in front of our bedroom door. My fingers held the knob but I couldn't turn it. I sat, my back against the wood. Arin, pale and ghostly, joined me in a wash of half-sleep as my head tried to find comfort against the hard surface. There was no comfort. I pulled my knees to my chest, wrapped my arms around them, and laid my head down to rest. In a few hours, I would sit at the bedside of the future Prime Minister of Jamaica and love her back to health.

———

Padraig Collins pulled four chairs into a circle and signaled his crew to take a seat. The Edge shot his lanky legs forward and crossed his ankles. Anwulika declined to sit, preferring to stand. She stood behind her chair and arched her back, working out the kinks and knots. Lihua pulled her legs up under her, making her seem more diminutive.

"I want to thank you for what you accomplished tonight. You can never discuss this with anyone. Lihua, Edge, I want you to think about somewhere you've always wanted to go, and I will make it happen. Anwulika is going first. She's leaving in a few hours."

Anwulika shot him a look of surprise.

"I just learned that Arin Murphy and the woman you saw with her at that press conference, Cat Fahey, were shot while confronting one of the conspirators. Arin will be fine. Fahey didn't make it."

Anwulika sat at that, nearly collapsing in the chair.

"I am flying to Philadelphia with Key's parents." Speaking to Anwulika, he said, "I want you to come with me and stay for Captain Fahey's funeral. We will visit with Arin when she's well enough."

Anwulika fought back tears and gave him a slight nod.

"You will then fly to Punta Arenas, Chile. A science expedition ship leaves for Antarctica in two weeks. You'll join them as soon as possible for training as one of the crew, lending your computer skills. You will be the first Nigerian to crew an expedition to Antarctica."

Collins watched for her reaction. She was neutral.

"I am sorry, sir. I want to laugh and dance at this great news, but my heart is too heavy for Cat and Arin." Anwulika stared at the floor.

"Mine also." Padraig searched the faces of his young geniuses. "I have never asked you to do this before and I know that you don't pray, but I want to say a prayer for them. Will you join me?"

Anwulika dropped to her knees. She reached for Padraig's hand on her left and The Edge on her right. The Edge turned to Lihua, who seemed utterly perplexed. He reached for her hand. Padraig completed the connection and took Lihua's other hand in his.

"Heavenly spirit," Anwulika began as each bowed their heads.

———

Buck and I walked into the intensive care waiting room just after nine a.m.. Arin's mother, Joyce, and brother, Joseph, were already there. My relationship with them was strained but we had worked on reconciling. Joyce embraced me and was slow to let go. Joseph shook my hand and draped his arm over my shoulder for a moment of warmth between us. They both greeted Buck. Joyce looked like she had aged ten years, her eyes moist and sad.

"Arin is still sleeping. They will let us know when she is awake," she said.

The door to the waiting room opened. Padraig Collins stepped through and held it for my mother and father, their arms begging for me. I pulled my mask down and fell into their comforting embrace.

After hugs and handshakes, Collins said, "This is Anwulika. She and her team were the ones who found the drones and helped save the VP. I wanted her to be here to meet you and be at Captain Fahey's funeral."

This woman was regal, tall, and confident, but a shyness overtook her. Her eyes were set downward.

"It is my great honor to be here. And my great sadness."

The ICU nurse entered.

"She is waking. Please, just one at a time, immediate family only."

My heart raced. I felt like I would explode. Only Joyce and Joseph were immediate family.

Joyce stepped forward and took me by the arm.

"You go first."

Some color had returned to Arin's face, a small sign of hope, like an unexpected spring day in early March. Her eyes fluttered, settled, blinked again. Her lips moved, dry, perhaps seeking water. Her head rolled slightly, then stilled, as if a desire to wake was quickly overrun by a need to sleep. Finally, her eyes opened fully, then slowly shuttered closed. Her body jolted; her eyes bolted open.

"Cat?"

I shook my head.

Arin's eyes fixed on me, pleading in them. I brushed tears from her face as her eyes closed. I leaned over her, allowing my cheek to rest against hers, then brushed away my own tear.

CHAPTER 42

Arin and I had only spent a few days with Cat. It's hard to say you know someone in such a short a time. But I did.

Cat would be remembered as a hero, a patriot. Her exploits would be and should be in the history books. But I knew the woman that traveled in the magnificent turbulence of memories, not her own, binding her in the simple and the profound arcs of time and history. I knew the Cat that meandered along the mystical notes of her harmonica, bending and twisting the sounds that enunciated the feelings of her heart. And moved my soul.

The funeral mass was held at the Basilica, where we had admired the golden cross from the FBI's rooftop bar just a few days ago. Agent Di Stefano beckoned Arin, Buck, and me to a quiet alcove.

"This is bad timing, but you need to know a few things."

"Tell us, Joe." Arin's left arm was in a sling and her weariness was evident on her face.

"Much of what we've learned is classified, but Arin, I need to talk to you and your mother and brother after the funeral.

Arin's body went rigid. "Why?"

"Morrison and Casey took their orders from someone you know from Jamaica. Li Chen."

Arin started to wobble. Buck put his arm gently around her and I held her right hand.

"We've uncovered some of Chen's files. He knew of your mother's ambition to have you become Prime Minister. He wanted you to be PM as well. That's why he had her shot in the leg. When the time was right, he would reveal himself. He planned to control you. He would tell you how vulnerable you are, that he could get to your mother. And unless you worked with him, he would let the world know that it was your mother that had Key shot and that your brother paid someone to take the missing pages of the Book of Kells from you."

I had no idea who Li Chen is, but Arin looked like she'd been sucker punched.

"He's disappeared Arin. Not a trace," Di Stefano said. "We need to find him."

———

The procession of cars following the hearse seemed endless as we made our way past citizens waving the flag on our way to the cemetery. I imagined no one in this Black middle-class neighborhood had ever seen anything like this. Children had stayed home from school, and families gathered around the fence that stretched the perimeter of the cemetery. The drum-line from the local high school marching band had been invited to lead the funeral march. The Honor Guard would walk behind them, young men and women who looked like America, and would offer a twenty-one-gun salute. An ensemble of Irish pipers in kilts would follow them. Behind them, a horse-drawn caisson would carry Captain Cat Fahey to her place of rest.

This large entourage had assembled at the Simon Recreation Center. We would walk east on Walnut Lane, then south on Limekiln to the entrance. It was a short walk from there to the grave site. Cat had told Buck that if anything happened to her, she wanted to be buried on these hallowed grounds, close to the section occupied by the United States Colored Troops who had fought so valiantly in the Civil War. For her, she explained, this would be in honor and memory of her great-great-grandfather and his kinship with Frederick Douglass. This was a military cemetery, and the military sprang into action to receive a hero. It was also where Arin and I had found the missing pages of the *Book of Kells* two years ago.

I learned that the Secret Service had pleaded with the Vice President to stay in her limousine for the procession. It fell on deaf ears.

Padraig Collins had agreed with the FBI that he and Anwulika should remain in the car, windows darkened, invisible to the world. There was no need for enemies to know of his role or of the Clontarf Team.

Arin's doctors insisted that she remain in her wheelchair with me pushing behind her. I had rolled my eyes. There was a better chance of me being in the wheelchair with Arin pushing me. I kept my arm lightly around her waist. She shouldn't have been out here walking; her body had not healed. Nor had she recovered from the shock of learning that Li Chen was the mastermind, a fellow Jamaican, who had once been a friend.

Arin stepped to the coffin before it was raised onto its carriage. Buck and I stood beside her. She reached into her pocket and cupped an object in her hand, then laid the

Claddagh ring on the nameplate that read "Nine - Semper Fi."

I laid my hand on Arin's, Buck laid his on mine and I felt metal touching my skin. Buck held Cat's harmonica. His hand closed around it and he forced his eyes tight, lest his tears escape. We bowed our heads.

The Vice President had asked Buck to accompany her and her husband. Fifteen former members of Cat's team walked beside the carriage. Maria Villanueva was one of them, the fiancée of FBI Agent Di Stefano, who was waiting graveside for the procession to arrive.

Buck and I had held a news conference on the Sunday before. We told the world about Cat and her ancestral memories, the tale of Frederick Douglass and Daniel O'Connell and Martin Fahey, and how the memories sparked revelations about the plot. The global press could not get enough of this strange and unique woman known by her unit as "Nine."

Word had traveled far and wide about Nine and the tales of her heroic actions that led to her nickname. One Veteran's social media feed said she was bringing nine flowers bound by a green ribbon. And so did thousands of people who lined the funeral route. As the caisson rolled onto the street, a father lifted his daughter and she tossed her bouquet onto the casket. And like a rolling wave, the bouquets rained down love on Cat.

The drumline played, then the bagpipes, repeating in a musical call and response. Faces young and old, the bodies, some trim, most not. Elderly Black men in their military jackets. Veterans of all stripes and colors in salute. Jewish men in yarmulkes and Muslim women in headdresses. Asian families, bouquets in hand, and the sound of Spanish families in prayer. And the Irish. The green, white, and orange flag resting against the red, white, and blue in one hand, a bottle of Guinness in the other. Each was raised as Cat passed; "Go *raibh maith agat,*" thank you in Irish, was said in reverential tones to the great-great-granddaughter of Martin Fahey.

As I searched the faces of my fellow citizens, I recalled that Jamaica and America had the same motto, the motto that Cat lived and died for: *E Pluribus Unum,* out of many, one people.

And I prayed, to whatever God might listen to the likes of me, that we might make it so.

CHAPTER 43

November 5, 2021.
The M Resort, Ocho Rios

I couldn't stop pacing. The calm turquoise waters of the Caribbean provided no tranquility. Though the sky was blue, the smell of rain carried on the warm breeze. Arin would return from physical therapy in a few minutes. We had moved temporarily to the Murphy-owned resort in Ocho Rios. The M was the crown jewel in the portfolio of resorts that Arin's family owned. Their all-Inclusive brands catered to mid- and upper-level vacationers, but the M was strictly for the super-wealthy. We occupied a two-story, three-thousand-square-foot home overlooking pristine waters. Paradise. But weeks of paradise can feel like its own prison to a city boy like me.

Arin's doctors told us to leave the world behind. Someone else would have to save it for now. The M Spa was the perfect place for her healing and recovery.

I had bouquets arranged on the veranda, rose petals strewn on the floor and furniture. A champagne bucket stood at the ready, the cork just removed from the bottle. I told myself to calm the hell down, but instead I fidgeted with the flowers and needlessly straightened the pillows on the sofa.

The buzzer rang downstairs as the door opened. I could hear Arin take the steps vigorously. Her strength and endurance had returned. I watched her turn from the foyer into the second floor living room, the large picture windows revealing me on the spacious veranda. She eyed me suspiciously as I watched her take in the floral display.

Arin stepped onto the veranda. She wore white shorts and a black workout top, *M Spa* embroidered on it. Her hair had been pulled into a band, but several curls had objected to captivity and danced across the side of her face.

I had practiced my lines over and over, but I just stood there with a dumb look on my face.

"Special occasion?" Arin surveyed my attempt at romantic.

My lines evaded my memory. I did the only thing I could remember and got down on one knee, took her hands in mine. I looked up at her as a smile spread on her face.

She looked at me with expectation. I looked back at her.

"Did you want to ask me something?" she said.

I responded by grinning more.

"Of course I'll marry you. It's about time you asked. Actually, you didn't ask." She was biting her lip, trying not to laugh.

I stood, wrapped my arms around her waist. The words I spoke to her in Irish two years ago, words I had heard Aedan say, the words I had practiced:

"Is tú an stór, stór m'anama." Her eyes lit up at the memory of it. I repeated in English: "You are the treasure, the treasure of my soul. Will you marry me?"

CHAPTER 44

December 3, 2021.
The M Resort

I t was a small wedding. If it hadn't been, Arin's mom said she would have had to invite half the island for fear of offending. No press allowed. Arin decided on December 3rd, the anniversary of the day we revealed the missing pages of the *Book of Kells*. That was a momentous occasion, she reasoned, although this day was even more momentous. When she proposed the date for the wedding, which was five minutes after I asked her to marry me, she added, "and you won't even need to change your name, Mr. Murphy." Clever woman.

White linen pants and shirts seemed the clothing of choice for a Caribbean wedding. I felt like I was wearing pajamas. Buck stood beside me, white linen, Panama hat with a red band. My parents sat in the front row. Mom kept squeezing Dad's hand. It was getting red.

A childhood friend of Arin's, Gabrielle, sat behind my mom. Arin had introduced her to Buck when he'd visited in October. He'd been back two times. She went to Philly once.

She was beautiful, and Buck had a hard time taking his eyes off her.

Padraig Collins sat across the aisle from them, next to the empty seat where Joyce would sit. They had been seeing each other quietly since meeting in Dublin in 2019, but they were now open about their relationship. Dr. Garcia was in the chair next to Joyce's seat. Joseph would remain standing with his sister at our makeshift altar.

Dusk was nearing, cooler now, as we stood barefoot in the sand. Festive outdoor lights had come on. Palm trees cast shadows. The Anglican Bishop stood in the designated area, and the musicians took their place. Harp, cello, violin, and clarinet. They played.

Then Arin was there. A crown of flowers, a sleeveless white linen dress, corkscrew curls brushing her shoulders. Stunning in her simplicity. Her brother Joseph took her right arm, her mother Joyce took her left. A bittersweet moment, I knew, yearning for her father to be there. She still missed him dearly. They made it halfway down the aisle and then Arin stopped, her face clouded over. She stood silently, eyes closed. When they opened, she hurried to me, leaving a confused mother and brother behind.

"Oh my God, Key. Doi Suthep."

The musicians stopped playing.

"What?" I leaned closer.

Arin's eyes fixed on me. "Doi Suthep. We must go there."

"I don't understand. What is it?"

"Key, I … don't know. Look it up," she said excitedly.

My mom had my phone. I stepped to her. She handed me her purse and I retrieved it. I entered "doy sutep" as I made my way to Arin's side. I looked up at her, an angelic smile, the crown of purple flowers resting on her head, the sweet smell of Jamaican roses rising from the nearby vases. And here I am doing a search on my phone.

I glanced back at the screen. Nothing came up with that spelling. It showed me *Doi Suthep* instead.

I clicked on the link and a stunning image of a golden temple filled the screen.

"It's a Buddhist temple in northern Thailand, close to China. Why?"

Arin's white dress seemed iridescent as the sunset tossed golds and blues and yellows into the Ocho Rios sky. She turned to our guests. "I'm so sorry, I got a bit carried away."

Something unexpected always accompanies Arin when she displays her devilish grin.

"I do," she said loudly.

"We didn't get to that part yet," I reminded her.

She turned to the Bishop.

"I almost died without saying 'I do' to my amazing, soon-to-be husband. I'm saying it now, as we start the ceremony. I do, I do, I do."

Our guests smiled, some laughed. Almost dying does focus things. It cuts to the essential.

Arin stood on her tiptoes, her arms on my shoulders.

"Key," she whispered, her voice strained with excitement. "My memories have begun."

THE KEY TO KELLS
SUMMARY

BOOK 1 IN THE KEY MURPHY THRILLER
SERIES

DISCOVERY UPENDS EVERYTHING WE KNOW ABOUT MEMORY AND GENETICS. IT MIGHT COST KEY MURPHY HIS LIFE.

Key Murphy is a freak, a prodigy. He has visions so real that he's diagnosed with PTSD. Key learns that his visions might be caused by a mutated gene which allows him to experience the memories of an ancestor.

Key also has a family link to The Book of Kells. Pages from the book were stolen in Ireland in the distant past. Those pages are believed to contain clues to the location of one of the most priceless treasures of Christendom.

Padraig Collins is one of the wealthiest men in Europe. He was an undercover operative for the IRA. He amassed a fortune. He wants those pages. His soul depends on them. He will do whatever it takes to possess them.

The race is on.

Fans of Dan Brown's Da Vinci Code, Steve Berry's Cotton

Malone series, and Clive Cussler's Dirk Pitt series will want to jump right into the action by buying the first book in an exciting new series of Key Murphy Thrillers.

> "O'Connor takes these familiar Dan Brown-style thriller elements—hidden societies, secret histories, shocking revelations buried in historical events (plus a certain cosmopolitan flavor; the narrative bounces from Philadelphia to Jamaica to Ireland and else-where)—and combines them to craft a thriller that will be pleasing to any fan of *The Da Vinci Code* (2003)."
>
> *—KIRKUS REVIEWS*

Available now to buy, and FREE on KindleUnlimited!

———

Join Key and Arin in their next adventure, from the barrios of Santiago Chile to the streets of Bangkok and the Buddhist Temples and jungle terrain of Northern Thailand:

Shake the Jar

Book 3 in the Key Murphy Thriller Series, coming in 2024!

AUTHOR'S NOTE

It was James Buffum, not Martin Fahey, that accompanied Frederick Douglass to Ireland. That said, I stayed true to the historical record as much as possible. Where I veered into fiction, I attempted to do so while maintaining the voice and ideals of the great Frederick Douglass and the indomitable Daniel O'Connell, drawn mainly from their writings. In reality, they met only once. It was the night that Frederick Douglass attended O'Connell's speech in Dublin. The baton had passed; Douglass arrived in Ireland as a single-issue campaigner for the abolition of slavery. He left Ireland as an international campaigner for human rights.

Thanks to the efforts of Don Mullan and Dr. Christine Kinealy, there is a Frederick Douglass Walking Tour in Dublin. Don Mullan is a prominent civil rights activist from Derry who now lives in Dublin. He kindly invited me to his home for an hour-long discussion that lasted four hours. I left a wiser man, with a greater understanding of the parallels between the perilous times that Douglass navigated and the danger to democracy that we face today.

ABOUT THE AUTHOR

Kevin Barry O'Connor performed and wrote for the stage for 12 years, built a global marketing business and has traveled to over 90 countries. He taught himself harmonica in high school and has guest appeared with bands around the world. As the grandson of Irish immigrants, he holds dual American and Irish citizenship. Kevin lives in Philadelphia with Lee Tracy, his traveling companion and spouse of over forty years. Threshold is his second novel with sequels on the way.

You can visit the website at www.kevinbarryoconnor.com

ACKNOWLEDGMENTS

For location research, I walked in the footsteps of Frederick Douglass in Dublin, had lived in Jamaica for several years, and much of the story is set near my home in Philadelphia. However, I needed to absorb the expertise of those who report on the dark web, hacking, and counterintelligence. I did this through more podcasts, books, and interviews than I can state.

Kris Spisak was my editor for my first novel, The Key to Kells, and I thank her for her guidance and editing expertise as Key and Arin faced their next challenge. I am married to my greatest critic and advisor, Lee Tracy. When I had her read and re-read the edited versions of The Key to Kells, she would tell me it wasn't ready yet. It wasn't until she gave a thumbs-up that I felt confident to have other readers. To my great surprise and delight, Lee offered an enthusiastic thumbs-up on her first read of Threshold. I hope you feel the same. If so, please leave a review by going to www.kevinbar ryoconnor.com/threshold

ALSO BY KEVIN BARRY O'CONNOR

Key Murphy Thriller Series

The Key to Kells

Threshold

Shake the Jar – coming soon!